Edge had botched the first proposal terribly. But he wasn't going to botch the first kiss.

He moved Lily slightly, turning her so he could savour every second and give her a feeling she would cherish.

'This is how it starts,' she said, whispering, shaking her head, turning away. 'It's not safe.'

'One kiss,' he said, knowing it was likely the biggest lie of his life.

'No.'

But she didn't push him away. She didn't move to her feet—she just sat and leaned closer against him.

'Half a dozen, then.' He didn't smile, again letting her hair brush his face. 'Twenty. And that's my final offer.'

Author Note

When the Duke of Edgeworth first appeared in *The Notorious Countess*, and felt irritated by his brother's choice of an adventurous wife, I wanted Edge to have his own chance for love. Only Lily Hightower would do for him. No one would be better for him than the reserved woman he'd known since childhood.

Writing Lily's story gave me a chance explore the path of having been friends with someone from such an early age that you can't remember first meeting him, and knowing he is right for you and yet not quite being able to get beyond the barriers inside and around you.

That path of discovery is what I planned for both Lily and Edgeworth—because when romance enters the picture, no matter how long you have known someone, you can realise you hardly knew them at all.

Lily and Edgeworth are characters of my heart, and I hope you enjoy their journey as well.

THE WALLFLOWER DUCHESS

Liz Tyner

First published in Great Britain 2017
By Mills & Boon, an imprint of HarperCollins*Publishers*
1 London Bridge Street, London, SE1 9GF

Large Print edition 2017

ISBN: 978-0-263-06780-4

Our policy is to use papers that are natural, renewable and recyclable products and made from wood grown in sustainable forests. The logging and manufacturing processes conform to the legal environmental regulations of the country of origin.

Printed and bound in Great Britain
by CPI Antony Rowe, Chippenham, Wiltshire

Liz Tyner lives with her husband on an Oklahoma acreage she imagines is similar to the ones in the children's book *Where the Wild Things Are*. Her lifestyle is a blend of old and new, and is sometimes comparable to the way people lived long ago. Liz is a member of various writing groups, and has been writing since childhood. For more about her visit liztyner.com.

Books by Liz Tyner

Mills & Boon Historical Romance

The Governess Tales

The Runaway Governess

English Rogues and Grecian Goddesses

Safe in the Earl's Arms
A Captain and a Rogue
Forbidden to the Duke

Stand-Alone Novels

The Notorious Countess
The Wallflower Duchess

Visit the Author Profile page
at millsandboon.co.uk.

Dedicated to my cousins.

Prologue

The future Duke of Edgeworth stretched his chin, and felt the nick he'd made on his first attempt with shaving. When he'd told his father how he received the cut, he'd been told never to touch the razor again. But some day he'd be Edgeworth—and no one would dare tell him what to do.

His parents' voices blended into the background as he worked with the mathematics. He liked mathematics and he liked that his parents singled him out when preparing him for his future.

His father sat at the other desk, and his mother read over his shoulder, but then returned to her sewing stand.

The Duke's voice broke into the quiet. 'The younger Miss Hightower?'

'She's a lovely little girl.' His mother nestled into her chair, picked up her sewing and studied it.

'Not the older one,' his father added. 'She scowls.'

'The older one is Lily.' His mother returned to her embroidery, grumbling at a stitch as she picked it loose with her needle. 'And she's not scowling. She's figuring things out.'

'That girl is quite well mannered, but not a duchess,' the Duke said.

'She is too serious.' His mother never looked up from her threads, needle again moving in and out through the fabric. 'But I'm sure she'll grow into a beauty. The least attractive babies make the most beautiful people, and frankly, I'd never seen such an ugly baby as Lily was. Her eyes were huge and her little arms so scrawny. Reminded me of a starved mouse. But she's more human looking now and one can do wonders with cosmetics.'

The Duke tapped his fingertips together. 'With her father living next door, it would be easy to keep up with the young one's upbringing. But I'm not sure… Their mother is such a…'

'But that doesn't mean the children will be. The

small one is an obedient girl. Did exactly as her older sister instructed.'

'Obedient.' His father nodded and Edge had looked up in time to see the wink his father gave his mother. 'I've never heard you say a duke needs an obedient wife.'

'Oh, most certainly,' she'd added, turning to leave the room. 'Sad your mother didn't tell you that.'

His father chuckled, patted the papers on the desk and said, 'It's settled, then.' He looked at his son. 'What do you think about the younger Miss Hightower?'

'She's a baby.' Lord Lionel continued with his sums. 'Babies can't marry.'

'She'll grow,' his father said. 'If we choose while she's young, we can see that she is educated and trained just as a duchess should be. Just as you want her to be. Once I inform her father that you're interested in her, he'll be certain she is raised exactly as she should be. The man understands the value of society even if he has only half a boot in it.'

Lionel shrugged. Perhaps he would wed Miss Hightower some day, but not the little one. After all, only old people married. They were twenty-five at least. Perhaps thirty. Yes, at thirty he could ask the older Miss Hightower to wed, because by then he'd be too old for it to matter.

And he didn't think she looked like a mouse, but even if she did, it was fine with him.

Last Wednesday, he'd been studying in the gardens when Miss Lily had called out to him and she'd curtsied. No one had ever done that before and he had nodded to her, just as his father did when people curtsied to him. Then she'd asked him to play dolls. He'd said no, even though it sounded better than studying. Then she'd called him Lord Booby-head. The governess had walked out and reprimanded her and Miss Lily had scrambled to her house.

He felt sorry for her. He'd overheard what his parents said about her and it was much worse than *booby-head* could be.

He didn't know what a booby-head was, but he was not it. After all, he was going to be a duke, just like his father, and everyone always spoke nicely to the Duke. It was a rule or law or something like that.

His younger brothers said they would never call him Edgeworth because that was their father's title and when he became a duke they would call him Edgeworth*less*. But their mother had overheard and shamed them. She'd told him they would have to be well behaved or it would reflect badly on the whole family. They were of the peerage. They must always remember that.

Chapter One

'Your Grace.' The valet's voice had all the bounce of a rock falling into a well.

The Duke of Edgeworth did not want to wake up. He'd worked too late into the night trying to pull his mind back into the ledgers he'd neglected.

'Your Grace,' Gaunt repeated. 'Your Grace.' The voice broke just a bit.

Edgeworth opened his eyes, mainly to assure Gaunt that he still lived.

'Yes,' Edgeworth muttered, half-rising. The wobbliness in his head nearly threw him back to the bed. The pain had almost taken him.

Gaunt's voice barely rose loud enough to be heard, as if he feared that the sound of it might damage Edgeworth in some way. Edgeworth clamped his teeth together. He was alive. Alive.

He'd survived twice. The first time he'd nearly drowned and then he'd been burned. The year had not started out well.

'The reason I woke you—'

'Yes?' Edge just wished the man would speak quickly. Gaunt's delicateness grated and only served to remind him how close he'd been to death.

'There's a woman who wishes to see you. That—we are sure of.' Gaunt's hands were clasped.

Edge pushed himself to sit against the head-board, ignoring the pain, then he put his feet on the floor and stood. The sulphur-scented poultice Gaunt had tried to suffocate him with still lay by the wash basin. He pointed to it and with a sharp jerk of his hand indicated it should be removed.

Gaunt snatched up the cloth by two fingers and held it at his side, away from his body.

'The housekeeper is with the guest now. The butler insisted,' Gaunt explained.

The housekeeper never saw to guests and for the butler to have someone stay with a visitor was unheard of.

'We thought it best,' Gaunt added, 'that the woman not be left alone. But we could not exactly escort her out as she claims to have news of a friend of yours from the country who has passed on to a greater reward.'

'Claims?'

'She does know your relative's name.' Gaunt's face remained immobile as he spoke.

Edge strode to the basin, splashing water on his face. The burns had left him weak, but not feeble minded. And Gaunt knew the family tree far better than Edge himself did. On one occasion he'd even helped Edge sort out just how a cousin came to be related.

'Why was she not asked to leave a card and sent on her way?'

'I will dismiss her.' His pause had a cough in it. 'She's dressed in black. Head to toe. Face covered. Handkerchief. Sobbed pitifully. I thought it best you decide. Something about her is… familiar.'

'I'll see to her,' Edge said, wondering if the illness had affected his mind.

'No carriage with her,' Gaunt added. 'Not even a hackney.'

'Maid?'

'She's alone.'

Edge shook his head. This sounded like a jest

his cousin Foxworthy would try. Sending some lightskirt on a mission of seduction and then waiting outside with a group of friends who'd wagered on how long before the woman left. Fox had done something similar in the past—more than once—but he should know better than to try such a thing on Edge.

Edge would give Fox a chance to gauge his own recovery skills.

When Edge stepped into the sitting room, the housekeeper's eyes darted from the sombre hand-kerchief-clasping form to him.

Pausing to think back to the mourning attire he'd seen, he didn't remember seeing anyone dressed so completely in black, although the veil over the bonnet did have a bit of yellow ribbon peeking through.

The woman's clothing wasn't dashed together and had no frayed edges or worn seams, and yet he didn't think it entirely new. She held a wadded handkerchief in each hand and moved the one in her right clasp beneath the veil to daub at her face.

'Someone has passed from this life?' he asked the grim form.

'Yes. Might I speak with you about it privately?' The soft, velvety smooth words fluttered the veil. A lightskirt's voice if he'd ever heard one. Foxworthy would pay.

At Edge's side, the housekeeper's arms tightened.

'No,' he answered.

Her fingers reached up, grasping an edge of the veil to lift it. But she paused.

'Tell me your news,' he said. 'I would hate to keep a grieving person about on an errand when she could be finding solace in her home with loved ones around her.'

He heard her exhale and her arms tightened.

She stood, one sweeping movement. 'Your Grace, I regret to inform you that your mother's fifth cousin, Lady Cumberson, has passed on.'

Edge remained motionless, sorting out something, but he couldn't quite place it. Lady Cumberson had died some months back. Then he let out a breath. 'Lady Cumberson passed on? For a moment I had forgotten her. A dear, sweet woman. About so high.' He moved his arm out to his side, indicating just below his shoulder. 'Sainted woman. Grey hair.'

Lady Cumberson had stood taller than any

woman he'd ever seen, had a vulgar sense of humour and coal-black hair.

'No. Quite stately. Dark hair. And I suppose you could call her a saint, but I didn't see her that way.'

He paused, recognising the voice. He forced himself not to react.

Lily? Lily Hightower? Fox would never dare send her. He had nothing to do with women like Lily. *And when did Lily get such a sultry voice?*

'Could you spare a moment to tell me about her last days?' he asked, turning to dismiss the housekeeper. The older woman scurried out.

'What is going on causing you to attempt a masquerade?' Edge asked.

She raised her veil just enough so that he could see a chin, a well-shaped mouth that caused him to take note and then two brown eyes peered out from under the edge of the veil. He swallowed.

'I can't visit you openly without my father knowing. I can't wait until your mother returns from the country so I can pretend to visit her and hope you *might* walk by and we *might* chance a few moments to talk privately…' She shook her head as if trying to remove unsure thoughts. 'I suppose I didn't think anyone else could help.

And I had no idea what to do if you didn't re-cover—soon.'

'Thank you for your concern about my health.'

'Of course.' The words burst out. Her voice tightened and she lowered the veil over her face. 'I heard of your accident—goodness, *another* one—but then the next thing I knew you were back in London, brought home in a wagon, and we didn't know if you were going to live or die. My family would have been so distraught if you'd...'

'Your...family...would have been distraught?' He managed to inflect the words with just enough emphasis to point the question her way.

'Of course, *all* of us would have been.'

The veil popped up again. The handkerchief bundled so that she could use two fingers to raise the covering and the dark eyes studied him. Then the fabric fluttered down again. 'I feared for the worst, but then your mother took me to your bed-side.' Her voice wobbled. 'You looked... But you recovered quickly after that.'

He waved her words away. 'I only had two choices and I thought this one the best.'

'It was horrible to see you so ill.'

A fogged memory of hearing his mother begging him not to die on his birthday surfaced, but he batted it away. Dwelling on those thoughts would do him no good.

'Your Grace,' she said. He leaned forward to hear her. 'I am very relieved you are yourself again.'

'If I had awoke to find that I was my cousin Foxworthy, I would not have recovered.' He had to lighten Lily's words.

He waited, watching for reaction. Blasted veil.

'It would be a shame to die after you finally grew into your boots.' Her voice regained strength.

'Pardon me?'

'Your boots. I remember looking at them years ago when you studied outside. It was as if someone had taken you by your ears and just stretched you right up from the boot-tops to the chin. You fit yourself now.'

'Thank you.'

'I did rather think you were quite handsome until that day you made me fall out of the tree.'

'I kept you from killing yourself.' And it hadn't been easy. He'd realised she was going after the kite which was tangled in a small, half-broken branch near the top of the tree. He'd shouted for her to stop. She'd moved faster.

He'd darted forward, getting to the trunk in time to grab her by the ankle, but she'd had a firm grip on a tree limb. She'd tried to kick free of his grasp. He'd explained, methodically, that he should get the kite by another method. She was going to break the kite's limb if she put her weight on it.

'Oh,' she'd said, looking up, eyes squinted.

He'd released her ankle, thinking she understood, and she'd lunged for the next higher limb. He'd caught her bootlace and she'd lost her grip, tumbling backwards on to him. He'd landed on his back, cushioning her. Spindly as she was, she'd plopped like a boulder on to his stomach. He'd laid on the ground, struggling for air while looking up at the kite fluttering happily overhead.

She'd screeched and jumped up, staring down at him. Apparently she'd bumped her face against the tree on her way down. He'd seen a split lip before, but not on a little girl.

'You booby-head,' she'd called out, eyes blazing into him.

Booby-head? He'd stared at her. *Booby-head?*

Apparently little girls swore differently from other people.

'You booby-head. You made me fall.'

'You—'

He'd been planning to explain again how she'd been going to fall from a much higher limb and he wouldn't have been able to catch her, but the blood on her face stopped his words.

At that moment, she put her hand to her lip, lowered her fingers so she could see the crimson liquid and wailed out a terrifying sound. She'd raced into her house before he could stand.

Later, he'd seen the thread-like scar, resting a finger-width from the bow of her mouth. Lip stain covered it when she grew older, but he always checked for it. Only now her mouth was hidden behind a gauzy screen. It irked him.

'Your governess should have been punished,' he said.

'Mrs Smith was a dear, dear governess. Not like the next one.' The bonnet tilted back and the veil dusted against the outline of her chin. 'I think I turned out quite well.'

'Of course.' He'd known she would. 'You don't have to hide from me.' He stared at the black cloth.

'I'm not. I'm being discreet.' Her tone rose.

'Then keep your voice down.' He moved closer and carefully reached out, lifting the cloth, holding it up like a tent between them.

He looked at the uncovered blemish on the challenging lips, then up at the brown eyes, and he felt like a youth—which was odd because even when he was a child, he'd never felt like one. 'Why are you here?' he asked and fought to keep his voice distant. He waited for her to say she'd wanted to see him.

'Edge,' she reprimanded and tilted her head back. The cloth slid from his touch.

She'd called him by the nickname his brothers and cousins had begun using right after the old Duke had passed on. Much better than being called a booby-head, he supposed.

'I'd hoped to catch you in the gardens for a word, but—' A prim sentence.

He nodded, frowning. The gardens. He'd not been into the sun since he'd been burned. He'd barely been able to move and he'd had no care about anything else. He'd put off leaving town for the summer, deciding he'd wait to see if he lived or died. If he died, he'd let someone else see to carting him to the family crypt.

She turned away. Inwardly, he smiled. She turned to hide her expression—as if he could see it under the gauzy fabric covering it.

He stared at her shoulders and his eyes drifted downward. At that second, he realised Lily had become Lillian. He took in a breath and turned his gaze to the wall.

'You are a determined person. You've always done exactly as you should and you have a considerable amount of duties to keep up with…' She cleared her throat. 'One in particular.'

'To what particular one might you be referring?'

'You really are the only person who can answer the question I have.'

His gaze washed over her. 'You are here to ask a question?'

She turned and lifted the veil again, staring straight into his face. 'I don't know exactly how I would word this and I would hate for a note to fall into the wrong hands, so I had to arrive myself. It's far easier to deny a spoken word than a written one.' She lowered her voice. 'And I suppose I did want to see for myself that you're up and about,' she added.

He kept perfectly still, his mind's eye seeing the

little girl who would stare at him when he studied out of doors. He soon discovered he could look at her, grumble a growl and she'd laugh and run back into her house, leaving him alone with his books the rest of the day.

'What question could you have for me?' he asked.

'Are you going to propose to my sister?'

The feeling of a boulder landing on his stomach returned. He leaned forward, staring. 'Pardon?' Confusion—then irritation—flooded him.

'Soon?' she asked.

'I've not given it any thought,' he said, snapping out the words.

'You nearly died,' she accused. '*Twice.* And where would that leave her? She's not getting any younger.'

'None of us is.'

Brown sparked in her eyes. 'I would hope our connection of knowing each other years and years and years would allow you to appreciate my honesty and understand my concern for my sister,' she said. 'I would think we have a bond.'

'We do.' His gaze dropped to her lips, again. That tiny vertical scar, hardly bigger than a thread and only visible at close distance, ran upwards from her top lip.

Her attention wavered and her black gloved hand touched the mark. 'Makes me look like a pirate,' she said.

'No. I can only see the scar because I know where—to look.'

Her eyes became solemn. 'Are you going to court my sister? I need to know.'

'Why?' He shook his head. He'd thought that nonsense of his interest in her sister had died long before. It had been his father's talk and he'd never encouraged it. Never. In fact, he'd thought it long forgotten.

He knew that on occasion when he'd planned a day at home, his mother had arranged things so the Hightower sisters would arrive for tea. But his mother planned a lot of teas with young, unmarried women when he was at home.

Her words about him marrying her sister slid in under his ribs and irritation bit into him. He didn't mind so much when his mother dangled the names of young women in front of him, but Lily—she should know better. 'You realise I nearly died,' he said, chin forward. 'Marriage has not been foremost on my mind.'

'You are all recovered now. Aren't you?' Her eyes locked with his.

'I'm alive, at least.' Not that it appeared to make a great deal of difference to her, except where her sister was concerned.

'Another reason for a marriage, I'd say.' Hopeful eyes stared at him.

'But if I die, it wouldn't matter to me whether I have a wife or not.' Well, it might. Lily should not wear black.

'But it might matter very much to your lineage and to a woman wanting a family. A duke needs an heir. Simple fact. But I don't expect you to die, however, I expect you to live a long and healthy life.' Her eyes sparkled in jest. 'You've no choice. Duty.'

'I hope you don't overestimate me, Miss Hightower.'

He'd wanted to make his mark in life by the time he reached thirty. He'd thought he'd be able to use his influence in Parliament to produce more jobs for the people put out of work by the mechanised looms, but his progress was much slower than he'd expected. Marriage had seemed the logical next step after his work. And he'd just assumed Lily understood. The few times he'd spoken with her as an adult and told her how much progress he was making, and had said personal duties would come afterwards, she'd nodded her head in complete understanding.

He'd thought.

Now Lily stood in front of him and she must have seen something on his face. She put her hand out, not touching him, but hovering above his sleeve. She smiled. 'So you will be at our soirée next week and consider courting my sister?'

'No.'

'No?' She stepped back, eyes widening before the lids lowered, her hand falling to her side. 'No?'

Neither spoke.

'Are you certain?' The words came out carefully, hesitant. 'You're not going to marry Abigail?' She examined him closer than Gaunt had when he'd been checking Edge to see if he had a pulse.

'I can't believe you ask that.'

She took in a breath and somehow managed to hold it. 'Do you have any plans for marriage?' Her voice rose, her arm moved out and she patted as if touching the top of small heads. 'A family

of your own. Little heirs. A little group all snug-
gled together at bedtime.'

'I do not think of it quite the same as going to a
litter of kittens and picking out the one with the
healthiest yowl.' Then he thought of Lily falling
from the tree and hid his smile. 'Although I'm
not opposed to a healthy yowl.'

'Agreed,' she said. 'But you have to admit my
sister would make a good duchess.'

'Your sister is a pleasant person. But I've never
seen her as a duchess. Ever.'

Mouse-brown eyes stared up at him and a flutter in the area of his heart gave him pause. His
mother was right. Lily had grown into her eyes,
although he did not think her comment about his
marrying her sister deserved explanation.

Because of his father's words claiming it to be
true, people had assumed Edge would marry the
younger Hightower sister. It had suited Edge's
purpose to let people believe the tale. It deflected
false hope in mothers angling their daughters to
catch his eye and kept him from having to dodge
flirtations. Besides, he'd always known he would
some day marry Lily. He'd decided it and the idea
had flickered through his thoughts on occasion,
seeming more perfect each time, and he'd just

known Lily felt the same way. How could she not? True, he always danced with her sister first, then Lily last so he could linger with her without Abigail fluttering around waiting for her dance.

And they'd not said much, but he'd not thought there was a need. They'd stood by each other, companionably, watching the others. If that did not signal a deep interest then he did not know what could have. He'd stayed late at a noisy soirée with music and chatter drowning out all words so he could spend a few moments at her side. Never had he done that with another woman.

'Stop looking so grim.' She mocked his face, a forced snarl to her lips. 'It hasn't hurt my sister to be considered as your potential bride. Quite the opposite. She received the best education and the envy of so many people.'

He shrugged internally, realising he didn't quite understand women as well as he'd thought. 'So, on the day you mentioned that your father would be so happy to have a duke in the family…' Well, he'd misinterpreted that statement. Her sister had been the last person on his mind as he'd waltzed with Lily that night.

He knew without question she'd always been pleased to have a private word with him. And when she'd spoken about how well Abigail was growing up, he'd noted it as a statement of how well Lily had taken care of her sister and how Lily would be a good mother…to his children. He'd not imagined her as assuming he had any interest in Abigail. *Abigail?*

'Edge.' This time her lips pressed firmly before speaking and he knew she didn't jest. 'I know you're an honourable man and, since you've said nothing, I started to worry we'd misunderstood. No one will court her because they think you have her planned for a bride. Father has frowned upon any other suitors. She's going to end up a spinster if she waits almost for ever for you and then after she's rejected everyone else you look in a different direction.'

'I have never once indicated any intention to marry *Abigail*.' He'd treated her with extra no-tice because he did plan for her to be family. His *wife's* sister.

'Well, Father has so much money I suppose we could purchase a husband for her later on.' She wrinkled her nose. 'I do feel you should have told me, though.'

'I thought I indicated my intentions to you.'

'That you intended to marry Abigail.' Her

words accused. 'Yes. And she's said she's tired of waiting on you and she's determined to wed before the year is out. It is on her list.'

'Her list, or your list?'

'It is on her list, above finishing the embroidery sampler. That sampler will never make it to the wall. However, Abigail will make it to the church… And it is on my list, too. Finding my sister a suitable match.'

'I will attend the soirée, but—' The same feeling of the ground crumbling beneath him he'd had when he'd fallen into the water overtook him. His breath shortened. What if Lily didn't— wouldn't marry him?

She walked closer, a form he could not decipher behind the dark clothing, and reached out, again stopping just before touching his arm. 'Thank you for letting me know,' she said. Her voice quavered.

'Lily—'

She smoothed the edge of the veil and the view of black covering her eyes shot into his body, the same as another brush with death. Darkness choked him at the thought of her not being in his life.

Lily moved away, walking towards the door.

The air stirred and a light floral scent swirled around him.

The whiff of the perfume jarred him to his boots. He couldn't have spoken even if he could have thought of something to say.

He kept from moving forward. He'd thought himself delirious after he'd been burned and when he recovered he'd shoved the memory aside, not wanting to accept that his mind had been so addled.

But it hadn't been an angel sitting at his bedside. He knew the second the trace of flowers touched his nose that Lily had been in his sickroom, comforting his mother.

He slightly remembered his mother leaning over his form in bed and wishing him a happy birthday and dripping a tear on his face and then smudging it off and bursting into loud sobs and running from the room.

Foxworthy had spoken from somewhere in the chamber and said that there wasn't anything to worry about because Edge's brother had three sons to pass the title to.

Anger had blasted over his last embers of life, giving him strength to move his hand. He was going to do one last thing and then die.

He'd tried to curl the fingers down, except for the middle one, but he didn't think he'd made it before an angel had taken his hand, pressing, covering his fist. A feminine touch held his fingers. The skin was cool—refreshing after the heat that smothered him. An angel to ease his pain and take him from life.

He'd squeezed the fingers twice.

The angel had grabbed him and jostled him, sending aches throughout his body. But then she'd hugged him, pressing closer. A wisp of her hair had tickled his nose and the flowery soap she used had masked the sickroom scent. Her touch worked better than laudanum and the pain had abated. He'd breathed in, trying to keep the scent of her locked inside him and the feel of her cheek imprinted on his.

'Hurry and get better,' she'd whispered, her lips at his ear.

The touch made his blood flow and his heart beat, but when her hands left him, he'd been unable to move to follow her.

He'd wanted her to stay. Ached for her to stay, but it was a different kind of pain than the jagged throbs that had sliced him.

She'd told him to get better and he'd done it. For her. For the angel. For Lily. And he'd be damned if he didn't ask her to marry him.

Chapter Two

'Gaunt.' Edgeworth stepped from the window when his valet entered. 'Are my things prepared?'

'Your Grace?' Gaunt tilted his head forward in question.

'For my neighbour's little…' he waved his hand in a circular motion and sat at his dressing mirror, pleased that his face had regained the look of health '…soirée. Surely you have my clothes ready.' Keeping his eyes on the mirror, Edge asked. 'You *do* have my clothing ready. You have not forgotten?'

'Um, yes, Your Grace. Of course.' Gaunt stepped away, feet brisk.

Edgeworth didn't move. In one brief moment, he'd seen Gaunt's eyes reflected in the mirror. Even as he answered with the usual unruffled respect, the valet's eyes had briefly looked heavenward. Exasperated.

Edgeworth stared at the looking glass. Gaunt had been Edgeworth's only valet—ever. And the servant never forgot a— Edgeworth thought back. He'd not told Gaunt of the soirée. No. He had no memory of mentioning it. He'd been busy catching up with all the duties that had fallen by the wayside while he recovered and he'd been planning his proposal. But it didn't matter. Gaunt was always prepared.

When Gaunt returned, he had the same stoic expression as always—except for the few moments before when he'd not known himself observed. Now Gaunt whipped things about just as if he'd been told earlier of their need. Warm water appeared. Clothes were readied. Shaving was quickly accomplished, with the little splash of the scent which Gaunt said was nasturtiums and Edgeworth suspected was merely an ordinary shaving soap put in an expensive container.

Edgeworth gave a final perusal of himself, though he knew the valet would have alerted him to any flaw.

'I can't believe you forgot the soirée,' Edge said. 'Nor can I.'

No flicker of irritation. Perhaps Gaunt did think he'd forgotten.

Edge took the comb and did another run through his hair, then set the comb on the edge of the tabletop, absently letting it fall to the floor. When he stood, he picked up the dry cloth on the table, brushed it at his cheek, wadded it into a ball and tossed it over the soap pot. On the way out, he glanced at Gaunt's expression. Calmness rested in his eyes.

The Duke paused outside the door, shutting it, but then he stopped and opened it quietly. Gaunt retrieved the comb, putting it in the spot it belonged. Then retrieved the flannel and his cheeks puffed. He wrung the cloth once, and then again, and again, as if it were—perhaps, a neck. Then he precisely smoothed it before returning it to the exact spot Edge preferred.

Pulling the door softly shut behind him, Edgeworth paused. The towel had not been wet, but if it had been his neck, he wouldn't be going to the soirée.

Lily walked to Abigail's room and peered in. Her sister had the face of her mother, a perfect heart shape, and her father's fair colouring and blonde hair.

Lily supposed her colouring came from her true father. At the one time she'd seen the blacksmith, she'd not been aware that men could pass their resemblance on to their children. She was thankful for that.

Her mother had jerked Lily's hand forward, pulling her into the invisible wall of heat and charred odours which separated the shop from the alive world. A blacksmith had appeared, standing like a gruff ogre at a fire where his next meal could be roasted—or a fire where a little girl who'd stepped too near could be tossed.

His eyes couldn't have been gleaming red-hot—he was human—but in her memory he'd had red eyes, blocks of huge teeth and his wet hair had spiked down the sides of his face into points.

When the stories in the newspaper were published about her birth and she fully considered what that really meant, she'd shuddered. Fortune had plucked her into a princess world where even her maid hummed. Being illegitimate wasn't nearly so bad as the thought of how different life would have been with the man whose walls hung dark with long pinchers.

She'd only had the one nightmare where he'd grabbed her with the pinchers and tossed her into the flames, laughing and telling her she didn't belong in the rich man's world. She belonged in the coals.

Now, Lily appraised her sister, thankful for the brightness Abigail brought into the world.

'You look like a princess.' Lily leaned around the doorway.

'I feel like one, too.'

Lily smiled and left, moving down the stairs to the ballroom. Tonight, instead of frowning at any man who stood too close to Abigail, she would smile and step into the shadows.

She took a breath before she walked into the ballroom, the scent of the specially ordered candles wafting through the air. She fluffed out the capped sleeves of her gown. The dress was three Seasons old, but the embroidery on the bodice and hem had taken a seamstress months and months to complete.

She paused when she took in the broad shoulders and firm stance of Edgeworth. The man to the left was taller. The one to the right had a merry face and narrow frame. Edgeworth was not above average in height and features, except for his shoulders and eyes.

Everyone noticed him, even if the ladies were cautious about it. No one wanted to anger Edgeworth. Even her. Usually.

But she had once borrowed his book when he'd left it outside on the bench. She'd known he was returning for it. She'd known—and she'd darted upstairs, nearly biting her tongue in half when she'd stumbled on the steps, then she'd rushed into Abigail's room to watch the events next door unfold. The hedge around the bench hadn't been so big then and she'd stood at the window, waiting.

He'd returned and stared at the empty spot.

Then he'd looked up. She'd held the book against the glass.

Edgeworth had pointed to the bench and she'd seen the set of his shoulders.

He'd moved one step in her direction. He'd waggled a finger. He wasn't smiling as she'd thought he might. One hand was at his side and clenched.

She'd put the book down because she couldn't manage a book the size of a chair seat and the window at the same time.

She'd pulled open the window, lifted the book and then held the volume in both hands and released it flat. Then she'd jumped back inside, shut the window and stepped from sight.

The rest of the day she'd expected to be summoned for punishment, but no one had mentioned it. Her father would never have forgiven her. A common girl did not irritate a duke's son.

And then he'd left that second book out and she'd taken it, knowing he left it for her. She'd laughed when she'd seen the title. She'd never read it, but still, she'd placed it in her father's library and it had made her smile when she walked by and thought of him leaving it for her to find.

She'd intended to tell him later that she'd burned it, but she'd forgotten about mentioning it the next time she saw him. She'd been too excited, telling him that her mother had decided to leave London. She'd not be pulled back and forth between her two parents' homes any longer. She and Abigail would stay behind.

She wondered why she noticed so much of Edgeworth. She always had. But she supposed it was just because she'd known him her whole life.

Now, he glanced around the room at the soirée and his eyes didn't stop on her. They didn't even pause. Her stomach jolted. She knew, without any doubt, that even though he'd not looked at her, he'd seen her. He'd seen her just as clearly as he had on the day he'd glared up and into the window, staring because she'd taken his book.

His eyes reminded her of the story of the man who captured the sun's rays and reflected them on to boats to light them afire—only Edgeworth's flares were blue. It was mesmerising, the way he used them, almost like a knight might flash a sword tip in a certain direction, ready to slice someone in two.

Pretending not to be aware of him, she moved to the lemonade table. She kept her back to the men so she would not be tempted to watch Edgeworth. Music from the quartet drifted over her, and she smiled. The night would be perfect for Abigail.

'Miss Hightower.' She could not help herself from turning towards the words right behind her shoulder and the voice she instantly recognised. The voice sounded in direct opposition to his eyes. Perhaps, she thought, that was what made him fascinate her. Cool eyes. Warm voice, at least some of the time.

He reached around her, keeping his balance and not touching her, and lifted a glass to her hand.

'Thank you,' she said, tone low and attention safely on the lemonade. She looked up for a brief second, taking care not to linger.

He reached out, touching her elbow. 'Would you like to dance?'

'No.' She looked at her feet and admitted, 'My slippers pinch.' But something was different. Something about him, and she couldn't figure out what. Dancing with him—it almost seemed too close. Not that it ever had before. And he'd not asked her sister to dance first, she was certain of that.

'You shouldn't wear something painful,' he said, looking in the direction of her feet.

'That's part of why I detest these events.' She stopped suddenly. 'I don't detest them, I didn't mean that.' She did. An interloper. One step above a governess—only she knew some of the governesses had a better lineage than she did. One had once told her that. A pang of guilt burned in Lily's stomach. She'd not so innocently told her mother what the woman had said and the woman had been sent on her way.

Now Lily held her chin level. 'You look like your old self—frowning from ear to ear.'

A grin did flash, but he quickly hid it. 'I don't think one *can* frown from ear to ear.'

'Oh, goodness,' she said, blinking awe into her eyes. 'You manage it regularly.'

'Thank you, Miss Hightower. Your presence makes me capable of things I didn't know possible. Such as my earlier recovery. I wanted to tell you that I remembered your visit to me when I was ill. I suspect I had so much laudanum in me I hardly knew what was real or imagined.'

'I had little choice but to visit you,' she said, a smile added. 'Your mother was pacing outside, weeping, certain you weren't going to make it. The temperature had turned back to winter and rain had started. I begged your mother to let me see you so I could get her out of the weather.'

'Thank you.'

'I may have been worried about you a hair. Just a hair.' She smiled again.

'As you had me planned for Abigail's husband.' His eyes iced over.

'Not just that—and you know it. I've known you and your family all my life.'

'Would you have been so concerned if it were my brother Andrew, or Steven, ill?'

'Of course—' she insisted. His eyes narrowed. 'Of course,' she added, speaking straight into the ice. But she softened her words with an upturn to her voice. 'But they never caused me to be scarred for life. Growled at me. Or tried to convince me that unicorns did not exist.'

'Fine. You win. The drawing you showed me did prove that unicorns are real and I hope you have finally saved enough to purchase one.'

'I bought a doll instead.'

'I did ask to see the unicorn when you purchased it.' His shoulders turned to her.

She lowered her chin. 'Even then, I was not fooled by your sincerity.'

The silence in the air between them was filled with shared memories of childhood.

'Well, I do thank you for visiting me while I was ill,' he spoke softly. 'It meant a lot.'

'Someone needed to make you mind your manners,' she said.

'What?' He raised his brows.

'When you were ill and Fox said that dreadful thing and—you—really shouldn't have done that, you know.'

He shook his head, not following her meaning.

She looked over his shoulder and stared into space. 'That gesture. The bad one.'

'Ah…' He shrugged. 'I apologise. I was out of my head from the pain and the medicine and I didn't realise you were there. Fox and my brothers and I don't always speak gently to each other.'

She shook her head and censured him with her stare. 'Your mother had stopped in the doorway. I had to make sure she didn't see it.' She leaned closer. 'And then you were whispering that very bad word.'

'I didn't whisper anything.'

'You did.' She locked on to his gaze. 'I had to speak to cover your words and get you quiet.'

She examined his face when she spoke to him, because he certainly wouldn't say what he thought, and if not for the little—well—spasms of emotion that she could imagine, she wouldn't have any idea what he might be thinking. His words didn't give much away.

But he had been quite the different person when he was ill. In those moments she'd sat at his bedside, he'd needed her. She'd known it. She'd known he wouldn't have wanted her sister—or any other woman—to see him sweating and restless, but he didn't mind her being there at all. 'You squeezed my hand and called me an angel,' she said. 'That's the nicest thing you've ever said to me.' She leaned in. 'And you had to be *out of your head* to do it.'

He didn't respond. Not even with his eyes.

'What are you thinking?' she asked.

'That honesty is refreshing.'

'Isn't everyone honest to you? Mostly?'

'If their opinion is what they think I wish to hear.'

'Don't let it concern you. Most people are like that.'

'It does concern me. Most people won't say what they're thinking to me and it seems your words are a reflection of what you truly believe. Not just what is the more correct thing to say to a duke.'

'Are you wishing you were born a second son?' She asked the question aloud the moment she thought it.

He examined her face. 'No. Not at all. I was born to be who I am. As we all are.'

Lily heard laughter break out at the other side of the room. She turned, forcing her attention from Edgeworth, but not truly noticing the others.

Lily wasn't meant to be who she was. It was just her good fortune *not* to be living in a home with a fiery pit. 'One would say your mother was born to be a duchess, too.'

'Yes,' he said. 'One could say the same of you.'

She gulped in air and moved so that she held her glass with both hands for a second. 'No. One couldn't.' Her heart warmed at his politeness. Edgeworth knew his manners.

'Don't disagree when I'm right,' he said. 'It's true.'

Music filled the air and Edgeworth watched her as if she should say something profound, but all she could manage was a pinched-sounding mumble of thanks.

'Greetings, all.' Fox appeared behind Edgeworth, popping into the conversation like a marionette might drop on to the stage to scatter the other puppets.

'Edgeworth dragged me from the country so that I might attend this evening, but when I realised that I would be seeing the two Hightower sisters, I thanked him most utterly and profusely—even though one of them...' he tilted his chin to the ceiling, batted his eyes and looked as if he might whistle '...may once have compared me to a piece of very important pottery.' He smiled. 'I tried to steal a kiss and you told me you'd prefer to kiss a chamber pot.'

'I meant it as a gentle reprimand,' Lily said.

'It was.' He chuckled and put a hand to his ear. 'Is that music I hear?' He held out his arm for her to clasp. 'Dance with me, please, I beg you, so that I might apologise for being so ungallant in the past.'

'You are not here to impress Miss Lily,' Edgeworth said.

Foxworthy's jaw dropped, but his eyes sparkled. 'I thought for certain I was here to impress every woman in attendance. I'm crushed.' He winked at Lily. 'So even if I cannot sway you to swoon with admiration, will you please do me the honour of dancing with me?'

Edgeworth's eyes narrowed and his jaw tensed.

Quickly, she returned her glass to the table and accepted the request, feeling the men must be separated immediately.

She glared at Fox and hurried to the dance floor.

Even with her back to him, her mind's eye could see Edgeworth watching her. Prickles of warmth flared. But he needn't have worried. Foxworthy was all nonsense. He liked a certain type of woman and she wasn't it. That she knew.

Fox turned to her, pulling her into his orbit with a half-hidden smile. He moved into the dance so quickly she had to pay attention.

'Edgeworth is watching us.' Fox leaned close and practically stumbled over her, but she was certain he was an excellent dancer. The cad. She hated to dance and it was hard enough for her to keep up with the steps without having a partner who purposefully stumbled.

His head turned and at that moment his eyes changed. 'Your sister just walked into the room.'

'She tends to do that.'

'I had not realised how long it's been since I've seen her,' he said, eyes locked on Abigail.

'She's not for you.'

'Really?' She had his full attention. His brows moved so that a little crease formed in the middle between them.

'She is only interested in men who have the most honourable intentions.'

'My intentions are honourable. Always honourable intentions,' he said.

She didn't answer. Honourable intentions written in air.

'Miss Hightower. You're starting to look at me the same way Edge does. Are there any sharp objects about that I should hide?'

'If we look irritated at you, it's for good reason and you know it. You are a disaster waiting to happen.'

Nodding, Foxworthy said, 'I've tried to keep my life amusing, unlike Edgeworth. He's just like his father. I can still hear my uncle saying to Edge, *"You are a duke first, you are a duke second and you are a duke third, and whatever of you that is left over after that is also a duke."'*

'That's Edgeworth.'

'Yes. And I see him being just like the old Duke. He'll settle into married life some day, because he does his duty. He will have his duchess. The perfect family. And then some years hence, he'll discover he's a man as well. Then you know what will happen. Just like his father.' Fox shut his eyes for half a second and shook his head in the way of a sage.

His words jarred her insides. The recollection of the old Duke looking over his nose at her ignited memories she'd rather forget.

'I want to experience life while I am young and get all the adventures I need out of my system.' Fox swirled her around. 'When I marry I will happily rot away, blissfully, in the arms of my beloved.'

He caught her eye, giving her another wink. 'Just wanted to reassure you.'

'Foxworthy.' She snapped out his name. 'You cannot possibly reassure me. You're constantly in that half-rate newspaper that scandalmongers delight in.'

'I've only been in it fourteen times and I count the Beany Beaumont incident even if I wasn't mentioned by name.'

'You are terrible.'

'I am not.' He glanced towards his feet. 'I've missed only one step and it brought me closer to you. So how can I be upset with myself?'

'Foxworthy. You wish people to talk of your missteps. You are a rake to the core.'

'But beyond that, I'm pure gold.' They turned around the room again. 'Admit it, you find me quite charming.'

'I would not exactly say that. I would say you have the very minimal charm necessary for a dance partner.'

'Ouch,' he said, and the dance ended without any more banter, but at least a dozen smiles from

Foxworthy. He did have a rather elegant way of looking into a woman's eyes, but it made Lily feel as if he expected her to swoon over him. She would be pleased when she could retire to her room, but she wasn't leaving Abigail alone with only their father and aunt for chaperons.

She didn't think it coincidence that Fox managed to stop them near Edgeworth.

'Miss Hightower has commented quite directly on my charm as we danced,' he said to Edge. 'I fear it has quite gone to my head. Near smacked me across the temples, in fact. But—' He spoke as he released her hand. 'She was quite the most wonderful partner and a treat to listen to.' He looked deep into her eyes. 'Thank you. I will never, ever forget these moments with you.'

Then his eyes turned to Abigail and he clasped his hands flat over his heart. 'Another Miss Hightower. How fortunate we are to have two in our presence. Please do me the honour of a dance.'

Abigail rose on tiptoes and proved women could not fly or she would have fluttered off the floor at that moment. 'I would be honoured, Lord Foxworthy.'

He swirled her away.

'Stop staring after him,' Edge said. 'He's full enough of himself as it is.'

'I don't like him dancing so close with Abigail.'

'It's not close.'

'He's looking at her much too lingeringly.' She turned to Edge. 'Are you going to let him get away with it?'

He didn't move, but she heard a snort of air from his nostrils. 'I insisted he accept the invitation for that very purpose.'

Her eyes widened. This wasn't the same Edgeworth she'd known her whole life.

He took her by the arm and led them from the music and back to the refreshments. He bent his head low so his voice wouldn't carry. 'When you told me that everyone believed I'm interested in your sister, I made sure Fox knew it wasn't true and insisted he attend to change the perception.'

She stopped, mouth gaping, and reached for a glass. 'You can't be serious? Foxworthy?'

He nodded.

'But you've always…I've heard the rumours—that you warned men to—'

'To take care around the Hightower sisters.'

'Around Abigail.'

'Lily and the sister she watches over.'

'Because we're neighbours. Because Abigail and I often were next door.' She put the lemonade to her lips.

'Certainly,' he said. 'And because I didn't want another man near you.'

She spewed droplets of lemonade over his coat.

She coughed, her hand over her mouth, choked. She followed with another sip to keep herself from coughing again. 'My apologies,' she croaked out.

'Not a problem.' He pulled out a handkerchief and offered it in her direction. She shook her head. He dusted off the front of his coat while he studied her.

'Could you repeat that?' she asked.

One musician began a softer tune and the other players joined in as background, the evening slowing down. On her right, a group of older gentlemen discussed the Chancery Court's recent decision deciding the guardianship of a child.

Edgeworth led her to the other side, almost behind where the musicians were, and used them as a buffer to keep the conversation quiet.

Lily looked at him. Gauging Edgeworth's thoughts in bright light wasn't easy and in the muted shadows she could see only the barest amount and had to rely on his voice. He examined her just as closely.

'I realised you haven't always known,' he said. 'Our understanding. I thought you did. I thought you would have told me, nicely, if you'd not agreed, so I accepted that we both thought the same.'

'Known? Understanding?' She spoke rapidly. 'I knew you—were going to court Abigail and I had to make certain she never stepped one foot wrong. You seemed to pay attention—'

'You were always together. I couldn't see you without seeing her.'

'Me?' She tilted her head to the side.

He looked at her, his eyes narrowing. 'Yes. Of course.'

'You know how different Abigail and I are. She's like lace and I'm more—' she couldn't think of a word that wouldn't be insulting to herself '—practical.'

'Practical. Sensible. It's all the same.'

'I'm...' She couldn't say the words.

All eyes watched a duchess. Her events were well attended and filled with lace-like people. A duchess would think nothing of meeting someone in the royal family. Other peers. Lots of people. People who couldn't help sharing little whispers.

She crossed her arms over herself. He'd never understand. 'Why did you wait so long to tell me?' she asked.

'We talked about it.'

'No.' The word whooshed from her lips. 'I would have remembered that. I know I would have.'

'Well, maybe I didn't say the exact words, but I could tell you are fond of me. You always spoke so honestly to me.'

'I speak honestly to everyone.' She leaned forward so he could not miss the emphasis in her words.

'No, you don't. I've watched. You're very kind, nice, and—' he moved so they stood at a slant to each other, mostly facing the room and shoulders aligned '—the most polite Miss Lily Hightower. With me, you're different. You told me when my voice squeaked like a carriage wheel and asked if I could please do it again.'

'I didn't know boy's voices did that.' She took in a breath and looked away. 'You could have explained it wasn't a new skill. I thought it fascinating. And the look on your face that day didn't convince me you were fond of me in any way.'

'I wasn't. At that moment.' His shoulders bumped just a bit. 'I thought my voice would stay that way for ever.'

Their eyes caught in memory.

She had to speak, to put words in the air between them and make the world seem normal again. 'What if I had courted someone else?'

'I would have swooped in like a hawk.'

'It would have been too late.'

'That's what I mean about your honesty,' he said. 'And it wouldn't have been too late.'

'And you have quite the opinion of yourself.'

'I was taught I should,' he said. 'And so should you. Have a high opinion of yourself.'

Her teeth tightened against each other. She couldn't keep her lips from forming a straight line.

Small muscles in his face tensed, making a statement of disagreement without speaking. 'We've known each other since childhood.' One shoulder moved in the closest he would ever get to a shrug. 'I thought you were keeping yourself hidden away...well, because you were waiting for me.'

'No. I wasn't.' She shook her head. 'I was just—
living. Next door.'

His lids shuttered his eyes, but then he looked
at her—the first whimsy she'd ever seen on his
face. His eyes weren't cold. Her toes squeezed
into her slippers and somehow her legs kept from
melting away.

'Apparently, when I err it's on a grand scale,'
he said.

'We've been friends for a long time, true. And
you're a lot like your…family.' She thought of
his father.

'It's a good life,' he said. 'I've known you since
I was six. Or something around that age. Why
shouldn't you be my duchess?'

He knew full well why. Just as everybody else
did.

'Is this a proposal?' she asked. 'Not a jest—not
a jest like when I took your book and you left the
volume of manners out for me to see.'

He moved closer. 'I knew you'd see the note.'

'There was a note?' Her voice rose.

'Yes.' He nodded.

'What did it say?'

'That you would need this for when you became a duchess.'

* * *

Edge watched her. 'Lily. Breathe.' She acted as if he'd told her he'd not marry her if she were the last woman alive.

Her lips moved. 'I have other plans.'

'What other plans?' He leaned in.

'I don't know.'

The first time he remembered seeing her she'd asked if he could growl. She'd walked to the bench on his parent's property, holding a biscuit in each hand.

And in his confidence at being the heir and needing to do whatever he must, he said, 'Of course. I can do almost anything.'

'Growl, then.'

'No.' He'd frowned. 'I'm studying.'

'Lord Lion can't growl. And you can't fly. You can't do most anything. You only read.'

'Lord Lionel,' he'd corrected her.

She'd paused, studying his face as if she didn't hear correctly. 'Lord Lion-owl. Lions growl. Owls fly. You don't do either. I've watched.'

'Lord Lionel,' he'd insisted.

She'd looked him over. Frowned. 'If you growl, Lord Lion Owl, you can have a biscuit. They're good ones. Cook makes them just for me.'

He'd held out his hand, but she'd stepped back, shaking her head.

He'd growled. She'd thrown the biscuit at him whilst sticking her tongue out. He'd caught it with one hand and growled again. She'd turned, running to her house, laughing.

That biscuit had tasted like orange cake.

Chapter Three

Lily stared. Edgeworth didn't look down his aristocratic nose at people—she was certain of that. But when one looked at the sky and saw one layer of wisped clouds floating lower, and then a second tier floating above the first, Edgeworth was the most distant level. He floated on the top tier.

'No,' she said, remembering her manners and then adding, 'but thank you so much. I'm so honoured to be asked. And it is a great compliment. I will cherish this moment.' She paused. 'For ever.'

His eyes still blared blue at her. And he did seem to be looking down his nose a bit, after all.

'I said thank you,' she whispered. All eyes would be on her as a duchess. And while she didn't take the responsibility for anything her mother had done, she couldn't bear the whispers about her being above herself.

He didn't move when he heard her answer. 'You said *"No, thank you".* One word too many.'

'Perhaps you could clasp your hands over your heart,' she said, 'and act as if an arrow pierced you deeply because I didn't respond with a yes.'

'I am deeply wounded.'

She lowered her chin. 'I believe so,' she said. 'I believe the shock has rendered you unable to show the deep grief you're feeling.'

'Exactly.'

She shuddered a half-shake in disagreement. 'Why do you consider me for a duchess?'

'If you'd said yes, I'd be inclined to tell you.'

'You're making a mistake. I'm—'

His lips firmed and he gave the slightest shake of his head. 'You're not a mistake.'

All the other sounds of the soirée faded away while she listened with her whole being for his response. The insides of her stomach bounced against each other, waiting. 'Explain.'

She could see it in his eyes. Few people insisted he speak when he didn't want to. He stared at her, but it wasn't the knife-cutting stare of his father, nor the biting glare of condemning eyes.

He seemed to be pulling the thoughts from inside himself, having trouble putting his feelings into the air.

'I know you.' Each word hit the air alone. 'I was at university and I thought of you and your sister's laughter, and I studied hard so that when I took my seat in the House of Lords I could do the country well for people like you.'

'Because of laughter?' She could hear the squeaking wheel in her own voice.

He bent his head towards her. 'Miss Hightower, never underestimate the sound of innocent laughter.'

She leaned forward. 'I wouldn't have ever assumed it worth a marriage proposal.'

'I did not propose,' he said. 'I merely discussed it with you.'

'Well, that is totally a horse of a different colour.'

'Not vastly different, I suppose.'

'Not vastly.' She spoke in the same tone, but with a smile at the end. 'And had I heard your laughter in the past, I suppose the answer might have been different.' Not true. But she felt guilt for refusing him and interrupting his plans. He planned so carefully.

He didn't speak.

'How long has it been since you've laughed?' she asked.

'No one can easily answer that question.'

'It's harder for you than for other people, I would imagine.'

'I never thought such a simple enquiry would lead to such a long conversation.'

'Your Grace, you might do well to expect a lot of talk to accompany a marriage proposal, years and years of it, and it shouldn't all be one-sided.'

'I try not to clutter the air with unnecessary prattle.' His brows moved. 'You've never once before called me "Your Grace".'

'I'm sure I have,' she said.

'I'm sure you have not. A discussion of marriage shouldn't distance us.'

'It hasn't, Edgeworth.'

'You don't call me that often. You call me Lord Lionel, or Edge—as my brothers do.' His eyes were walled. 'And not long before my accident, you called me Edgy, which served its purpose and took days to forgive. I usually have no reason to forgive anyone.' He stood like a pillar beside her.

'That was childish of me. Please forget I said it.'

With the barest of forward movement, he leaned in closer to her face. He'd not really needed to. No one could possibly hear his voice but her.

'I do have a question. Something I've wondered for years,' he said.

She waited.

'What is a booby-head?'

She squinted and leaned towards him. 'What? What is a—?' She could not fathom what he was thinking.

'Never mind. I suppose I know.' She heard a smile in his voice and this time she was included but she didn't know why. 'I think it best to forget the question.'

His eyes showed nothing. No humour. No irritation. Just the calm demeanour of a man who might as well have been alone.

If she could change one thing in her life, it would have been the moment she told the newspaper man about his father's illegitimate child. Edgeworth must never find out she was the one who told. He'd never forgive her.

He left, leaving her with a polite manner groomed from centuries, and she felt as if she had been jilted at the altar.

* * *

Her sister dashed into the room without knocking. 'Did you notice Foxworthy must have looked into my eyes for a full minute, when our dance stopped?' Abigail sat on the bed, depressing the mattress. 'I suppose it could have been longer. What do you think?'

'It was a night to remember.' She couldn't recall much about Abigail's actions at the soirée. Different memories lodged in her, creating a pleasant and unpleasant feeling mixed deep inside.

Her sister waved a hand. 'Lord Foxworthy... Really, did you notice how he looked at me? And after our dance we stole away to the library and he kissed me.' She shivered. 'That lasted much longer than a mere five seconds.'

'You do not need to tell me all the gory details,' Lily muttered. 'And you are not to be alone with Fenton Foxworthy.'

Abigail sighed. 'Isn't Fenton the most elegant name?'

'No more elegant than, I don't know, Lionel.'

Abigail grimaced. Then she spoke softly. 'He looked deep into my eyes. Deep. Something happened. It could have been love. On his part.'

Lily snorted. 'Don't fall in love with him. He

has had so many women's names linked with his it would be easier to count the few he hasn't romanced.'

'Love.' Abigail smiled and her eyes lost focus. 'I could not say *I* am entirely in love. But enough. Just deliciously in *like*.'

She whooshed up from the bed and her gaze locked on Lily. 'I hope you're not jealous of my friendship,' Abigail said. 'I noticed you standing very close to him.'

Lily's heart thumped an extra beat. The Duke's face moved through her thoughts.

Abigail's face peered close. 'Yes. What *were* you and Foxworthy talking about?'

Lily glanced at her sister, then answered, 'Foxworthy?'

Abigail chuckled. 'That was much more pleasant than when you spoke with the Duke. It is a good thing your faces didn't get stuck that way.' She moved to the door. 'On the other hand, if Foxworthy's face had locked for ever when he looked at me…' She took in a deep breath and didn't complete the sentence.

'It's time for breakfast,' Abigail said. 'Father's

already at the table and probably finished eating by now.'

Abigail left and Lily rushed through her morning ablutions.

By the time she stood at the table, her father was lost in his paper. Abigail sat on his left side, hardly touching her food, her fork designing shapes in the jam. 'Fox seemed to think the Duke is truly not interested in me,' Abigail said.

Lily slid into her seat. 'I received the same conclusion.'

Their father lowered his paper, but didn't speak.

'Fox says I am too lovely and too vivacious to waste my time on his stuffy cousin.'

'Nonsense. He's a duke,' her father said. 'He is not a waste of your time.'

'Perhaps we misunderstood His Grace all these years,' Lily said.

'Couldn't have,' her father said. 'I saw the book.'

'What book?' Abigail asked.

'The deportment one. The one Abigail put in the library.'

'I put it there, Father,' Lily said.

'What were you doing with Abigail's book?'

'Book?' Abigail's voice challenged.

'Edgeworth gave me a book on deportment.' Lily shrugged the words away.

'He did?' Her sister's head snapped around to Lily and her eyes widened. 'You never told me.'

'The note...' Her father studied her. 'It was for you, Lily?'

'I never put any note in a book.' Abigail's nose wrinkled. 'What did it say?'

'Something about you becoming a duchess,' he answered.

'Oh,' Abigail put her hand over her mouth. 'Oh.' She looked at Lily and then at her father. Her eyes gleamed with laughter. 'Lily. Lily's note.' She jumped to her feet and leaned over the table. 'Father.' She stretched her arm and pointed her finger almost into Lily's face. Lily batted it away. 'It was hers.' She laughed. 'The Duke. They were whispering in the corner. Foxworthy was trying to distract me and tell me how beautiful I was—right out of the blue. We all know that's true, but Foxworthy kept saying all his normal balderdash, and all the while Lily and the Duke were nose to nose in the corner. You didn't notice?'

'They've always—' He stopped, irritation fading. He tapped his fingertips together, staring at Lily. 'It was your note.'

'A jest,' she said.

'Well…' He stood and perused both his daughters. 'This may change plans for the two of you. But it doesn't really change mine. I want your fortunes to increase with marriage.' He rested a hand on the back of a chair. 'Remember, money can't buy happiness, but a rich person who is miserable has to work at it.'

He turned. 'I want Edgeworth for a son-in-law. I don't care how the two of you sort it out.'

Lily watched him leave the room.

'So…' Abigail swooped, laughing. 'You are all set to steal my beau.'

'No.' She shook her head, wishing Abigail would stand still enough to swat. 'Edgeworth has—had a misunderstanding.' She couldn't have so much attention on her. People would sneer. *The blacksmith's daughter who married a duke.*

'Well, I should be upset that he prefers you over me, but I'm really rather relieved. Particularly since I prefer almost everyone over him.' Abigail grimaced. 'Edgeworth is a little—I mean, he acts ancient. I prefer someone more lively.'

'He's just serious.'

'Yes. He is,' Abigail said, leaving. 'Too serious. Just like you.' She tapped her finger against her lips. 'I never noticed that before.' She turned, her dignity leaving as she called out, 'Father. Is the note to Lily still there?' Her voice rose. 'I must see it.'

Lily clamped her teeth together. Abigail could look all she wanted. The book was now hidden under Lily's bed and the note had been folded into a bookmark and now resided in a recipe book.

Standing behind the open curtains in Abigail's room, she watched for the Duke to step out of his house. The nightly jaunt into the gardens had been a tradition of sorts. His father used to walk out in the evenings and smoke occasionally—and always when Edge was home from his studies. She'd eavesdropped several times, impressed with his father speaking so much. But after a few nights, she'd lost all interest in what a duke should do and how he should do it.

When Edge was injured, she'd known he was very ill, because his forays into the garden had completely stopped. Not once in eleven days had he stepped out.

Now, she waited.

Finally, a lone figure moved into sight. If she'd

not been watching for movement, she wouldn't have seen him in the fading light. He stood, eyes taking in the night. He'd been named well. She'd never seen a lion at night, just the one in the menagerie, but it hadn't seemed to care who watched it, or what they thought, because it had a powerful build and the force of generations of strength bred into it.

She took a wrap from the dressing chamber and put it around her shoulders, and sat a bonnet on her head, leaving the blue ribbons to flutter.

A flash of memory caused her feet to slow and a pang of guilt to hit her midsection. She'd lived so carefully, avoiding every opportunity to be like her mother.

Before stepping outside, she gave an extra tap to hold her bonnet in place. She paused when the fresh air hit her face. But it was dark enough no one would see her.

She'd had to wait until the sun set because otherwise when she moved forward, she would be in view of all the windows, and it simply could not appear she was engaging in anything of questionable nature. She'd been fortunate with the mourning attire, but one servant had seen her returning to the house and met her with a broom, concerned a stranger was lurking about.

She'd explained that the sun had given her a headache and she'd wanted to shield her face, and she'd donned the darker clothing. That had caused a furrowed brow, but hadn't been questioned.

If she said she'd suddenly taken an interest in horticulture at night time no one would believe it.

She could not let anyone think she was like her mother, particularly Edgeworth.

Not one word had been mentioned in print about Lily's family in such a long time and she didn't want it to change. The words didn't seem to stick to the people who'd been generations in London, but it landed on her family like the stench in the streets everyone stepped around and it lingered. Everyone thought her father had bought his way into society and, in a sense, he had.

She took in a breath and moved away from the house. Perhaps she was like her mother.

Her footsteps didn't make noise in the dew-dampened grass. She forced herself to slow, the wafting honeysuckle perfume of the night sur-

rounding her. When her eyes locked on Edgeworth, she could have been the predator.

When he saw her, his shoulders turned while he
pulled in a normal intake of breath with the same
fluidity. With that movement, their positions re-
versed. She couldn't even see into his eyes, but
still he mastered the space.

She curtsied, but didn't lower her head. The
bench, hidden in the daylight by the semi-circle
of hedge around it, was at her left. Edge had sat
there so many times with his books.

Even though she couldn't see it until she stood
near, she moved directly to it and sat.

He walked to her as if he'd invited her into the
garden and had been waiting.

She saw not a man, but a monument to one,
carved like the figures that jutted from the towers
of some castles to warn intruders. She wanted to
tap at the stone, study it, look for divots caused
by weather or age, and see how the shape had
been formed.

The thought flitted through her mind that if she
didn't speak, he wouldn't. The ability to outlast
another person had been bred into him, perhaps
from some warrior grandfather of his.

But she could tell this wasn't a contest to see

who could outlast the other. He merely waited for her.

'You have to discourage Fox from my sister,' she spoke quietly. 'Now she's enlisted Father in her plans for marriage.'

'He should take part in his daughters' futures.'

'He never did particularly before. But now it's as if he's thought of it as business and he's taking it as seriously as if it's something on a ledger sheet.'

'Has my name been put into the accounting?' he asked.

'Of course. But now he knows you're not interested in Abigail.'

'What did he say about your prospects?'

'That,' she said, 'is immaterial, as I do not have a list for such a thing.'

His breathing tightened. 'It's nature to want a person in your life who thinks you above all others and you think above all others. Selfish, perhaps. But nature.'

She ground her teeth against each other and the moment was so silent she could hear the sound from inside her head. 'If people followed their nature—'

'Most people do.'

This time she didn't mind the long silence. His words remained in her thoughts. 'Do you?'

He could have given a soliloquy in the space before he answered, 'My nature is precise. Planned.'

'Methodical?'

The silence fluttered around them again.

'Your Grace.' She spoke more softly, taking the bite out of her words.

'Miss Lily.' His voice, little more than a whisper, rumbled into the night and had no sting in the words. 'Speak as you wish. You always have. To me.'

She stood. 'I don't particularly care what your cousin does. But I do care if my sister is hurt.' She moved closer—which would have been improperly close in the daylight, but she needed to see his eyes.

She raised her arm, keeping it close to her body so she wouldn't nudge him and clicked a fingernail against her incisor. 'Did you notice he has white teeth?' The wind fluttered her bonnet and she grasped the untied ribbons with her other hand, holding both in one grasp.

'Teeth?' He narrowed his eyes, questioning. 'I don't care about Foxworthy's teeth and that isn't a concern of mine at all.'

'My sister noticed. She thinks he has the love-liest mouth she has ever seen.'

'His teeth are just teeth. He's lucky someone hasn't removed them for him.'

'That would devastate my sister.' She sighed. 'She notes every little detail about him.'

'Fox encourages such nonsense.'

Her brows rose and her chin tilted down, and her lips turned up the merest amount. 'I asked her about you.' Again she watched for the divot or a clue to show inside the immovable stone.

He leaned his head forward, but she sensed only a mild curiosity about her sister's opinions. In fact, Lily felt he studied her report of her sister's talk to judge her view of it, not to form an opinion of Abigail. 'She thought you have nice teeth, too, but she wasn't certain.'

Brows flicked the words away. 'Nice enough.'

She could sense he found the moment humorous, but she couldn't see a smile.

'And I asked her about your hair since she noticed Foxworthy's hair turns up in darling little curls when it gets wet.' The words tumbled over each other. 'She said she once saw him come in from the rain.'

'So he comes in from the rain. That shows he is more intelligent than I thought.'

'You can't let him near my sister.'

'They would make a good match.'

This time she heard decision. She gasped. 'No.'

'I believe Foxworthy is ready to settle in to marriage. Your sister could keep his attention.'

'*No* one is that enchanting.'

'Marriage will settle him.'

'You're willing to ruin my sister's future.' She wanted her words to jar him, yet he didn't move.

'Underneath it all, Fox is a good sort.'

Edge would just dig those boot heels tighter into the ground if she kept mentioning his cousin's flaws. But she couldn't stop. 'I don't believe that. Underneath his heart, lungs and liver, there's a part lower down that is not virtuous. He's a scoundrel. But I suppose if you are talking about his knees and his toes, he has quite an amount of quality. Those are not the parts which cause trouble.' She grimaced. 'I must correct myself. They are the parts which lead him to trouble as he dances from one woman to the next.'

'He is maturing.'

'And in twenty years he'll surely make some woman the best of husbands. But I'm worried about tomorrow. Before she left to visit my aunt, Abigail said Father has asked you and Fox to our house to discuss an investment. It is a thinly disguised attempt at matchmaking.'

His eyes widened. 'I am so shocked.'

'Sarcasm? Your Grace?'

'I sent my man of affairs over to ask your father if he knew of any business ventures Fox or I might invest in. A simple query.'

'Oh, my.' She put a hand to her cheek. 'You cannot get his hopes up like that. To have a duke and the son of an earl at his home to discuss business.'

'He is very knowledgeable about investments.'

'Yes. And he will be considering a very long-term one for his daughters.'

'What is so wrong with that?'

'It's Abigail I'm concerned about. She's the one interested in marriage.' She levelled a gaze at him. 'And Foxworthy is interested in an entirely different arrangement.'

His face became bland again. He stepped aside, putting a foot on the bench, adding more distance between them, yet not. He leaned her way, one arm on his propped leg and his fingers clasped. Almost subservient. Except, not. A lion taking a step away, yawning, pretending not to see the prey, letting it get closer and closer. 'So tell me. What exactly would it take for you to risk a long-term investment?'

'I don't have to take any risks and see no need to. I am able to live my life as I wish, without upheaval.'

'A life without upheaval might not suit you for ever.'

'Then I will worry about it when that time arrives.'

'I have arrived at that time in my life. As I won't live for ever, I've decided I might wish to marry some day.'

'You only have to say you're a duke.' She increased the distance between them and could tell by the barest flick of his head that he noticed.

'Not worked so far.' His voice fell, fading into nothingness. A low rumble.

She didn't move closer.

'Describe a suitor's best qualities. Knowing them might help me impress someone.'

She caught the emphasis he put on the word someone and the subtle lightness that appeared in his eyes as he looked at her, and her heart beat bird-like. She clasped her skirt in her hand, clenching her fingers on the cloth. 'It would not do you any good to be putting on a pretence while courting a future wife.' She pushed forward, moving close, her body directly aligned with his face. 'You must be true to who you are.'

'I agree.' His words affirmed in a way that said no one should doubt it. 'Tell me about what it would take for a man to interest you as a husband.'

'I have never given it thought because the nature of marriage seems false to me. I have no pressing need to carry on the lineage as you do.'

'It's a shame because you would make a good mother. You watched over your sister so closely.'

'I had no choice.'

'No one would have faulted you for not.'

'But she is my sister and I could do it. I would have faulted myself. And now I fear I can't keep her from that rake Foxworthy and he will break her heart or ruin her.'

'You cannot manage someone's life for them. And they may be good for each other.'

'Will you help keep Foxworthy away from Abigail?' she asked.

'No. It's their lives.'

'But she's my sister and I don't want her

being—' Miserable. Miserable like their mother had been. Separated from her husband and society. Locked in an unhappy marriage.

'Let the romance finish on its own. You can't keep them apart.'

'I thought you would help me.'

'I am. Let it be and Fox will tire of her soon, and if he doesn't then it may be a good match.' He took his foot from the bench.

Edge no longer stood in front of her. His Grace watched her. But it was the Duke she wanted to question. 'Why did you notice me?'

He moved his palm only slightly, indicating her house. 'You live—'

'So does Abigail.'

'So she does.'

She tried to pull every memory of him to the forefront of her mind. 'Do you remember shouting at me?'

'I did not shout.'

'You told me you had to study and for me to play in my garden. Not yours.'

'I had to be top in my studies. I couldn't grasp the Greek language. It was hard to concentrate with you asking me what each word I said meant.'

'I had to go back to my mother's house that day

and my grandmother had been telling me that Mother didn't love us or she would have stayed at the estate. It was a very bad day.' Lily had been almost ten when her mother moved into a nearby house. But the separation was as failed as the marriage in many ways. Her parents hadn't truly been able to stay away from each other until Lily's late teens when they'd had one quiet argument—a courteous one—and something had turned bleak in both their faces.

'I would have been kinder had I known,' he said.

'It wouldn't have mattered. I had to get used to the arguments. My parents could not live together and couldn't live apart. Until, well, you know the story.'

'Yes. I remember. Your mother left town when Sophia's memoirs were published.'

'Just before. They'd been friends, but had a disagreement, and I'm sure Mother knew Sophia would use the book as a chance to get back at her.' She shook her head. 'I didn't know how peaceful a day could be until she finally moved away.'

'You stopped going out so much.'

'I've not been invited—not that it mattered.'

'I meant in the garden. You used to spend hours and hours outside.'

She laughed. 'Part of it was a quiet rebellion. Mother had told me that my skin would blemish in the sun and no one would want to marry me.'

His grumble barely reached her ears. 'I thought you were spending time with me—because you were interested in becoming a duchess.'

'You did make my rebellion more enjoyable.'

'And you made the studies more tolerable.'

'Did you envy others their freedom?'

He shook his head. 'I was fortunate. *With privilege there is responsibility.* My mother said it over and over.'

Another silence surrounded them, but didn't separate. This time, he spoke. 'I was curious, though. To not have a purpose would have been strange and I didn't want that. Everyone's future is mapped for them to some degree, so I didn't rail against my good fortune of having the best of life. But the common life—the *rest of* life is so foreign to me. How can I represent the country well without understanding all of it?'

'So *that* is why you noticed me. My commonness?'

'Lily. Don't put words in my mouth.'

'I want to know what you really think.'

'Then don't jump to conclusions about what I say.'

She let the skirt she still clasped fall from her fingers. 'You have been so trained to be a duke and lived it so long—that I wonder if what you say is what you really feel or what you have been trained to feel?'

'Does it matter?' Each word could stand alone.

'It might some day. If you are deciding on your marriage now because it is what you are supposed to do.'

This time she heard his inward breath, slow and measured. 'On my sickbed, I could hear the voices around me, but I didn't want to speak or even open my eyes. My brother Andrew asked, "Do you think he will die tonight?"

'I heard my brother Steven answer. He said no, I wouldn't die that night.' He continued to face her, but didn't see her. 'I didn't care one way or the other.'

The honeysuckle touched her nose again and this time the sweetness churned her stomach. He'd been so pale and the pupils of his eyes so strange.

'My family gathered around me, but at a distance. My mother would move close, but only for a second. My burns weren't contagious; they all had to know that. They all kept their respectful distance. Respectful. Distance.'

'But they were with you. You could not have wanted them to smother you with closeness.'

'I didn't. But my life felt wasted. All the work I'd done didn't matter.'

'So now you worry about having an heir?' She called him back from his memories.

'No.' The quiet word slashed the air. 'I only want to do the best I can with the time I have left. I was trained to be a duke, so I did precisely as I should. Motions. All the right ones. I still believe in them. But I want more from life.'

'You want a touch of commonness? A wife who has lived on the edge of society, one foot in and one foot out.'

'Is that wrong?'

'It could be if you look around in a few years and discover that you are a duke through and through, and these moments are a reaction because you almost died. Then you might wish for a wife who is completely in society and has the same strength in her bloodlines as you do.'

'I might wish for a wife who'd be willing to

hold my hand when I lay dying and who would miss me.'

'I don't think marriage necessarily provides those things.'

'It should.'

'Yes. But, if anything, marriage seems to move people apart, instead of closer together.'

'My parents had a good marriage—mostly.'

She shook her head, disagreeing. 'You can hire someone to hold your hand and you can live a life so that others miss you. Marriage is tiresome. I understand your need to have heirs. And you should find someone who can stand with you in public and create the world you wish to have around you.'

She stepped back. 'But don't invest your heart in someone. It's too risky and the return on the investment is dismal, from what I've seen.'

Chapter Four

'I saw you return from the garden.' Abigail swooped into Lily's vision when she topped the stairs. A smile glittered in Abigail's eyes. 'You were *talking* with the Duke.' She bounced on her heels. 'What were you speaking about? The date for the wedding?'

Lily's mind almost blanked and she moved past her sister. 'No. We won't wed. Just speaking of things. The past. How he studied so hard. Did you have a good time visiting Father's sister?'

Abigail followed behind. 'No wonder you had to know whether Edgeworth would court me. You have a fascination with him.'

She stepped to the sitting room. 'Well, he is fascinating. But distant. You know how distant he is.' She looked around. 'Wouldn't a cup of tea be good?'

'I do know how he is,' Abigail said, ignoring the suggestion of refreshment. 'That's why I'm relieved he doesn't want me for a duchess. I've always much preferred his cousin. Foxworthy is an adventure. Edgeworth is more like a tutor.'

'It's just Edgeworth's look. He thinks a lot.'

'He's like his father. You know how you said the old Duke always looked at you as if you had breakfast on your face. Edgeworth has the same stare.'

'No. He's not so superior.' He couldn't be if he'd considered asking her to marry him.

'Well, the old Duke might not have been either. Remember the time he had the coachman leave the carriage out so we could play in it.'

Lily nodded. 'It was the first time we'd been back after Mother took us.'

Abigail moved to the sofa. Her reticule lay on it, and two parcels, one opened with gloves scattered about.

Lily paused, thinking back to Edgeworth's face. 'Edgeworth takes *life* seriously. His father took *himself* seriously.'

'The old Duke didn't hate us as much as you thought. The time he realised we were at Mother's when he was meeting his mistress, I thought he was going to choke.' She held her arm out, showing Lily the purchase. Lily nodded absently.

'I don't remember that.'

'You didn't see him. He left as soon as he started breathing again. He just glared at us afterwards because he felt guilty. We knew his secret. Maybe he wanted to intimidate us. He surely didn't like it when the Duchess had us for tea.' She slipped the glove from her hand and threw it with its mate.

'He should have been kind to us.'

'Yes.' She wrinkled her nose. 'But you didn't exactly look well at him once you found out he was not true to the Duchess. You thought him terrible. Terrible. And you were so angry when Mother's friend visited us and told us about the baby being on the way.'

'But I couldn't say a word. Mother would have been…unsettled. It wouldn't have been worth the upset. Mother actually thought it a grand jest that her friend had had a romp with the old Duke. She encouraged it. Did all she could to push them together.'

Abigail snorted. 'I know.'

'She exhausted me.' And when her parents lived together, their father had been little better where his wife was concerned. He'd acted as if it hurt to have her on his arm. His smile had condescended. His wife was beneath him. He wanted everyone to know he thought her a mistake.

Lily knew her father had once been smitten with her mother. But that hadn't lasted. A grand love turned into an even grander liability. Lily's grandmother had filled her granddaughter's ears with tales of how her son thought himself in love with the first woman who sidled up against him. Married her, and then her grandmother's eyes had become slits as she'd stared at Lily. 'And *that* has been a *delight*.' The older woman had nodded and turned away, sniffing into the air and leaving the room.

Abigail rolled her eyes. 'Do not let the past hurt you. It's over.'

'It doesn't hurt me.'

'You have always been mature.' She wriggled her nose. 'And staid. Or is that stale? And do I smell mould?'

'No. You just smell.'

Lily dodged Abigail's pretend slap.

'That's what I mean,' Abigail said, 'you always use the oldest jests.'

'Go away.'

'You can't be that fortunate as to have both Mother and me move. But I am happy Mother left. Now I can fall in love without worrying she will cause more tales.'

'Love,' Lily muttered. 'Mother and her friends showed me just how wonderful that is.'

'Lily—'

'Can you name one person happy and in love?'

'Well, no,' Abigail said. 'But it exists. I'm sure of it.'

'Would you like to buy a unicorn?' Lily asked.

Abigail laughed. 'No.' She dragged out the word. 'And you'd still be saving for one if Father hadn't told you that they cost over a million pounds.'

'I wouldn't,' Lily said. 'I finally outgrew that stage of my life.'

'Maybe you shouldn't have.'

'I can't imagine how I could have believed in them so much.' But she had. Her mother had told her story after story about unicorns and true love and golden slippers and all kinds of nonsense when she'd been in one of her folderol moods.

'Not all men cause such problems.'

It was true. They didn't, she supposed. But Edgeworth's father had caused his family problems. He'd so infuriated her and, because of that, she'd hurt the Duchess without meaning to. Without thinking things through. She'd let her own emotions escape, just as the old Duke had, and her conscience hadn't cleared since.

She wished the unicorns had been real.

Abigail glided into the main sitting room and Lily followed behind, her skin tingling at the thought of seeing Edgeworth again.

Their father sat in his usual chair, wearing the same clothes he would have worn for dinner with the King. He rose.

But the other two were already standing. Fox lounged against the mantel, every one of his teeth lit up like stars in a night sky shining only for Abigail. Lily's vision locked on the third male in the room—the one with a placid, thought-free stare. Edgeworth.

He met Lily's eyes. His head dipped just a hair in acknowledgement and he lifted his glass in a salute only she could notice.

'Ladies,' her father said. 'Edgeworth and Foxworthy have so kindly agreed to stay for dinner.'

Abigail beamed into Foxworthy's eyes. 'Oh, how wonderful.' Abigail sat on the sofa.

Lily had two choices. Sitting across from Edge, or with him standing behind her. She chose across.

She tried not to look in his direction, but her eyes didn't want to co-operate.

He watched the person speaking, adding little to the conversation. His superior stare was probably learned early. She imagined his nursery maid holding a spoon of porridge in front of him and withholding it until he scowled.

The men discussed the speed of carriages and the mail coach, and Abigail informed them of how she'd like to travel in one because it would be so much fun to hear the trumpet sound and see the gates open, and to dash through at such a speed.

Fox told her all about his journey in the coach and her father mentioned a different trip, but somehow Fox's far outshone his. Everything Fox talked about had a flair of adventure in it, possibly because Fox didn't play by the rules.

Her father beamed and Edge just looked on, seeming somehow to guide the talk with his nods of approval or lack of response. Lily didn't think anyone noticed but her. A little plume of irritation flowered inside her.

She picked at the arm of the chair and the talk faded from her thoughts, and she remembered telling Lord Lionel once that she wanted to learn what was in his book and so he'd started talking about someone named William of Orange, and wars, and kings and queens. He'd kept talking about fights between families and she'd stood up and said she'd changed her mind. She didn't need a tutor because she'd learned all she needed about the past. People were mean.

Then he'd tried to explain how important history was and she'd felt scolded because he'd sounded so fierce. But she'd let him scold her while she stared at him. She blinked and he'd tried to explain more, and she'd blinked some more and he'd tried to explain more.

Then he'd jutted his chin and blinked at the end of a sentence, only it was more of an explanation point. And then she'd blinked six times. And he'd laughed.

Now, she looked up and straight into the fathomless blue eyes she'd stared at while he told her all about history.

He stood, back stiff. Ever so ducal. And he said something about fines and penalties, but she'd not really been paying attention to his words. But he sounded so above everyone else.

He caught her watching him. She blinked. Three times.

He tilted his head just a bit, pausing briefly mid-word before he continued.

The look he gave her could have wilted her eyelashes and maybe hers did fall just a bit, and then her eyes widened in question.

She didn't know how he smirked at her without moving the muscles of his face, but he did, and then he turned his head towards his cousin and his tone became conversational. 'Fox is not sharing the story of the time he was caught by the thief takers.'

'Nothing to share,' Fox muttered. 'I was in the wrong place and the wrong time with the wrong woman. I had to send for Edge to vouch for my character.'

'Hardest thing I ever did,' Edge said.

'A woman was the thief,' Fox muttered, 'and she used me as a decoy. I lost the best pocket watch I ever had that day.' Fox tilted his head down 'It would have been terrible to be punished for a crime I didn't commit.'

'I doubt you would wish to be punished for a crime you did commit,' Edge said.

'Too true,' Foxworthy admitted, grinning.

Lily's father patted the arm of the chair twice in quick succession. 'I've asked Abigail if she might entertain us with one of her poetry readings tonight. She's quite good.'

'And what of you, Miss Lily?' Edge asked, no smile on his face. 'Do you have a poem selected as well?'

'No. I didn't prepare anything.'

'Pianoforte?'

'I gave up on it years ago.'

'You cannot get Lily to read or sing for others,' Abigail said. 'She prefers to listen. She's a very good listener. And she is…' Abigail paused, smiled at the Duke and spoke as if mentally touching a finger on a list while she recounted, 'Kind. Neat. Loves kittens. Has wonderful handwriting, reads recipe books, helps Cook plan delicious meals, donates to charities and has the best speaking voice.'

'Be quiet, Abigail.' Lily tried to shush her sister with a private stare.

'She's such an example for me.'

'You need no example.' Lily smiled and peered at her sister.

Edge nodded, emotionless. 'I've always admired Miss Lily's manners.'

'Thank you, Your Grace. That's very gracious of you. Your book helped immensely.'

'Abigail,' her father inserted. 'Why don't you recite that poem you prepared now?'

'I can do so only because Lily spent so many hours helping me practise.'

Then Abigail recited her poem.

But nothing diminished Lily's awareness of Edge, even as the dinner progressed, and Fox and Abigail told tales, each one leading seamlessly to another.

After the meal, the men didn't wander to another room, and Fox's cache of adventures seemed endless. Her father listened, an elbow on the chair, and one finger resting across his upper lip, investing forgotten about as the evening moved of its own accord.

Edgeworth had no tales of his own, except occasionally he would remember details Fox omitted and share them, bringing Fox to laughter.

When the clock struck midnight, the men took

that as a signal to leave. Abigail stood, getting in a few last moments of conversation as they all walked to the doorway.

Edge and Lily lagged behind as everyone else moved away.

'You never did read that book, did you?' Edge asked.

A laugh burst from inside her. 'No.'

'I bought it especially for you.'

'You should have purchased a unicorn.'

His hand touched the small of her back and he didn't speak. Edge saw the quick glance Lily's sister gave them, but he didn't take his hand from Lily's back. 'You've always preferred to stand at the side, watching your sister flit around,' he said.

'Because it was my place. My role.' She stepped from his touch. 'People call it being a wallflower, but I think of it as being an audience. Not everyone should be in the centre of the stage.'

He let his hand fall to his side and he gave her the same look she'd given him when he'd been caught up in his own words.

'Events exhaust me. I dread them,' she continued. 'I'm pretending the whole time I'm there.'

'Nonsense.' He didn't want her to feel inferior.

'You are equally as welcome at the events as any other lady is.'

She didn't answer. 'I'm not. In the past years, I've been invited to so few. It's rare.'

He took her hand and pulled her so that she looked into his eyes. 'Lily. You're a part of society, too. You're an heiress. You've lived here your whole life.'

'An heiress. So I purchase my place.'

'Still your place, all the same. And you can dig your heels in—with your choice of husband.'

'I could,' she said. 'But at what cost? And why should I try to enter something that doesn't wish for me to be there? My sister—if you watch her, you can see the differences between us. I can see them. She savours the attention. It's her place. And I thought her to be your duchess—all these years. I thought you'd planned it, too.'

'Were you disappointed that I hadn't?'

'It wasn't something to consider. You were to wed Abigail.'

'You have a closer bond with her than I do with my brothers.' He spoke softly.

'I watched over her when we were young and that gave me something important to do.'

'You were hardly older than she was.'

'But she was my little sister.'

He chuckled softly. 'I felt a decade older than my brother, Steven, instead of the year difference. And the same with Andrew.' He stopped. She turned to him.

'Do you still feel the difference?'

'No. I feel much, much older now. More like their father than their eldest brother.'

'Perhaps you should have more relaxation.'

'Well, I planned it. I thought it would be relaxing and important to go to the country and learn about how others lived their lives. A country gentleman invited me to go fishing with him. And then my horse stumbled when a rock turned under his foot and tossed me into the water. I couldn't swim, of course. I'd no time for such a frivolous and useless experience. The gentleman pulled me out, but I thought I would drown first.'

'You were fortunate.' She crossed her arms over herself.

'Very. I think of it every day.'

'So do I,' she said.

He stopped.

'Your mother,' she added. 'She would have been devastated. And your friends.'

'My friends. I don't notice any of them particularly caring one way or the other.'

'They just don't show it. That's the way men are.'

'We can be rather distant with each other.' His hands were clasped behind his back.

The others had reached the door and Fox was lingering over a farewell to Abigail. Then Foxworthy noticed his cousin missing. He turned. 'Edgeworth. You've a long walk home. Hurry along.'

Abigail draped her arm over Fox's elbow. 'Did you see the moon? It's enchanting. We must make a wish on it.'

'A wish on the moon?' Fox asked.

'Yes,' Mr Hightower said, practically shooing them out the door. 'It's a tradition in our household.'

Edge kept talking, ignoring the commotion at the door. 'The next time I tried to experience the life of my tenants—I was with them while they were rendering lard, only it was more like a festival than a chore, and the ale was flowing heavily and the next thing I knew, my legs were burned by a man who'd had more ale than he should have.'

She stopped. The others had walked from sight. She touched his arm.

'I almost had more freedom from work than I bargained for,' Edge said. 'While I recuperated. As soon as I could think I had the ledgers brought to me. I didn't lay on my bed thinking of all the joys I'd missed, but of all the work that I still need to do. And then I called myself a fool. An angel had appeared to me and I had let her get away.'

'An angel?'

He nodded. 'I decided a man should not lay on his near deathbed thinking of the work he missed and note how far his family stands from him. Two brushes with death. So close. And I'd never even kissed your cheek.'

He reached out, twining a lock of her hair around his forefinger. 'I told your father earlier that I must speak privately with you tonight.'

Her eyes widened and she took in a breath. 'He will be expecting a proposal.' After a pause, she said, 'You should be considering the overall role of a duchess. It doesn't suit me.'

'Are you as forthright with everyone as you are with me?'

'Not in the same way.' She cocked her chin. 'You're a duke. You can take it.'

'Perhaps one should ladle it out a little more nicely as I am a peer.'

'You are also the person who grew up in the house next to my father's. Who studied in the garden shade hours on end and who batted me away. I thought you'd pursue my sister. Your father once mentioned it. We were summoned after your father said that Abigail might make a fine duchess. We had tea with your mother. My father beamed from ear to ear for a whole year.'

'I didn't know that.' Didn't surprise him, though. When thinking of Edge's future, his father had tended to look years ahead. He'd told Edge to make a goal and plan a strategy to achieve it, and if things moved a different direction to change plans, but keep his goal.

'You always followed what your father said. In the winter, when you were home on holiday from school with your brothers, he would take you with him and leave them behind. He never took Lord Steven or Lord Andrew.'

'Of course not.'

'And he chose Abigail for you.'

'Idle talk. Years past.'

'Not so idle. My father put a great store in it for a time.'

He took in a breath, dismissing the thought with his exhalation.

He reached out, took her fingers, pulled them close to him and took a ring from his smallest finger, the one where he usually wore his father's family seal. He reached for her finger to slide the circle on to, but she clasped her hand. He opened the fingers and put the circle in her clasp.

Her eyes studied his face.

'Edge. Why do you have a fascination with me?'

'Your absolute and utter awe in my presence.'

The movement of her face would have been better viewed in bright light, but he'd seen it before when she'd called him a booby-head. He didn't care. He loved the way her face moved when she looked at him.

On a day when he'd thought the pain too unbearable to live through, she'd touched his hand when he wanted nothing but darkness and escape. Her caress had given him the only solace he could cling to. He'd pulled his strength from the moment of her skin against his and he'd been able to believe the agony would stop.

Chapter Five

Without a doubt, Edge had lost his mind. Lily looked at the gold band. It had a lily engraved on it. She had to strengthen her resources to be able to stand.

A lily. Engraved. One of those flowers she hated. But he meant well. 'Again…' She had to gather her strength to think of the word and push the sound from her body. 'Why? Have you ever heard that it is excess to paint the lily?'

'The saying is true. Because a lily doesn't need it.'

She didn't raise her eyes.

'When I accepted my seat in the House of Lords, I knew what it meant. I had a responsibility to my country to help guide it in the direction best for England. It is a lifetime commitment. I will not be successful in every speech. But enough of them will influence.'

'That is politics.'

'Marriage is the politics of daily life. A couple makes a vow. They agree to act in the manner of marriage. A commitment to make a family. Every day will not always bring about the exact results hoped for, but it is the overall direction that is important. Guiding the children so they can make the world better for those less fortunate. I have an obligation to society.'

'I'm an heiress. I don't have to marry.' She couldn't. She couldn't do like her mother had done and place herself in a world she didn't belong. Her mother had never managed to fit into her husband's world. Never made friends there. She'd moved back to the world she felt best in and the people who didn't look down their nose at her. But then, she'd not fit there any more. She'd had a wealthy husband and tasted a better life. Her friends didn't welcome her back as she'd expected. They'd thought her above them. She wasn't upstairs and she wasn't downstairs.

'Lily.' Exasperation tinged his voice. 'Don't you feel a need to do all you can to make the world better?'

'That, Your Grace, is your department.'

He leaned closer. 'You're taking this far too lightly,' he said. 'And stop calling me that.'

'I'm not taking this lightly. You are. The injury affected your mind.'

He put his fingers around her hand, causing her to clasp the ring and the metal to warm against her skin.

For the first time in her life she understood her mother's transgressions. He released her and then she could speak again. 'You know what my mother—'

'Yes. I do. But you're not like her.'

'The venom… You didn't hear the worst words my parents said. They talked quietly when they spoke of killing each other. Marriage is like that.'

'You and I are nothing like our parents.'

He could not know that to be true and she didn't either. 'At least…your parents had a calm marriage.' She whispered the words.

'Until that rubbish was printed.'

The words iced her body, momentarily freezing her so she couldn't move. Her fingers clenched the ring in her hand. She stepped away, turning towards the staircase to the family rooms. 'I must be going.'

In one long stride, he covered the distance,

stopping her before she reached the bannister, resting his hand on the wood. 'Don't let what your mother did concern you,' he said.

'I don't belong in the world I live in.' She spoke without inflection. 'I've known that since I can remember. And besides, marriage is a foolish institution that brings much misery. My mother and father hate each other in a way that affects everyone around them.'

'You didn't warn me in this way when you thought I might approach your sister.'

'She's my father's child. She has a claim to this world through him—besides, she likes soirées and all those times when eyes are on her. And she looks like a duchess should look.'

'And just how is that?'

She stood taller, straightened her shoulders and waved her hand in a circle. 'You know. That social look.'

'I've never noticed my mother appearing all that much different—except she does wear larger earrings than other women. But she wasn't a duchess all her life.'

'She might as well have been.' She shrugged the words away. 'It's natural to her. My sister would have worn the title like a glove. But people can't say the things about her that they can say about me.'

'I understand. I wasn't happy when my father's life was shared with the world,' Edgeworth said.

She'd recounted almost every conversation of her life to her sister, but this one she would not. She squeezed her hand around the ring.

She glanced in the direction the others had left, knowing her father would keep Abigail away as long as possible, but Lily wanted to be certain she wasn't interrupted.

She returned to the dining room, his footsteps close behind.

Lily placed the ring into his hand. The warmth of his fingers felt like a hug around her heart. She didn't raise her eyes from their hands. She put her hands behind her back, clasping them, hoping to erase the imprint of the metal and his touch. It stayed.

She tilted her chin up, but didn't look into his eyes. 'I feel badly that happened to your father.'

'Your origins don't matter to me.' He put the ring on his smallest finger again and they both watched as the movement stopped. 'But what you say, does.'

He looked at her.

'I couldn't escape it before and I didn't know what it was like to have any peace in my life until my mother and father no longer lived together. She was difficult to live with and he made her worse.'

'Did you know of my father's life?' he asked.

She didn't answer. Of course she did.

'All the things in life were handed to me, but I worked to be worthy of them,' Edgeworth said.

'The etiquette of a duke should be flawless and the person on the other side of it appreciates the notice,' he added. 'With my heritage comes the opportunity to make others feel taller by my notice. To give them a certain boost. I'd just not realised how setting myself apart distanced me from everyone, even my family. I trusted myself smart enough to gauge the truth of life, and of people. I discovered, after the fact, that my brothers both knew of my father's mistress and spoke of it among themselves, but didn't tell me. Even the men at my club knew. I didn't.'

'Well, I know of my family secrets. I vote for being in the dark.'

He took her elbows and eased her arms from behind her back. He clasped her fingertips.

'I can't be in the dark any more. I have re-

sponsibilities. And you can help me. You are an
extra set of eyes and ears.' He rubbed his thumb
against her palm. 'And a friend.'

She should pull away, she knew, but she
couldn't. Friends didn't pull away. They didn't.

Letting out a breath, she stepped back, watching as their hands slid apart. 'You don't need
another person. You can find out easily enough.
Just ask people. If you ask the right person or the
wrong—or wronged person—they spit out the
words as fast as they can.'

'I don't know that I prefer to associate with
those people.' He turned, sideways, and looked to
the window, his face completely from her view.
'And I couldn't fit into the world of others. To
absorb their culture and understand their ways
would take so much more time than I have. I
could feel the wall between us. The wall between
me and most people.'

'The same wall I feel.' Tendrils of hair curled
at his ears, softening only the back of his head.
'How can I help when I am no different in that
sense, except you are on the top side of it and I'm
on the bottom?'

'You choose to keep your distance, Lily Hightower.'

* * *

He couldn't cross that gulf alone. He'd tried. The people weren't themselves when he was in their presence. They either wanted to impress him or resented him.

Lily walked to face him. He moved only his gaze. Her eyes challenged. 'I was curious once about what my life would have been like if I hadn't been born into this house—but not any more. Last summer, when Aunt Mary and I went to the shops, I pretended I wanted to see the house my mother had been raised in. I knew it would take me by the blacksmith's shop. I didn't want to see him, but I wanted to see the life that could have been mine.'

'What did you find?' He searched her face, knowing he could not take his finger and soothe away the concern edging the corners of her lips and eyes.

'The carriage passed too quickly for me to see much. A simple building. The huge doors in front open to let the heat escape. Fire from inside glowed, but the rest was dim. I couldn't imagine what it would be like to live in that world and yet it should have been mine.'

'I own a world I cannot be a part of.'

He remembered the other trip to the country that had started easily enough because he'd wanted a chance to understand the people he served. Then the accident and scent of his own skin mixed with the hot fat when the tenant had stumbled. The renderings had splashed over Edge, from feet to knees and on one thigh.

Pain took everything from him. In those seconds he could not see, move or live anywhere but inside his burning body. He'd thought a human could not feel so much pain and live. He'd been wrong.

A simple quest to see how his tenants lived and the man had been nervous at being so close to a peer and stumbled. At one ankle, the skin had fallen away.

'One of the maids cared for my blisters,' he said. 'She's worked at my home for years and I hadn't seen her before. She didn't grimace at anything I said or did, only at the burn. She never spoke more than necessary, stayed as long as needed, but then disappeared instantly. Below stairs is a foreign world to me and it is owned by me. If I were to ask about their jobs, I would get all the correct answers. No grimaces or hidden feelings.' He thought of Gaunt. 'No rags wrung out in front of my face.'

'Our housekeeper mentioned that we recently hired a maid who'd once worked for you. A ginger-haired woman.'

He knew of no changes in the household. 'Why did she leave?'

'The woman had hardly worked for your staff a fortnight. Apparently she had committed some error.' She waved away the words. 'My housekeeper said it was not of any importance and she had learned her lesson and our new maid would be certain not to be underfoot.'

His teeth tightened against each other. He remembered asking the housekeeper to let a maid with ginger hair know that she need not clean the library when he was in the house, even if it meant days might pass. He'd been trying to walk away the pain in his leg and she'd stepped in. It had irritated him that she'd seen the strain in his face and his movements.

But she should have known to wait.

'I think, in my memory,' Lily said, 'we have three people in my father's employ who have worked for you. I believe one didn't know how to make tea properly, but my housekeeper said she could teach anyone to make tea.'

'Tea?' He leaned forward. 'Tea?' His voice tightened. He remembered his father's demands on the servants and had always considered himself much more compassionate.

'Yes. But we have had no trouble with her.'

'I am sure you have not.' Every bit of his ducal training surfaced in the words.

Lily stepped away, which drove into his body with the same force of hot oil. He kept standing. 'The servants have a world of their own and I know so little of it, yet I'm sure they are aware of every moment of mine.'

She nodded. No more emotion on her face than the maid had shown. He wanted to pull her to his chest, but he didn't dare. She'd handed back the ring. He didn't want to be handed back his heart.

'Yet I have always known that I am in this world by mistake,' she said. 'First, my mother entranced a suitor above her station. She married, but didn't have the constant nature to remain satisfied with the responsibility of a husband and family.' She shut her eyes for a second. 'She needed the servants because even with them she was hardly capable of survival.'

'No one holds you responsible for her actions.'
She didn't answer.

'Lily.' The rumble of words couldn't have reached far. 'I know—some of—how you feel. When my father's scandal was published in the newspaper for all to see, my mother was crushed. She still bears the scars, even though they aren't visible. It almost killed her. And my father died not long after. Their marriage ended on that day.'

Air trapped itself in Lily's throat. She used extra force to talk and appear unaffected. 'If he were alive, would you even speak with me?'

'Of course. I spoke with you often when he was alive. He knew.'

'And did he ever mention it?'

Nothing in his face changed. But the first word he spoke lasted longer than the short word should have. 'Why do you ask?'

'He thought so little of me. I was a lesser person.'

'He saw most of the human race as lesser than the ducal family. A flaw. I saw it. I saw it in the way he spoke to the staff when they displeased him.'

'Did he ever tell you to avoid me?'

'Lily. Don't talk of things that don't matter.'

'It may matter most.'

He frowned, his eyes warning her that she'd asked the question and might not like the answer. 'Mother told him that when your sister grew up,' he said, 'I would forget about you.'

She smiled. 'Not entirely accurate.'

His eyes met hers. 'I just let them think what they wished. I mentioned Abigail's name in passing a few times and nothing more was said.'

'You were being sly.'

'Father was teaching me about diplomacy at the time. I found it helpful.'

'I never imagined you going against the wishes of your father,' she said.

The words hit him with the force of a hammer, sparking the twist of regrets that could gnarl itself around him. 'My father's wishes guided my life. The overall point of them. Not his words, nor his actions, but his wishes. Accomplishing them is my life's goal because they are the basis of everything I believe.'

He formed words he would never say to any other person. 'He guided me until he lost his way. Then I became the Duke even though he was alive, in the same way the Prince Regent had to assume power from his father. His father lives.

Mine does not. It wasn't our choice; but necessary. There is a certain tragedy in that.'

He'd wrested his father's power from him while he was still alive. 'My father died in the same room I now sleep.'

That night, Edge had seen his father's eyes sharpen and lock on his son. Edge hadn't woken his mother, but stood at his father's bedside.

His father died surrounded by splendour, but desolate. He'd awoken, his mind strangely clear, to ask Edge what had happened to the boy and Edge had told him the woman had left with the child. The curse on the Duke's lips wasn't directed at his mistress, but at Edge. Because he knew. In those last moments, lucidness had returned and his father had known his son had taken everything from him while the old Duke lived. The estate was in his son's hands. The mistress had been sent away. Only the title remained in his father's name and that only by a thread.

'I was the favoured son. The heir.' The son who would always have the disappointment of his father in his memory. Until those last, dying words, Edge had not realised he'd sent away his own brother.

* * *

Lily reached out, brushing her fingers over Edge's knuckles. She wanted to give him comfort.

The thought flashed in Lily's mind that the only reason she hadn't been like her mother in the past was perhaps because she'd never really been alone in a room with Edgeworth. She breathed in the scent of his shaving soap and it warmed its way into her chest.

Her mother's weakness had seemed unfathomable in the past—but that was all crumbling now. She moved, standing behind the table.

One of Edge's eyebrows quirked. He'd noticed her putting the distance between them, and a hint of a smile flashed and disappeared.

She grasped for something to speak of besides the old Duke. She didn't like thinking about the way his life had ended.

'Even with all the diplomacy, you could never have improved my mother's life,' Lily said. 'She had all she could wish for and she couldn't remain happy. She would mire herself in despair and only raise her head in a search for attention from her family, friends or a man. When she walked into a room, she kept moving, talking and flitting about. She had to be noticed.'

'You should have been kept with your father.' His face was like thunder, as if her pain were his own.

'If we didn't return to her house when she sent for us, she would arrive and take Abigail by the hand. I had to go as well. If we'd said we didn't want to go with her, tears and curses would have jabbed the air.'

'Theatrics.'

He'd heard the shouts.

'I didn't want your family to know and she would have continued until she won. Father would agree to anything to keep her from shrieking or running out of the house in her chemise. Mother's emotions controlled her and it wasn't only pretence. She wouldn't know I was aware of her and she would be dancing or crying.'

'But she's away now.'

'Yes.' The last Lily had heard, she'd followed a love—married as well—to somewhere near Manchester. 'I hated Mother's outbursts, but Abigail didn't seem to mind as much. I tried to keep her from the worst. I tried to make it sound adventurous.' She chuckled to herself. 'It must have worked. She wishes to wed.'

'You don't have to have that kind of a life.'

'Of course not.' But she could already feel the spirit inside her bubbling to life when Edgeworth just leaned in her direction. She couldn't let herself teeter on some brink because of a weakness in the emotions inherited from her mother.

Even now, keeping the wall between herself and the giddy, foolish side of nature took all her effort. She didn't have the same grasp on her thoughts when he stood near.

And if she were to step into a duchess's shoes, she could imagine that more people than just a governess would be speaking of Lily's mother's life and Lily's birth.

'I wish I had asked my mother before she left about the other man. The one hinted at in the newspaper and mentioned again by name in the book Sophia Swift wrote. The blacksmith. Mr Hart. But the time never seemed right and she could be so…volatile. And each time I thought of it, I told myself it didn't matter. I am who I am regardless.'

'You could speak with him.'

'No. It would be disrespectful to the man who has sheltered me my whole life.'

Silence moved between them. Whatever he made her feel, she could never let Edge into her heart. She'd seen marriage from the eyes of her mother's friends. The shouts. The tears. The husbands living in one place. The wife in another. Or the one marriage she'd envied. The one perfect marriage. His parents—until his father's mistress showed up at her mother's house upset because she and her beloved had no secret place to meet.

Her mother had commiserated. It was no mistake she lived in a home where visiting carriages couldn't be easily observed. A small house her husband purchased for her residence and with no particular merit except seclusion.

Lily and Abigail had been sent to their father. They'd been so happy to be back at the estate.

Then the old Duke had escorted his wife out to a soirée one night soon after, ever so perfect. Just like before. Lily had been standing outside. She'd heard the Duchess's laughter as she'd stepped into the coach. The old Duke's eyes had raked across Lily as if she'd been so much refuse.

Her heart pounded in her ears and reminded

her of her mother's despair. The romances had always started simply enough.

'He spent an extra moment talking with me. He touched my hand. We are so in love.'

And then…

'He hates me. I wish I didn't exist.'

Her father and mother were in love once, she'd heard, time and time again. She'd heard it shouted and whimpered.

One of her earliest memories was of her mother taking her by the hand and leading her into the blacksmith's shop. Lily had felt she walked into a cave. A hammer clanged and she'd thought it swords clashing. The coals glowed like dragon's teeth and she'd looked around, expecting some sort of winged creature to dart at her.

She pushed the memory aside to speak. Her breaths raced, fighting each other for dominance. 'I saw the blacksmith once when I was young. A sweaty beast of a man waving a hammer, swinging it in my direction. He told us to get out and never return to his sight.'

'Lily.' Edge's voice soothed. He moved around the table now, taking her by the arms, sending her insides into frazzled, unfamiliar pulses. 'That was a long time ago.'

'It doesn't matter. I'm—' She pushed his arms aside. She stepped back, propping herself against the wall. Her body trembled. She didn't have to hold out her hand to see the tremors because the ones in her heart were bigger.

'All my life I've known I don't belong in your world. My sister does and I watched over her so she would be comfortable anywhere—I told her she belonged with kings and queens over and over.'

She'd not felt the least envious. But, now she wasn't sure.

'I'll tell my father I refused your request. He can't force me to marry you and if he tries, I'll leave town,' she said.

'You don't have to. I will tell him I haven't asked.'

'No,' she said. 'He must know. I'm not only refusing your request for now—I'm refusing it for ever. I'm the blacksmith's daughter. I've earned my place in this home by caring for my sister, but I will never be a duchess.'

'What of our friendship?'

Cold air washed over her. She hugged her arms around herself.

To lose the moments she had with Edge and

make them only memories would gnaw at her for years, but she'd known all along he wasn't to be hers. Always she'd known. He could never be hers.

'We can't have a friendship now,' she said.

Nothing moved in his face. Nothing. But his eyes could not have been bluer or colder. Then they changed and he didn't seem to see her as he turned away.

Chapter Six

He only slept fitfully, waking often to think of Lily. When the sun rose, he took the ring from his smallest finger and put it back in the box.

Her words kept floating through his mind, or at least the part of her lack of interest in what would be a perfectly sensible marriage, with some shared insensible moments to make it worthwhile.

He thought of the valet, a perfect servant. Gaunt didn't need an extra nod. The wage he received proved his worth. Some of the lesser servants might appreciate a kind word, however. He'd tell Gaunt to pass the news along. Or better, he'd tell them himself.

He dressed without ringing for his valet, then he walked from his room and moved to the top of the servant stairwell, hearing a murmur of voices. Taking a few steps, he could almost hear his father's voice telling him that a duke did not go into the servants' quarters. It was unseemly for the Duke and the servants would be affronted, thinking he assumed them incapable of doing their job and seeing to his needs.

He listened. Instructions were being given to someone. 'This is an excellent house to work in, and you'll like it here…'

Exactly.

'But His Grace must never see you. Nor his guests unless it is a moment when you've been summoned or it can't be helped. We must always be invisible to someone so lofty as him. The housekeeper will let you go if he mentions you to the butler.'

The voices moved away.

How could he represent the country well if he didn't even know what happened under his own roof and if the people he paid couldn't even be seen by him?

He returned to his room and rang for Gaunt, telling him to search out disreputable clothing.

A stable boy sent on an errand to the blacksmith's shop had found the tavern the blacksmith frequented, and Edge had been given a good description of the man.

That night, leaving behind a valet who wouldn't sleep until Edge returned, Edge stepped from the carriage. The scent of roasted meat reached his nose. A violin wafted through the air, mixing with shouts of laughter. An oaf stumbled along, talking about his aches, with a female companion guiding him by pulling on his arm.

Inside the Bear and Boar, no familiar faces stared back at Edge and after a few grunted greetings no one paid him much attention.

A man with a full head of white hair and an overgrown scattering of whiskers walked in, matching the lad's description. The blacksmith sat in a spindle chair by Edge, the scent of burned coals clinging to him. 'New visitors with coin in their pocket always buy me a drink,' he said.

'That so?' Edge asked.

'I would suppose, since you're the first one I ever remember seein' in here.' He tapped the chair leg, scooting it in Edge's direction. 'You lost?'

'No more so than on any other day.'

'Then sit and tell me where you're from. Got a toff's voice.'

'My past is my business.'

'Ah.' The smith smiled. 'So tell me the nature of your crime.'

'I've committed none.'

'You mean you've not been caught.'

'No. I've committed no crime.'

The man's eyes wrinkled at the sides and his face lit again. 'Well, I don't suppose you have to be honest to buy me a drink. And I can talk for a while. I've got a fair share of words stored that I've been saving and it seems like they're getting so clogged in my head I can't pull out the right one every time.' He finished off the last of his liquid expectantly. His shirt sleeve had a neatly seared hole in the arm. 'Or I could be just foxed.'

Before Edge had finished his first mug, the older man waved to the barmaid to bring them another drink, while rambling on about the forge.

'I started when I was a lad at my father's knee. Or perhaps earlier. I was born with a hammer in my hand, best I remember.' He glanced over his shoulder at Edge. 'Remember what I said, lad. First rule of blacksmithing is you don't have to be honest with people, but you do have to be honest with the metal. It won't let you lie. You follow its rules or you start over. I never get tired of the beauty of steel. You can heat it until it's soft, pliable. The more care it gets, the harder it becomes. Just like a man with a pretty woman. Only the metal's smarter.' He chuckled. 'And what do you do with your days?'

'Mainly work with ledgers.'

'Other people's money.' He shut his eyes and looked dreamy. 'Probably the most beautiful thing next to a warm woman or hot steel.'

The buffoonery continued on, with the man waving two more mugs their way. He rambled with no seeming purpose to his words except during pauses.

'So whose ledgers do you work with?' he asked.

'A man on St James's Street.'

'And who might that man be you work for?'

Edge had been waiting for the question. 'One of the toffs.'

'He have any work done on his carriage wheels of late?'

'I wouldn't remember.'

'You're a man of numbers. Wouldn't you have seen the bill?'

'I see so many bills.'

'So tell me something about yourself. You have heard all the stories I tell and so has everyone around us. Wife you love or can't tolerate? Mistress who wants marriage or to see the last of you?'

'What of you?'

'Wife some ten years. Says she loves me like a pinch o' snuff, whatever that means. But she does like her occasional pinch.' He laughed. 'Just as I do.' He leaned forward, the mug grasped firmly. 'So what of your sweetheart? She ready to shoot out your heart? If she was still in the flush of love, I doubt you'd be here.'

'I've no sweetheart.'

'Shouldn't you be out searching?'

'You've only been wed ten years. It seems you got a late start.'

'Third wife, but who is counting? First wife died in childbed with our babe. Second wife run off with a tailor, but died of a fever. Gave up on marriage, until I met this one. She's eight years older than me and has outlived a fair share of husbands. Perfect wife. She could move an anvil with one arm. Can melt steel with one glance if she's in a temper.' He raised his brows high. 'I do just as she asks.'

'Are you the man who once courted the Hightower woman?'

The man's wife wasn't the only one who could

melt steel with a stare. 'I believe you know more about me than I know about you.'

'You're the man mentioned in the Sophia Swift book?'

'I am, but you're peddling old dirt that does no one any good.' He stood, calling over his shoulder, 'Martin. Daniels. This man asked to leave.'

One of the scruffier men, hair hanging around his face in a never-washed mop, looked up. He wore a coat too warm for the night and stuck his hand in the pocket, grasping something. Another man poked his head from a small door, holding a fowling piece.

In a distant part of his mind, Edge realised he was finding out how it felt not to be a peer. If he'd suddenly introduced himself, he suspected that wouldn't help him stay in the room any longer. 'I'll be on my way,' he said. Reaching to the weapon in his boot would have been the most senseless thing he'd ever done.

But now he knew for certain he'd found the right man and tomorrow he'd visit the man's shop so they could speak alone.

Stopping his horse at the blacksmith's, Edge tied the reins loosely to the hitching post. He didn't have to worry about the horse straying. He gave her several light pats on the neck and knew she understood. She'd wait until he returned.

Flat rocks set flush into the ground surrounded the shop, making a comfortable walking area, and the man's house connected to the forge.

Walking into the forge reminded him of his scorched skin. The memory of the pain flared—and the leeches. As long as he could move, no one would ever put one of those creatures on him again.

In the night, Edge had recalled everything he could from his conversation with the blacksmith and, even though the man had called for reinforcements to dismiss Edge, he'd not seemed the kind of man who'd shake a hammer at a child. And if he was, Edge could take the hammer from the man. Lily would never have to know and it wouldn't appear in the papers. No one even knew who Edge was, or his purpose.

The wide-open doors of the shop did little to brighten the enclave. Inside the forge glowed, flickering in his direction, blinking jewels of death. He walked inside the dreams he'd had while the laudanum dulled his pain and flared his imagination. In his pain and nightmares, he had stood inside death.

As he pushed forward, his footsteps didn't slow nor did his heartbeats. The scent of coals and heated leather moved through his nostrils. He could taste the smoke and, when he swallowed, it rested in his stomach.

The blacksmith's hammer banged, reverberating in his head. The scars on his legs shot fresh pain to his temples, making the fabric of his trousers scrape against his skin.

The blacksmith hadn't heard him, but kept clanging on the metal, a tolling bell that could have gone on for ever.

Edge took a step closer.

Before Edge could move, the blacksmith turned, swinging the serious end of the pinchers which held the red-hot blade tip towards Edge. Edge stepped back to keep from being seared, the heated air smothering his ability to breathe.

The man stopped, eyes narrowed in thought. 'Aren't you the ledger man from the Bear and Boar?'

Edge nodded.

The man shook his head. 'Don't ask me questions I don't want to answer.'

'It seemed to me like you'd answer anything until I spoke of the Hightower woman.'

'You wouldn't answer anything, though. Didn't say a thing about yourself.'

'I wasn't there to find out about me.'

'Well, if you'd talked a little more, I might have felt like telling you what you wanted. But I didn't then and I don't now.'

He stepped to the forge, laying down the metal and hammer. He exchanged the pinchers he'd been using for a longer pair. Then, using the ones with the lengthier handles, he pushed the scythe blade back into the flames.

Edgeworth didn't step closer. His jaw locked. Heat danced along his cheeks like devil's fingertips.

'You know anything about smithing?' the man asked.

'I know it's hot, hard work,' Edge said.

He saw the burning glow of the forge and he could feel the pressure from its heat.

'First rule of blacksmiths is don't walk up behind one when he's working. Second rule of blacksmithing is… Well, there's so many rules I forgot the second one.' He looked at Edge, holding the blade into the heat. He examined it.

'Imagine what this blade could do to a man's softer skin.'

Edge stood solid. 'Imagine what the forge could do to a man should he go into it head first.'

The man pulled the glowing metal closer, examining it, the darker room making the hues of the hot metal easier to see. 'I don't have to imagine where metal is concerned, or the fire. I've been doing this so long, I don't have blood in my veins, but molten steel. Makes it hard to get the bones moving on a cold morning.'

He glanced at Edge, pulling out a wadded, blackened cloth he'd had tucked at the back, under his apron ties. He dotted his forehead and put the rag back in place. 'Why'd you return?'

'Unanswered questions.'

'Just 'cause a man asks don't mean another man has to answer.'

'True.'

Edge pulled the stool near the table, wiped the bead of sweat from his brow and listened to the clanging of the hammer meeting metal again. The man continued, repeating motion after motion.

Edge studied the man, noting him taller than most, the same as Lily. The brown eyes. The studious face. The white shock of hair dripped water on to his face and his shirt clung wet against his body, and the leather apron protected him from flying embers.

'You want to try this?' the man asked Edge, examining the glowing metal.

'No.' Edge stood. 'But I will.'

'Might as well,' the man said, putting the metal on the anvil and giving Edge the pinchers. 'I'm not speaking about myself and you're not speaking about yourself, so you need to earn your rent to stand in my shop.'

He'd walked in the garden twice and she'd not stepped out. Of course, she could have been unaware he was there. The houses were side by side and her window faced the back, not the side as her sister's did.

He took the handkerchief from his pocket. White. Embroidered initials.

Every day that he reached into the pocket, he always found a precisely folded handkerchief. Always looking new. Folds ironed, he suspected, so it would lie flat.

He'd never asked Gaunt to provide the handkerchief because he'd never needed to. He wouldn't have thought of it. Edge looked at the initials, wondering if Gaunt did the stitching or someone else did.

He raised his eyes to the home, the handkerchief in his hand.

Lily's house showed no hints of life. On occasion he'd see a carriage leave or return. At times he would see activity beyond a window or a servant rushing out on an errand. But except for Lily, and sometimes Abigail with her, the house kept to itself, much like his own.

He could remember her mother living there. Lily's mother didn't merely leave or arrive. She parted the way in front of herself and dangled a parcel or a servant or a child along with her. A plume. A dash of red. Something gold.

He hadn't paid attention when she'd moved out because he'd really only paid attention to Lily. Even though her parents had separated, they'd each moved back and forth between the two houses at first.

No one had bemoaned Lily's mother leaving, not even the Duchess. And—on the day when he was a child and his parents had mentioned the possibility of Abigail being his wife—his parents had said something about it being only a consideration because Mrs Hightower left the care of her daughters to the staff.

He examined the house once again. He wasn't waiting.

At the hedge in his gardens which concealed the bench, he stepped to the back, towards her window. He wrapped the fabric loosely, but knotted it enough to hold it to the greenery. He was reduced to a surrender when there wasn't even a war.

Abigail stood at the window of her bedroom. She clasped the edge of the curtains and her head darted about like an indecisive turtle. 'He's looking this way. He's frowning. He's staring at his hand. He's—'

'Get away from the widow,' Lily ordered. She turned the page of the recipe book. She sat on top of the covers, her back against the headboard of the bed, her ankles crossed and rocking her stockinged foot. 'Violet Wafers. Have we had those?'

'He's tying something,' Abigail muttered. 'I think.'

'Get away from the window,' Lily commanded again. She didn't look up.

'Something white. He tied something white on the hedge.' She put her head closer to the glass. 'He's walking around the hedge. He paced in front of it. Maybe someone is sitting on the bench. But he's not talking.'

Lily read the contents page. 'Bergamot Drops. That sounds medicinal. Or like something a man might add to shaving soap.'

Abigail tilted her head from left to right. 'I think it's a handkerchief.'

'Yes. Could be.' Lily read. 'What about Damson Drops? The plums won't be ripe until autumn, though.'

'Why would anyone tie a handkerchief like that? Maybe he wishes his gardener to trim the hedge and he's telling him just how deeply he wants the cut.'

'Peppermint Drops?' Lily skipped over the Orange Drops. Too much like orange biscuits and no doubt they would not compare.

'It just seems odd...'

'Barley Sugar Drops. I think the person who wrote this just needed another recipe. Barley sugar? Not for me.'

'He's sitting because his head dropped from view. Remember when he used to read there?'

'Not really.' Lily looked up. 'I don't care what the Duke does.'

'I do. He's Foxworthy's cousin.' She let the curtain fall into place. 'And don't tell me you don't care what he does. You've always watched him when he was in the gardens.' Abigail peeped around the merest edge of the cloth.

'You really made Father angry when you told him what you said to Edgeworth. That was the only time Father ever threw anything. It was always Mother before. You shouldn't have told him what you did. You should have said Edgeworth changed his mind.'

'I didn't want to lie.'

'Well, you should have. It would have been the right thing to do.'

'I know.' Lily kept her book in front of her face.

Abigail put her hands on her hips and walked over to her sister. 'I cannot believe you. Sitting alone in this room all day when there are shops to be visited. Babies to be adored. Perfumes to sniff. New fabrics begging to be made into dresses.' Then she looked back to the closed curtains. 'Odd. Just odd. Tying something on a plant like that.'

'I'm reading.'

'Recipes.'

'You will appreciate this when Cook makes something absolutely divine.'

The door shut as Abigail left the room.

'Orange Drops. Seville Orange Drops. Orange Wafers. Orange Prawlongs…' Lily spoke to the book. 'Orange Drops,' she repeated. 'Seville Orange Drops. Orange Wafers. Biscuits. I would so love some orange biscuits…'

Chapter Seven

The Duke sat on the bench, tapping each finger of his left hand against the wood, one at a time. He'd had enough of this average-man business. He did not like being ignored. Not after he'd put out the white flag.

He could not believe it. He might have to enlist Napoleon's help. He'd heard the Frenchman had written quite a scandalous love letter that had been stolen and published. Not that he, as a duke, would ever write such nonsense. It was unseemly.

Stilling, he listened. The door to Lily's house closed.

Ah, he didn't need a general's help. The flag wasn't a flag of surrender, really. An invitation. His invitation had been accepted.

The hedge rustled with the handkerchief being

extracted and he stood. He heard rustling and footsteps. Miss Abigail walked around the hedge.

He did not move.

'Oh, Your Grace.' Her eyes widened. 'I didn't realise you were about.' She thrust out her arm, holding the silk to him. 'Somehow this was tangled in the greenery. I was going to send a maid with it, but…' She looked at it, eyes perusing the stitches of his initials. 'Oh,' she gasped. 'It's yours.' Her hand fell to her side and her nose wrinkled. She turned her chin away, but her eyes stayed on his. 'Why is it on the hedge? Lily and I were watching from the window. She couldn't stop talking about it.'

'Thank you.' He took the silk from her hand and didn't blink when he stared into her eyes.

She curtsied and dashed towards her house. 'You're welcome. Any time.'

Perhaps his look wasn't as nice as he'd thought.

He glanced at the Hightower windows, certain he was being watched. He waved his hand out in a strong gesture, then swung his arm towards his garden—a very un-ducal way to request someone's presence, but still commanding—much like he would have imagined Wellington doing to a single soldier who might need to be silently moved from one direction to another.

He waited. The window opened and two feminine arms reached out, grasping a book, then releasing it to fall on to the ground.

He didn't need to see it to know it was a book on proper manners.

'Lily,' her father's voice challenged. He held a note. 'From the Duchess. She asks if you might visit. Today.'

Lily didn't move.

'My father would have traded me away for an invitation such as this,' he said.

'Are you going to do the same?'

He shook his head, and read the paper again. 'I suppose I'm wealthy enough. Abigail is going to marry well. There will be someone to pass my business to. Do as you wish. I did.' He stared at her and tossed the paper into the waste bin. 'You see how well that turned out.'

Lily took one last glance at the paper before she left the room. In the past, the invitation had included Abigail. Lily's stomach tumbled at the thought of visiting the Duchess alone. Her entire life, she'd been invited to have tea with the Duchess six or seven times. But always with Abigail. She sighed deeply. In truth, there was no avoiding it. She must go to the Duchess.

Choosing the dress with the silk ribbons on the sleeve, she called her maid to help her dress. But she didn't tell anyone else where she was going because later she might have to tell the truth and that hadn't ended well the last time.

The maid brought out the slippers for Lily to wear. The pointed-toe ones that were impossible to dance in. Lily frowned at the maid, and the servant smiled and put the shoes on the floor. Lily sighed. Of course she would wear them. They were *elegant*, according to Abigail. They matched the dress so perfectly, according to Abigail. But still, Lily had only worn them the one time and all the tricks the maid knew about stretching them or cushioning them hadn't kept them on Lily's feet more than a few seconds.

Lily walked gracefully to the house next door. She had no choice. If she hurried, she'd fall on her face or leave a slipper behind.

The ducal sitting room had to be the largest room in the house because if all the other rooms were the same size, fitting more than one or two under the roof would have been impossible. Glittering orbs hung from the sconces, reflecting the colours in the room and falling like drops of gold.

The brightness of the Duchess's earrings and her simple dress could have looked out of place, but they didn't because the Duchess wore them. She greeted Lily, thanking her for sparing the time to visit.

As Lily sat, a servant appeared with a tea tray.

'Recently I've been staying with my son Andrew and his wife. She is painting my portrait.' The Duchess smiled. 'She's quite good.' She patted the lines at her eyes. 'But she forgets to add nature's lace. Took all these out, smoothed out my skin.' She held up her ring. 'Made the jewels bigger, though.'

'I've heard she's quite talented.' And that somewhere a quite naked portrait of Beatrice's husband existed, although for the life of her, Lily just could not imagine Lord Andrew allowing such a thing.

'My wish is that she might paint a single large portrait of my three sons standing together. They wouldn't even have to pose at the same time, but individually, and Beatrice could place them in the same room. I gave three polite hints politely missed from the men so I guess it isn't to be. I'm sure they'd do it for me if I insisted, but I don't want to be that kind of mother.' She twitched a shoulder and smiled. 'At least, I don't want to be that kind of mother on a daily basis. I suppose I am allowed one insistence on their time per adult child each year so I try not to squander it.'

'You have it worked out mathematically.' Lily sipped the tea, the temperature warm, just slight of being too hot. Exactly right. The blend wasn't the same Lily usually tasted, but a mix all the Duchess's own.

'Realistically. My sons were taught to think for themselves, except the Duke. He was raised to think for other people...' She paused, her head-shake filling the air with a medicinal-scented hair tonic. 'If I have made one error in my life, it was in how firmly I raised Edgeworth.' She lowered her voice. 'Remember, Foxworthy is not my son so I take none of the responsibility for him, although he is a dear, dear nephew.'

She continued, returning to the previous topic of her conversation. 'Edgeworth was never punished for his mistakes because he wasn't allowed to make them. From morning until his bedtime, he had a person at his elbow guiding him.'

'But a little child sometimes rebels.'

'He couldn't very well. Imagine when you're only this high...' she held a hand out to indicate the height of a small child '...and a servant whisks you out of bed to do your lessons and if you are to sit on the floor and refuse to go further—as he once did—two servants lift you and deposit you in front of your father. Your mother is called. The tutor and governess attend and all the adults stand around you, discussing how this type of behaviour is to best be handled in the child.'

The Duchess shook her head. 'He was my first. He was to be perfect. The whole family's future rested on this young child should something happen to his father.'

'He seems perfect.'

'Oh.' The Duchess smiled. 'He is. He is perfect. He is so perfect. He is so perfect he doesn't understand imperfection. His tolerance for others' errors is learned. He doesn't feel it, but knows that his duty is to expect less from others and be benevolent about it.'

She laughed softly. 'I cannot be satisfied. I have the most wondrous children a mother could hope for and I complain they don't make errors.' She touched the earrings. 'Even my youngest son, Andrew—that little mix-up with the portrait was not his fault.' She discreetly turned her eyes away, as if even speaking of such a thing was improper.

Lily looked at her tea cup.

'You'd think I wouldn't like his wife, Beatrice. She's…' the Duchess searched for a word '…exuberant. But I adore her. She's exactly what Andrew's serious side needs. And my other son, Steven, his wife lightens his day.'

She continued. 'Think of it, I raised Edgeworth so carefully—a little boy whom it took six adults to convince to do something he didn't wish to do and each of us spoke openly about which privilege we should remove from him if he wouldn't behave. And we could come up with nothing. No favoured toy. No game. No treat. He finally looked at us, stood and said if we would leave he would do his lessons.' Her eyes watered. 'That night, my husband and I scheduled his Sunday afternoons so that he and his brothers could go to my sister's house to play with their cousin Foxworthy.' She crossed her arms over herself. 'That took courage for me. My sister is not exactly the same kind of parent I am. I promised myself if the boys came back alive I wouldn't complain.'

She uncrossed her arms, one hand resting atop

the other. 'Edgeworth came back alive and the games with the toy soldiers didn't go quite as planned. They were furious with each other. Foxworthy just wanted to blast ahead with cannons and didn't go by their rules. Andrew planned the supply lines so precisely that he needed more soldiers than allotted. Steven was upset because he wanted the troops to lull the enemy in for an ambush. And Edge could not enjoy it because the troops kept arguing with the general and he felt they should forget supply lines, march forward and do their duty.'

She waved a hand. 'We finally enlisted the groom who had had six children and told him he must take them to the country for a bit and teach them to be boys—but it never quite worked for Edge as it did for the others.'

Lily wondered if the Duchess knew about the ring with the lily on it and couldn't figure out if the older woman was trying to encourage or discourage her.

'He's the perfect son. The perfect Duke. The perfect man.' A smile drifted across the Duchess's face. 'Is that an imperfection? I admit I enjoy being a duchess,' his mother said, smiling into the distance. Then her eyes rested on Lily and she took a sip of the tea. She'd once sent a parcel of it to the Hightower house with Lily and Abigail.

'Not that there's anything not to enjoy about being a duchess,' the older woman said, 'except sometimes I feel my family is scrutinised a little closer than others. It's the cost of the privilege, I suppose.' She held her head perfectly in line with her body. 'You can't walk away from being a duchess.' She frowned. 'At first, I was a little unsure, but I accepted the task.'

The cup clattered when the Duchess put it on the saucer—the most un-peerlike movement Lily had ever seen from her.

'You have to know,' she added. 'Those moments—in the past—my husband's problems—were the most difficult of my life. I still had to be a duchess every moment I stepped out of my bedchamber, and it's much harder to remain in a position of example when your life is being portrayed as a farce and you are in the centre of the jest. You have to carry your head high and you feel it is only raising you above the ranks so you can be targeted easier.' She moved the handle of the tea cup, aligning it with something only she saw. 'I wouldn't wish that on anyone.'

She laughed, leaning forward. 'Forgive me for talking about the past. I've just thought about it a lot since Edgeworth was ill. He's seemed different since he recovered. And I wanted to thank you for visiting me on his birthday and telling me he would survive.' She shook her head, the earrings bobbing, and she touched one, steadying it. 'I didn't really believe he would make it to another day, but it was glorious to be wrong.'

The Duchess chattered on about her grandchildren, the completeness of motherhood and other things that gave Lily the opportunity to smile and nod, and smile more and nod more. But her thoughts never completely returned to the conversation. She kept seeing Edge in her mind's eye and feeling disappointment that he'd not been in the room and wondering how she'd let herself get so close to the spider's web.

Boot heels thudded in the hallway.

And the Duchess's eyes suddenly held the same innocence as Foxworthy's.

Edge walked into the room, even though he didn't move outwardly, his eyes studied the situation.

She'd not known how much she hoped to see him.

His mother stood. 'Well, Edgeworth... You're late.'

'Because I did not receive an invitation,' he said.

His mother walked towards the door, giving him a pat on the elbow as she left. 'A written invitation works better than a white scrap of cloth.'

Chapter Eight

Lily met his eyes after the Duchess left the room, fighting both irritation and attraction at the same time. 'Stop looking at me like that.'

'How?'

'Just like your father did. As if I am beneath you.'

'I am just irritated that you did not—' The ice didn't stop at his eyes.

'That I did not jump to your bidding at first summons.'

'You didn't.'

'I am here now. So be happy.' He stood broad and angry, yet she felt no intimidation from him.

'I don't want *you* to be unhappy and from the way you are looking at me—' he leaned closer 'which I must say is remarkably like my father used to stare when I displeased him—shows your annoyance.'

'I am not annoyed. I am summoned. I am here.' She pursed her lips and gave the most forceful whistle in her repertoire, a little bird chirp of a sound instead of the one the groom used to call the horses.

'Could I hear that again?'

'Why did you—?' She stopped. She smiled. 'You put a handkerchief out. A white one.'

His eyes darkened. 'Yes. That worked.'

'And then your mother's note…'

He held up a palm. 'I had nothing to do with that. I just returned from your father's house and he had plenty to say on the subject of understanding, tolerance and how much he would like us to get along. He finally sent for you and discovered you not at home. He went to your room to make certain.'

'He can be thorough.'

'Lily.' His chest moved with the breath he took in. 'I appreciate your helping me understand what it is like to be in a different world. People are more irritating than I realised.'

'Yes. Isn't it grand?' She stood and moved closer, pulled by the force of his presence.

'I didn't expect it to be completely enjoyable.' His tone lightened and flowed around her, luring her closer. 'I expected it to be much like observing a raindrop running down the window pane on the other side. I didn't plan to feel that I was standing in the midst of the rain. But, I have been observing from the outside all my life. I need more. I stopped at the tavern again last night. The men at first appearance seem a bit dull, however their jests are sharp.'

'You wanted to see if you could handle the hardships of someone else.'

'I've endured listening to the variety of aches, pains and complaints of the men. I would have thought they visited the tavern for enjoyment.' He put a palm to the back of his neck.

'Is that different than the clubs you frequent?'

'Not much.' His hand fell to his side. 'I'm not comfortable with the men at the alehouse, though.'

'Why not?'

'They have known each other from birth and I can see them regarding me from the corner of their eyes. I could have stepped from a moonbeam and I doubt they would regard me any less suspiciously.'

'You do look a bit—' she frowned '—suspicious.' He would to men outside his world. His cravat looped exactly right. He could have been presented to any member of royalty without so much as a comb being brushed across his hair.

'You've taken your whole lifetime to become who you are. Wearing a less costly shirt isn't going to take away that toss of your head.'

He moved a bit.

'Yes. That one.' She laughed, studying him openly.

Nothing about his face was particularly handsome and yet his eyes could make him so. With just one glance he could send pinpoints of light into her body, or shoot sparks of command. Yet the command never seemed forceful to her.

He snorted, but their eyes joined in the way of two clouds melding into one.

'Trust isn't easy to gain,' he said. 'Distrust is even harder to overcome.'

She pulled herself back from his eyes. 'You wanted to know how people are when a peer isn't present. You know now and you don't particularly like it.'

'Lily.' He reached out, trailing his forefinger

over the back of her hand, filling her with a flash of that cosy unstable feeling she wasn't sure of.

'The blacksmith wants to meet you.'

The words hit her with the force of a hammer. She jerked, dodging.

He examined her face, not retreating.

'How dare you speak to him?' she said. She moved to the window, pushing the open curtains even further back.

'I had no trouble with it—after a short while.' His voice softened. 'He won't speak of the past with me. But he said he'll talk with you.'

She put her head down. All her life she'd tried to forget about the man. She'd only wondered why her mother had been swayed—she'd not wondered much about the blacksmith. A man who'd stained her in a way she could never undo. It didn't matter who he was. It truly didn't. He'd merely appeared on the scene long enough to cause grief and then move on.

'I don't want to know anything about him.'

She looked out over the gardens and heard a bird singing in the distance. A horse neighed. Everything in front of her appeared as perfect as nature and man combined could make it. Everything inside her felt as jumbled as nature and man could make.

Edge moved beside her, stopping to look through the panes. They were as close as if they posed for a portrait, yet not touching until the wool of his coat brushed her arm, sending pinpoints of light into her body.

'I met him once. That was enough.' She pulled the words from the most secret part of her mind.

Edge turned to her and, with the gentleness of touching fragility, moved her to face him.

He pulled her fingertips to his face and brushed a kiss against the back of her hand, then pulled it to his cheek, and a roughness tingled her fingers that she'd not noticed on his face.

'He asked to meet you,' Edge repeated. He lowered her hand, but still kept her fingers clasped. 'The decision is yours.'

'Life was simpler when other people made my decisions for me.'

Edge shook his head. 'They never did. You only let them think they did.'

Sitting on her bed, Lily wove the handkerchief around her fingers, the aroma of the lavender sachet it had been stored with floating in the air.

She stopped, studying her own precise initials on the cloth. She had a handkerchief to match the colour of every dress she owned.

Abigail and Aunt Mary were visiting a distant cousin who had a new baby and Lily had pleaded a distressed feeling in her stomach which wasn't a lie. The unease flared in her every time she thought of Edgeworth.

The blacksmith wanted to see her. Her curiosity had doubled each day since she'd discovered he wanted to talk with her. She couldn't remember anything about him but the hammer and how she'd wanted to hide behind her mother, but she'd known not to.

If something happened to the blacksmith before she ever spoke to him, she'd never know him.

But Edge could take her to the forge and no one would have to know. She could keep it a secret. A real one. Not the usual kind of secret which meant everyone knew and no one talked openly about it—they just whispered or talked around it.

She spread the handkerchief, and examined the size. It wasn't too small to be viewed from a distance. She walked to Abigail's room. It faced the Duke's.

The window was open to let in the fresh breeze.

She draped the cloth over the window sill and closed the window, trapping the cloth mostly outside. Then she moved where she could see the door of his house.

The handkerchief had hung from the frame less than an hour when Edge stepped outside. She opened the window and retrieved the cloth, completely aware he'd watched her take the cloth back inside.

Then she clasped the handkerchief into a ball and proceeded down the stairs.

When she stepped outside, his impassive glance greeted her and jolted alive the fluttering things in her stomach. She tensed. He wasn't even smiling and her body reacted to him. The instant he caught her regard, warmth reflected from the azure before a shutter passed over his thoughts. But she stored that half-moment of intensity into her memory.

'I'm ready to see the blacksmith,' she said. 'I don't want Abigail or anyone in my family to know about my seeing my father. You're the only one I trust to keep it a true secret.'

'Lily. You're aware there's no guarantee of anything remaining private. In fact, it is best to expect everyone to know and be surprised when something doesn't become public knowledge.'

'Will you help me or not?' Exasperation tinged her words and it wasn't wholly directed at him.

'Of course,' he said. 'If you doubted it, the handkerchief wouldn't have been in the window.'

Edge looked to the front of her house. A hackney pulled into view, stopping precisely between the two residences. 'I sent someone for a carriage as soon as I saw the handkerchief. I can't use my vehicle or it would be recognised.'

He led her to the carriage and helped her up the steps. The leather gave a soft creak as she became comfortable. When he stepped inside, the springs hardly moved and the seats accepted him without protest. She wondered if a tutor had taught him how to sit without stirring anything, or if it came naturally to him.

When the vehicle left, she stared at the cloth in her hand and asked, 'Did you ask your mother what we spoke of?'

'No.' His face emotionless and with no flicker visible, he said, 'I assumed the two of you spent the entire time talking about—not me.'

'Of course.'

'As I thought.'

'I half expected her to warn me away from you.'

'Why?'

She raised her brows.

'Lily, you weren't the only child with parents who didn't spend their nights together. You need to forget about what you think...' he paused on the word '...others are thinking of you. Society as a whole has given you hardly any notice. Your mother kept their attention. Not you. You only attended the minimum of events—enough so that people noticed how demure you are, but drew no negative thoughts for yourself. If anything, you gathered sympathy because you struggled under the weight of your mother's...'

'You said you have walls around yourself and can't see the way others thought, so don't expect to convince me no one noticed my mother's indiscretions.' The steady pace of the horses' hooves reached her ears.

'They noticed, but I'm sure they didn't dwell on it as much as you did. You had to maintain the calmness in yours and your sister's life. Your mother's actions burdened you, but a few moments of bantering tales was all the time those indiscretions meant to others.' His shoulders moved. 'It's a little hard to escape that kind of talk in this life. Even for the peerage.'

'Especially for the peerage.'

She let the words fall away and chose her next words carefully. 'So you just rose above the whispers when your father's secrets became known?'

'No. Not at all. In those moments, I was the same as you when you tried to hold your mother's life together, only older. I cleaned up my father's mess and moved on.'

'Did you really?'

'I will carry those moments with me for ever. Knowing I have a half-brother that—' His voice stopped. 'I did what I did to make things the best I knew how for my family. Just as you did.'

She didn't speak.

'When I saw you in the sitting room, I realised the Duchess knows of our conversations,' he said. 'If she does, then it is spreading about. I need to think of you, Lily. I don't want your reputation harmed.'

'I don't either.' She had no plans to marry so her reputation wasn't important for that reason. But she didn't want to cause problems for Abigail or be considered the same as her mother.

The thought made her ache. 'I don't want to be like her.'

'You aren't.'

But he couldn't feel what was going on inside her body and she didn't know if she could control it. She wanted to change the direction of her thoughts.

She rested the handkerchief on her lap and turned closer to Edge. 'What is he like? The blacksmith?'

Edge thought. 'A man toughened by the metals he shapes. He's not educated. He's not many things I'm used to seeing. But he's genuine and good-hearted, for the most part. The friends he has at the tavern think highly of him.

'You're doing the right thing,' he said.

Lily remembered the agonies of her mother's tears and tried to recount the men that her mother had believed herself in love with. On occasion, she wasn't even sure they were being more than polite, but if one looked her mother's way, her mother claimed him in love.

'It's odd that I feel unsettled,' she said. 'I owe the man nothing. Less than nothing. I've reconciled with it long ago. I'm the person I was born to be. Births are not an accident. We are somehow planned to be alive and who we are. It's that simple.'

'Life is never that simple.'

'As the first-born you should believe what I said. Otherwise, why are you entitled to be the Duke more than your brothers?'

'I don't know sometimes that I am. If something should happen to me, Steven could easily take over where I've left off. But I've been trained to lead the family. If he'd been trained from birth to do the duties, then the role should fall to him.'

'Would you have minded?'

'I doubt it. We were given our roles—my brothers and I—almost from the beginning. Mine was to lead. Steven lives in the countryside and has a quiet life, except for the three sons, and now he's taking in two orphans. Architecture calls to my brother Andrew and he buys structures needing work and after he makes them new again, he rents or sells them. We all do as we are meant.'

'I was fortunate to be born in a world above the station I should have been in. I shouldn't complain at all and yet I feel wronged. I was born into a wealthy nest when I could have been born in the back of a shop. I'm not sure if I'm a hypocrite with myself or not. Life is unfair and I received a bigger portion.'

'Lily. If life were precisely fair, then we could all look exactly the same. We would all be the same height, have the same muscles and the same straightness in our teeth.'

'I was very fortunate.' She straightened the handkerchief as she talked. 'If given a choice, do you think I would have chosen to be the blacksmith's daughter and live in a small home and wash my own clothing? My surroundings aren't so different from yours. Except you were heralded. I was whispered.'

'If you'd been born there, you might feel differently.'

'I doubt that. The day in the shop, I thought him frightful. I couldn't see that I was anything like him when I discovered what others said.' Her eyes stayed on the cloth in her hands, but she didn't see it. 'I didn't understand why she betrayed her vows with him.'

'I think that question is one I could have answered. The attraction two people feel for each other can be so strong.' He touched her chin and pulled her view to him. 'Strong.'

'Vows are vows.' She needed to hear what he thought.

'I agree. But to make errors is to be human.'

The carriage swerved as he spoke, jostling her, and helping fuel the anger inside her. He defended her *mother*. She wondered if he excused his future self from stepping outside his marriage vows. 'Did you feel that way about your father?'

'He was ill. He wasn't himself. He was weakened.'

She challenged him with her eyes.

'He was.' He didn't explain.

'Everyone could say that. People have weaknesses of some sort.' She closed her lips for a moment. 'Except perhaps a certain duke. Who is so near perfect he has to step outside himself to see what others are like.'

'You know I'm not perfect, Lily.' He spoke from his heart, but then he gauged her reaction. 'I learned French, Italian and the Greek you heard, but cannot carry a tune in any language.'

'Well, an inability to sing is frightful,' she said, using her hand to fan her face. 'That certainly is a blot against you. It will probably cause you to be tossed from White's instantly if the men find out.'

He shrugged. 'I let everyone think I consider myself above it.' He leaned sideways, his mouth close to her ear. 'That is my true secret. When others talk of something I am totally lost about, or wish to do something that I don't know how to do, I claim ducal responsibilities or take in a long breath, look bored and tell them to enjoy themselves.'

'You fraud.' She forced her smile away and completely forgot about the blacksmith for a moment.

'No. Most others do the same.' His whisper caused the tendrils of her hair to tickle her cheeks.

She reached out, palm flat against his coat and resting above his heart. She pushed, and he moved an inch.

'So you are terribly imperfect.'

'Shh…I can't hear such talk. I cannot imagine myself not on a lofty perch. What if I might doubt my decisions in Parliament, or somehow misconstrue the needs for our future? That might become weighty. Besides, I'm certain I had all the answers only a few years ago.'

'Before your father died?'

'Yes. I thought he was perfection itself. But my father was ill. His mind. He would be confused. The coachman told us later that Father had stepped out of the club and, instead of going to the carriage, walked away from the club. The servant enquired when he realised Father was gone and someone recalled Father leaving on foot. The coachman went searching and found Father, confused, but so happy to see a familiar face.'

Thoughts blasted through her head so quickly she couldn't sort them. No one had said his father was ill. No one. And he'd not acted ill when she'd seen him with his mistress. He'd not been himself, perhaps, but he'd been overwhelmed with the prospect of seeing the woman.

She remembered the last times she'd seen his father and knew she'd been unable to detect any change in him outwardly.

The carriage had travelled about half an hour when Edgeworth thumped the roof, alerting the driver to stop the vehicle.

Helping her alight, they walked to a small structure in the distance.

The blacksmith's shop looked exactly as Lily remembered. A wooden building of no special shape, except the two doors in the front opened like a carriage house in order to keep the temperature from building beyond bearableness.

The ring of a hammer pounding steel reverberated, the rhythm steadier than most clocks.

When Lily and Edgeworth reached the clearing to his shop, she stopped. Edge caught her arm, guiding her forward.

She took in the whiffs of burning coals and clanging metals, not wanting to continue. Edgeworth touched her back, but his hand moved almost to the side of her waist, pulling her along with him.

Walking closer, she could see the blacksmith working in the forge, a sweat-soaked linen shirt draping his back.

The blacksmith stood tall, with permanently stooped shoulders. His forearms hadn't withered with age, looking a match for any task. Using the tongs, he turned the short bar he held in the forge. The bar glowed red. He removed the bar from the heat. Placing it on the round part of the anvil, he beat the bar into a U shape with the hammer.

Then he left the metal, and the hammer, and pulled a cloth to his face, wiping it dry before tucking the rag back into the ties of his apron.

Wet strands of spiked white hair stuck out and he didn't fingercomb them back into place.

'Mr Hart.' Edge walked from the sun into the darkness around the forge.

The blacksmith looked their way. He took in Edge first and then Lily.

'Miss Lily?' he asked, his voice gentle.

She examined him, searching for familiarity. She found none. He was a stranger. The blood didn't bind them at all. She favoured her mother. She'd always known that. But she'd expected some instant moment of—something. But she felt nothing for him.

He turned to the planks making the wall. 'What I did was wrong.' The back of his shirt moved with his efforts and he hung the tongs near the others of various lengths.

The blacksmith returned to his anvil. 'I've always thought you a fine lady,' he said. 'I want you to know that above all. I felt bad for my part in what happened to you.'

'I understand.'

'Not completely,' he said. 'You're not my daughter. You couldn't be.'

The heat from the forge beat into her lungs. He

watched her and she repeated his words in her mind, making sure she heard them.

'But my mother—the stories.'

'I spoke with her. Others saw her about. We laughed together. We jested. But we were never more than that. It could have been, but it wasn't. We played at being unfaithful, but we never were.' He made a fist and rested it on the anvil. 'I may have thought to love her, but then when she told me a babe was on the way, I didn't wish for that any more. She was married. Someone else's wife. The child she carried wasn't mine. The game wasn't a game, but because we'd thought it a lark we'd hidden none of our laughter. None of our meetings.'

'You were just…pretending?' Her mouth opened. This pretending that affected her life.

'Don't get me wrong,' he said. 'I enjoyed her company. She enjoyed mine. I wasn't married. Figured she could handle her side of things and I could handle mine. I was young then and didn't see the harm—because I knew I would take it no further. She was married.' He shrugged the words away, picking up his hammer and tapping the anvil to bring a reverberating ring.

'The men around thought it and I didn't argue. I

boasted about how manly I was. But then a child was on the way and I realised too late—I realised it could hurt you and I had no more to do with it. None. So, I told my friends you weren't my child. They laughed. Didn't believe me. I looked like I was trying to deny my blood and I didn't like that either.'

'You're not? You're certain.'

His lips pressed into a line and his chin rose. 'Your mother should have told you. She knows I can't be.'

Lily had feared the despair or anger or remorse or joy her mother would have expressed if she'd asked about the newspaper story or the book.

'We never spoke of it,' Lily said. 'When it was in the newspaper, I didn't want to dwell on it. But when it was printed in the book—people keep copies of books. How do I know if you're telling the truth?'

'No reason not to. But you cannot be my child. You cannot.' He used a blackened fingernail to scrape at the anvil. 'At this point, it wouldn't matter to me much one way or the other. I have more reason to say you're my daughter than not. I get a laugh on the rich man and a daughter who might feel obligation to me.' He met her eyes. 'But it's not true. It cannot be. Plain as that.'

'If my mother told you she was going to have me, then you spoke of such things. Who is my true father?'

'The man who raised you. Hightower.'

'Did he—? Does he know?'

'Can't speak for him.' He again smoothed his hand across the anvil, a wistful smile flickering on his face. 'Before you were born, your mother told me that your father was the only man she'd had in her life. She wasn't happy in her vows, but she told me she'd kept them. I don't know if she always did after that, but she did when visiting me.' He rang the hammer down upon the anvil again, so close to his fingers she didn't see how he missed.

'Your mother.' He took in a breath. 'We were friendly and she caught my eye. She had a spirit that kept me laughing. She laughed so much. The happiest person I ever saw and full of spirit.' His eyes turned wistful. 'I didn't love her—in the way people thought. But I loved her in my own way. I wanted her near for who she was and that was all. I wanted nothing more from her.

When she told me about you, I distanced myself quickly.'

'When she brought me here, you told us to get out and never come back.'

He nodded. 'I'd married by then. My wife was dying. A little girl was standing in my shop and supposed to be mine. I couldn't hurt my wife. I didn't want you dragged into something you didn't belong in. Time had passed on and bringing you to me was like putting a lie on top of the truth.' He grasped the head of the hammer. 'I couldn't believe she did that.'

'Thank you for letting me know.'

He nodded towards his house. 'I told the woman I'm wed to now that you might be visiting. Told her the truth of it. She laughed. Says I deserved it.'

Chapter Nine

The silence that began the return trip was a different kind and his knee rested so near that the bumps in the road jostled her against him. She wondered if this was what it felt like to take every ride as a duchess. If she belonged in society... If she really had a place in it...

After a large move of the carriage springs, she noticed he watched her, an openness in his face she'd never caught before.

'Can he be lying? He must be,' she answered herself. 'Making me think I'm legitimate, when I'm not.'

'No gain for him in that now.'

'He's married and might want his wife to think better of him than he is.'

'I doubt that. He talked with me about his wife.' Edge reached out, touching her chin and guiding her face closer. He studied her. 'You have no re-semblance to him that I can see, other than you both have brown eyes.'

'But some people hate to admit errors and lie when the truth is—' She put her hand briefly on her cheek. 'I always supposed I looked like him.'

He ran a finger over the top of her lips, touch-ing the hairline scar she'd received from falling out of the tree after getting her kite caught.

'I'm certain you look nothing like him.' Hu-mour tinged his words and he kissed her, the warmth cascading into her and evaporating her thoughts.

He pulled away. 'To me, you look like no one else in the world. Just yourself.' His fingertips ran over the planes of her face, exploring, even touching the tips of her lashes, making all her skin feel new.

Only she didn't feel like herself. With Edge looking at her, and touching her, she was a duch-ess.

He kissed her, his arms cradling her so gently that she could sense his muscles more than feel them.

When he stopped, her mind slowly returned

and stillness surrounded her. The carriage had parked. No more sounds of hooves.

'Now you can put all the whispers behind you.' Soft words spoken in a deep voice. 'You have no reason not to go forward with your life.'

His words chilled away the peacefulness. She shook her head, answering even more quietly than he spoke. 'I heard my mother and my father fighting. He said I was the blacksmith's—child.'

The driver opened the door for them. Edge gave him a coin and waved him away. She couldn't see the response of the other man, but the door closed, making a small snap.

She'd overheard the conversation between her mother and father and knew of the tales. She didn't remember a single moment of discovery, but had always known the stories. Perhaps it was her father's mother who'd mentioned it in her presence when she was small. Certainly the woman had despised her son's wife.

'It doesn't matter.' His voice lacked emotion.

'It matters the world to me,' she said. She tapped the tip of her finger at her chest. 'All my life I've believed that the man who raised me did so out of compassion, or pity or something. I was the little bird that didn't belong in the nest,

but he kept me anyway. The whole town believes
that. Everyone. What if the lie I lived *wasn't* that
I didn't warrant the Hightower name, but that I
did? Another moment when my mother had a
laugh on us. Everyone thought my father good, or
foolish for having me about. Only Mother knowing I was his daughter and letting everyone believe the lie.'

'A child born within a marriage is the responsibility of the husband.'

'Correct. I was the responsibility. Not the
daughter.'

But she didn't know for certain. Even if Mr
Hart had never touched her mother, it didn't exactly prove her as being her father's.

She put a hand to her face, feeling the need to
hide her thoughts from Edge.

He could never understand. She didn't. Every
day she'd reminded herself that it didn't make a
difference. She was her own person and nothing
else signified. Her life was no different than if
she'd been born legitimate—that was what she'd
told herself while growing up. Over and over
she'd told herself it didn't matter.

He leaned forward. 'Lily, let it drop now. Mr
Hart knew your mother at the time of your birth

and he believes you to be born completely within marriage. You should be pleased.'

She shook her head. 'No. I can't let it drop. Granted, it's best to be a child of marriage. But why should I believe him? He can say that easily enough. Pretend innocence. Or he could be doing it out of a kind thought, trying to protect my mother.'

'Then forget it all. Leave it a question in your life, but not one you ask yourself.'

'That's like telling me to forget I have arms and legs. First the newspaper mentioned it as if it were no consequence and then years later the story appeared in the Swift book that my mother was unfaithful to my father and I resulted from her infidelity. Those words can never be erased.'

'You only need to remove them from your mind.'

She reached across, putting her hand over his. 'Whenever I visited someone after the publication, I wondered if somewhere in the house a copy of the book rested. I accepted it. After all, I was different. I was Abigail's half-sister, not whole. She was the true child and I wasn't. My parents should not have caused such a thing.' She thought of the blacksmith. 'Mr Hart knows he wronged me, too. He understands. Because all along he knew that a child wasn't his, yet the world said it and he let them.'

'Perhaps you should be angry at the world, then.'

'Perhaps I am. But, I don't feel angry. Particularly.'

'Lily.' He took her by the shoulders. 'You can't go back and change the past. I can't remove the scars on my legs. You can't remove the scars in your life.'

So easy for him. No one saw his scars. They were hidden. And the ones that were caused by the newspaper article concerning his father, no one would dare approach him about it.

'What others did has no bearing on who you are.' His voice barely carried to her ears.

'It's what I believed that had meaning. Has meaning.' She looked at the carriage top, shaking her head.

'Don't care about it. Accept whatever you wish. Mark it as a day on the calendar and move on.'

'You have spent every day of your life on the pedestal of society's eyes. Every day.'

'Not the moments in the tavern.'

'You could enter the life in the tavern and exit

back into a carriage with a crest on the side. You've always been able to ride in a carriage with a gilded symbol showing the world you're one of the few. For every second of your life you've known you are important.'

'I've known I was important because of my birth. Not because of anything I did. And now I am ready to change that. I can. I can work to improve the lives of others. But I only have a short span in which to work. My injuries this year showed me that. Third time I might not be so fortunate.'

'My role has been to be Abigail's sister and I was determined to protect her from the things I overheard from Mother's friends. I watched over her as close as the governess and the governess could do as she wished most of the time, because I couldn't risk anything happening to the one person who looked up to me.' She'd never realised it before. Abigail took Lily exactly as she was.

'You can think of yourself now. And your future.'

'Yes, I can.' She examined her fingers. 'Abigail will be marrying soon and starting a new life. Father prefers solitude. Mother is away. I'll be comfortable at home.' She raised her head.

'Mother said it was my fault. My fault my parents argued. She said her life would have been so much better if I'd not been born.'

She could have slapped him many times over and not seen the steel return to his eyes so quickly.

'You have very solid reasons not to marry.' He picked up her handkerchief that had somehow settled on the floor of the carriage.

He handed her the cloth, but their fingers didn't touch. An ache settled in her heart. She needed to make him understand.

'Don't think I believed her when she blamed me. I might not have spoken the words, but I put it right back on her. It added another blot to her actions—her blaming me.'

'She was doubly wrong to do that.'

'When I heard the tales of Lady Caroline Lamb trying to gain Byron's attention, I thought of my mother's actions. It pleased me that Mother wasn't the only woman who caught herself up in the drama of love.'

She'd been so thankful her mother hadn't attached herself to Byron or Wellington or someone like that. Her friendship with Sophia Swift had been disastrous enough. The two women had both become fascinated by the same man and had

had a falling out. The *Memoirs* had been published not long after.

She'd never asked her father how he'd felt to be
mentioned in the book, but by the time the book
had been printed, her mother had left.

'I never once thought about what it would be
like to not be the bastard child,' she said. 'Well,
not often. That would have been like telling myself I wanted to feel different about who I was.
You wanted to see what it was like to be on the
other side of your life, but I didn't feel that way.
I wanted to be happy with who I was.'

'Perhaps it would help to talk all this through
with your mother.'

Lily considered the words. 'I don't want to be
around her.'

His brows flicked in acknowledgement. 'Every
family has tales. And they should remain within
the family.'

She knew he thought of the newspaper.

'I am sure you read of my father's little blun-
der,' he said.

The words jarred into her. 'Yes, I knew.'

She knew much more of Edge's life than he
realised. He'd even had an attachment once and
she'd not known the woman, but she knew of her.

'Did you know of the babe before it appeared in the paper?' he asked.

'Yes.'

'And you didn't tell me?'

'Of course not. Would you have thanked me?'

'No.'

'Would you have believed me?'

'I don't know, but I certainly would have later. My father confessed to my mother after she'd read about it. A nice quiet conversation behind closed doors, then he walked out and she didn't have the strength to leave the room.'

'The mistress was no happier. She was at my mother's home before the baby was born.' The words hurt to speak them, an admission of the world she lived in when she wasn't at her father's. A completely different world of gaiety, misery and celebration of doing as one wished without regard for others.

'You knew her?' Clipped words.

'Yes. My mother wasn't welcome in many places. She tended to know everyone in the same situation as she was. Any married woman who hadn't strayed outside the marriage would never have stepped foot in Mother's home. So the women Mother welcomed were usually mistresses of society men. They shared stories. My mother had a husband who supported her and the other women often didn't. So I saw the mistresses and heard the tales of their life.'

All the stories were similar. Adventure. Love. Abandonment. The search for another man to ease their pain or house them. Lily had heard them over and over. The names changed, but the stories didn't. Heartbreak. Jealousy. Wives having more children and husbands having more mistresses.

Edgeworth paused, debating on his words. 'I saw that the woman had funds to leave the country.'

He'd seen no other way. His mother needed to survive. His father couldn't abandon her and start a different family. How could she go to any social events where her husband might be present? The Duke would have been welcomed as always and one couldn't invite his wife if he'd shunned her. But the Duke could have retained his friends, or at least, most of them. Sides would have been chosen and his mother would have been tossed away. Only his father would have been allowed to walk the same paths, albeit, alone.

And his father wasn't the same. He'd changed over the course of a year—became confused. His temper had floated below the surface where it had never been visible before. He'd planned to leave to be with his mistress, but he'd been unable to go.

Edge had taken the decision from him.

Edge had paid the woman to leave and that had taken some wrangling on his part. His father—his mind had been so unfocused. Edge used it to his advantage.

He'd thought he might have to put the woman and her son on the ship himself, and he'd been kind to her. Compassionate. Wanted to see the baby. Agreed with her plight. Bought time. Bought the woman a husband and shipped the woman and child to the Americas. Told her she could be a part of the growing country. He'd done what was best for all of them, her included. Hadn't he?

It needed doing. His mother could not look anyone in the eye, but she'd pulled herself together.

Finally they'd all realised his father's mind had been waning for a long, long time. At first when they'd looked back, they'd thought his father's increasing silence had been due to the duplicity.

But later, when he was dying, they realised he'd been failing and hiding it from his family.

For his mother, that had made the betrayal easier to bear.

For Edge, it had been harder.

He'd wondered if his father had crumbled under the weight of his duties, or if fate had stepped in and twisted things to blemish his father's life.

'You will be able to put it behind you,' he said to Lily.

But he'd not been able to do the same. The past lingered worse than the scars on his legs. He felt guilt for manipulating his father's life. Guilt he'd not realised what was happening until the paper had blasted the words into peoples' minds.

If he'd discovered his father's mistress earlier, he could have intervened before his mother was devastated. Before the rubbish was printed for his mother to see.

'I should go.' She turned to leave, but his fingers tightened on hers. She pulled her hand from his, moving back. 'I have to.'

'Meet me in the gardens tonight.'

'I need to speak with my father.'

'And then meet me again.'

Chapter Ten

After asking the valet when her father would be home, Lily sat waiting in the sitting room. Whenever she or Abigail wanted to know their father's whereabouts, they'd always asked his valet. The answer was always the same. *Working.* Sometimes the valet left the house—taking food, clothing and a shaving kit to her father.

Several days could pass without seeing him and no one would think anything of it.

Then she and Abigail might be eating dinner and he would walk in. Or they might pass him in the hallway carrying the brown satchel stuffed with documents.

She held the recipe book and took out the bookmark—the Duchess paper she'd folded into a kite shape with red threads stitched through it to give it a string.

All the food in the book sounded tasteless. She put the place holder in a random spot, closed the book and kept it in her lap.

The sun painted the outdoors with an evening glow and she heard the door downstairs close and her father speaking with one of the servants, their voices a rumble she couldn't make out.

The beauty of the evening made anything seem possible.

She pictured Edgeworth as her husband—the broad shoulders holding her. The possibility of their children. The little ones playing in the same gardens their parents had tramped through as youngsters.

She shut her eyes, imagining the home she wanted. A home. Peaceful. She could stare down all the condescending society women of the world with Edgeworth at her side. He would protect her from their barbs, just by his very presence.

One stair creaked and her father's shoes padded on the carpet. Passing the room, he stopped when he saw her.

Years of sitting in a room concerning himself over bank notes and money he'd been entrusted to safeguard had stooped his shoulders and masked his height. She wondered if he reached her shoulder.

She looked at him. His brows had greyed and the drooping lids shaded his always tired eyes. She could see nothing in his round face that she recognised in herself.

Nothing.

'I only have a few moments,' he said. His frown apologised. 'I'm needed at the club. I promised I'd sit in for a few games tonight. I'd rather be home working, but I said I'd round out the table.'

She tightened her hold on the book. 'Who is my father?'

His throat worked. 'I am.'

'That's not what you once told Mother.'

He stepped inside and shut the door behind him, the quiet click reverberating, and his hand still on the knob. His chest heaved out. His head shuddered when he shook it from side to side. 'I cannot discuss it.'

'Then you are the only one who can't.'

'Lily,' he snapped.

'You shouted it to Mother so that all the servants could hear.'

'I don't remember that.'

'What do you remember, then?'

'I told you I will not discuss it. Is it not enough that I fed and clothed you all these years?'

'Just tell me I am not your child, then. I want to know.'

'What difference does it make?'

'I asked myself that a thousand times. But for some reason I cannot fathom it seems to make a tremendous difference.'

His head leaned closer to the door and his chin trembled. 'You're my daughter.'

'You don't know for certain. Do you?'

He pushed his hand over his forehead, before waving his palm between them. 'I thought this had long ago died away and then that courtesan's book brought everything back.' Shutting his eyes for a moment, he opened them on a deep breath. 'You're my daughter. But it was hard to look at you when you were a child. I would always be looking for someone else's face in your smile.'

She couldn't remember how old she was when she'd heard the argument, or how old she'd been when she'd figured out what it meant. But she'd felt a fraud for living in her father's house, pretending to be Abigail's full sister. She'd been so angry at her mother.

'I looked in the mirror and examined my own face for resemblance,' she said. 'Many times.'

'I can't blame you.' His fingers clenched in the air, but didn't close into a fist. 'It ate at me for years—wondering.' He put his hand at his side. 'When you were about four or so, I went to see the blacksmith. He didn't know who I was. I wanted to see him for myself. I asked directions, simple enough, and left.'

'What did you think?'

'I—I confronted your mother. That had to have been the discussion you heard. She refused to tell me. Refused. I took it as an admission.' He shook his head. 'I didn't want to think about it. But then, I started noticing you'd taken to turning your chin just like my own mother did.' He laughed. 'The day I saw that, I thought you must have copied her. But it stayed in my mind. Over and over I thought of it, then I decided you learned the movement from the visits.'

'I cannot remember anything I do similar to her.'

'I studied you every time I was in the room with you, trying to find the answer. But the more I was near you, I decided you were your own person.'

'You do not know.'

'I do. But I didn't believe it at first. Not at all. Your mother and I—it was almost impossible for you to have been my child, but not entirely. We fought and returned to each other so many times I could not keep up with the dates. Later, I thought she'd returned to me when she did because she'd suspected a child was on the way and wanted to be certain I could think it mine. Because at the start of our marriage, she would return to her parents' home and it was so close to the blacksmith's shop.'

'Why do you think I am yours?'

'Put your hand flat on the table.'

She held the book in her left hand and placed her right on the table. All her fingers aligned straight, except the little finger, which crooked a bit.

'One day I noticed that. My own father had the same bend of his fingers. It's not much, but with the movement of your head like my mother… And then my great-aunt came for a visit. You were her all over again. I realised you are my own, but even that didn't bring your mother and I closer. She demanded so much attention. I couldn't concentrate on my work. I couldn't. Not with her upheavals. You know what she's like.'

'Yes, because I was with her more than you were.'

'She is your mother. Mothers and daughters are meant to be together.'

'You never liked having us around.'

'I did. I truly did after I realised you were mine. I knew it shouldn't matter, but it did.'

'Are you certain, or are you telling yourself what you want to believe?'

'Lily. I believe you are mine. I treat you as such now, whether or not I have found that difficult in the past.' He shrugged. 'I cannot do better than that.'

'Sophia Swift's words are written in ink.'

'She has financial incentive to stir as much mud as she can.' He looked away and downwards. 'Do not blame her entirely. Your mother and I set the stage for her. Your mother and I betrayed you first. There should never have been a question.' His hand slid away. He looked at the painting over the fireplace, then looked towards the rug. She could see his profile. 'The fault was mine. Mostly. I didn't want to be with her, but I couldn't bear the jealousy. She is the only woman I have loved with such passion and the only woman I have hated with equal passion.' He looked up and for a moment his stare faded. 'I would say she felt the same of me.'

His head wobbled. 'Time and time we tried to forgive each other. But the memories couldn't go away. We couldn't shut out the past we kept repeating.'

'You did nothing but fight when you lived in the same home, and even when you only saw each other for a few minutes, you'd be at each other's throats. I feared you might commit murder.'

He took in a breath and the memories took his vision from the room. 'I miss her.'

'She swung a candlestick at you.'

'You warned me.' He smiled. 'I dodged. No harm done.'

'*Father.* She could have killed you.'

He shook his head. 'She would have missed at the last moment.'

Lily stared.

A spasm of pain crossed his face. 'She was not the only one at fault. I knew exactly how to en-rage her.'

Lily shut her eyes, thinking of all the clashes and how they'd dug into her. Then she peered at her father. The lines in his face seemed to have been there for ever.

'We should never have married,' he said. 'Yet I couldn't imagine myself wed to anyone else. We can't be together, but…' He held out his hands, palms up, and his shoulders rose. 'I cannot explain to you what I don't understand. I don't regret the marriage. Or my daughters. I regret the hatred. But your mother…' He paused, shaking his head. 'Can't throw worth a flip, though.'

'You should not have married. Neither of you. To anyone.'

His brows furrowed. 'I'm not sure of that. Your mother—when she laughs, she laughs with her whole heart. Her being. She doesn't just see the colour in life, she lives inside it.' He shook his head and looked at the ceiling. 'Lily, she loves you and Abigail both. She told me that's why she had to leave. Because she had made such a hash of things and wanted to take her reputation with her so the two of you would not be harmed by it any more.'

He walked over, leaned down and kissed Lily's forehead. He straightened. 'I love both my daughters equally. And I care for your mother. She gave me my daughters. But it's more than that. I love her. I don't know why. But I do. I have from the first moment I saw her.'

'Couldn't you have fallen in love with some-one…quiet?'

'I wish, but it just didn't happen that way.'

'But if you decided I was yours, why didn't you refute Sophia's book?'

'And who would believe me? Your mother was likely to say something to spite me. Or if she claimed you were mine, it would only look as if she hid her unfaithfulness. The blacksmith and your mother were seen together many times.' He shook his head. 'Everyone would have believed I was merely blinded to your mother's infidelity. Saying nothing was best. I mentioned in conversation to friends that you took after my side of the family and I could see the waver in their eyes. I could have put out broadsheets and no one would have believed me.'

Emotions shut out her words before they could reach her mouth. She took a moment to push her thoughts far enough away so that she could speak them. 'Did you think that I would have liked to have heard you say I was your child? Did you not realise how it would affect me?'

'I never expected you to have heard the tales. You kept to yourself.'

'Page fifty-four.' She'd read it.

'I didn't realise you knew.' He stared at her. '*How* did you find out?'

She balled her hand into a fist. 'What is that witch's name?' She thought for a moment. She could remember a page in a book, but couldn't think of the woman's name she'd known of since childhood. 'Agatha Crump. Mrs Crump told me how sorry she was that such a thing was printed about me in the Swift *Memoirs*. I didn't know what she meant. So I found a copy. Paid for it. I paid well for that book. And on page one, I realised it would not end well for me.'

'I've never read it.' He sneered. 'Rubbish.'

'I burned my copy. A page at a time.'

He ran his fingers through his thinning hair, his knuckles thick and his fingers permanently curled. His lips pressed up. 'You should know, now that you and Abigail are older and things have settled, your mother asked if she might return.'

Her throat tightened, preventing words for a second. 'No.' Disbelief flooded her. In that heartbeat, she could have thrown a candlestick.

Her mother's emotions had flashed inside her. She clutched the chair to keep upright.

'I said yes.' He straightened, the stoop of his shoulders leaving. 'Years ago, I only agreed to let her go and provide for her because she was causing you and Abigail so much grief.'

Now, she wished the blacksmith had been her father. Everything would have made more sense to her.

Her question had been answered, but it wouldn't make a difference if her mother returned. All the old stories would resurface and her mother would fan them hot again.

Lily would know the truth, not that it really mattered. All her life she'd been in the right household, but she'd lived a lie in her own heart. She'd thought herself making the best of a bad situation, but she'd not been. If she had, finding out the circumstances of her birth wouldn't have been significant. But she'd felt differently about herself the moment the blacksmith said he could not be her father. The man who was her father had betrayed her more than the blacksmith.

Her father had not claimed her. He'd let the Agatha Crump vultures sit back on their perches and devour tales about Lily and her mother. Flesh had appeared to remain on the bones, but it hadn't really. The years of tamping down anger and smiling and not caring and not letting anything bother her flowered into one lone thistle inside Lily's heart with barbs that felt like they were sticking out of her skin from the inside and she really wanted to fling something somewhere.

But she couldn't rage at her father—that was how her mother would have handled it. And a lifetime of clamping her lips together kept Lily's mouth shut, but only barely.

Lily turned, taking a lamp as she left the room, and marched to the stairs. She grasped the side of her skirt and lifted enough so the cloth didn't hamper her decisive steps.

She should be happy. She should. She could hear the sensible side of herself saying all was well. That now she didn't have to feel any concern over not being the same as Abigail. She could tell Abigail what nonsense they had believed all these years. They could throw back their heads and chuckle at yet another time their mother had upended their lives. What a jest.

At the bottom of the stairs, Lily breathed as if

she had moved up and down them a dozen times. The light still shone in the sky, but the heat of the house smothered her; heat she'd not noticed until the past few moments. She glanced at her hand and realised she carried a lamp. She stared at the closed door in front of her, noting the outline of the light on the wall. It quivered.

The movement took the heat from the room around her and from the object in her hand and pulled it into her body.

Thrusting the door open, she moved into the night air, letting the breeze push air into her lungs, unaware of anything but the feelings strangling her.

She flicked away the dampness on her lashes. Dropping the gripped fabric, she brushed a hand over her eyes.

She wanted to move to some foreign country where everyone talked differently than she did and she could walk by and hear their chatter and not be a part of what they were saying. They would go about their daily lives and do their routine and she would move about alone and do what she must to get through her world.

She had already lived in a world like that for twenty-five years—why not continue?

* * *

Lily sat on the bench, trying to pull relief from the night air. The light didn't flicker from movement any more, but kept a steady glow, and she placed it beside her, trying to enjoy the moonlight.

She needed to let Edgeworth know that she wasn't at all considering the role of duchess. Her father might be her father, but the stain on her name remained. She did not wish to court. And she would not see him alone again.

But she wasn't going to tell him her mother might return, because it wasn't going to matter. This time, her father could take care of her mother's tempers and if one of them killed the other, she would not shed a tear.

Edge stepped from his house, silhouetted by the moon.

The light washed over him, adding shades which should have made him severe and sombre, but didn't. He moved with a purposeful stride and fluidity.

The glow from the lamp encompassed them, bringing them together in the night. But the light glimmered in a way that showed his clothes silvery and she remembered the armour shapes she'd seen in houses—relics from the past.

'He says I am his child.' The words cracked across the air, moving through the stillness, bouncing back to reverberate in her head.

'You should be pleased.'

'Of course I should.' Of course. Of course. But her parents—both of them hadn't taken the time to even think how their squabbles and lies seared into Lily's life. She'd been invisible to them for the most part. A convenient daughter to watch over the younger sister.

A door shut—the front door of Edge's home— and she jumped, jostling the lamp.

'That's just Foxworthy,' Edge said, reaching out, a reassuring tap on her arm, while he glanced towards his door. 'He's hiding from someone or up to something, or he'd be at his own home. He never shows up without reason.'

Lily leaned over, touching the knob on the lamp, lowering the wick and extinguishing the flame. She didn't want Foxworthy to see her. Or anyone else. She'd not been thinking when she brought the lamp out with her.

A curl of smoke seeped from the top of the glass, a whiff of it touching her nose. When she released the knob, the lamp tilted, sitting too close to the edge.

Instinctively, she reached to keep the globe from falling and her palm slid on to the hot glass. Pain shot into her palm. She jerked her hand back and cried out from the pain. 'I've—I just burned my hand.'

He lifted her from the waist, put her on her feet and bustled her to his house. 'I've some burn medicines.' He said the words over his shoulder, continuing forward.

She scrambled to keep up with him and he didn't even seem to hurry, but kept her on her toes.

'It isn't proper for you to lead me into your home and into the family quarters,' she said. 'What if I'm seen?'

He stopped, and the momentum carried her against him, but he didn't loosen his clasp, but caught her and held her steady.

'If anyone in my household hasn't figured out that we're meeting by now, I would think it only because they are sleeping through their day.'

'I don't want to be my mother's daughter.'

He moved close enough so she could see the

quirk in his lips. 'You're stuck with that one. I'm pretty sure.'

Giving up the resistance, she followed him, moving up the stairway, into the private rooms of the house.

He led her through a doorway and with her free hand she grabbed the frame and put the brakes on her feet.

He turned, momentarily paused. He looked at her. 'The only room with lamps lit. I can't see the burn in darkness.'

He led her into a room scented with all the things which reminded her of comfort. Starched curtains. Lemony clean table tops and oaken furniture, and a chair even the largest man could fit comfortably, its leather aged from years of life. A wooden carved stand of the sort a lady might put a wig on sat on a table, but atop it was an older hat, tilted at a rakish angle, and she remembered his father and realised the hat was most likely his.

The bed almost appeared an afterthought, close to a wall, a covering over it in forest hues. She held the wrist of the burned hand. 'This is a masculine room.'

'I would hope.'

She looked at her palm. 'Oh. My mistake. I didn't burn myself at all.' She raised the hand she'd been using to hold her wrist and tucked the other hand at her side.

'Wrong hand, Lily. Do you think I've gone senile?'

She moved inside 'If anyone sees me, I will be branded just like my mother.'

'No one will see you,' he said. 'I should call Cook. She's an expert on caring for burns. Better than our physician.'

'No. Don't wake her. It's only a small burn.' This time she held out the correct palm.

He huffed out a breath. '*Those* are always painless.'

'I can barely feel it,' she said and it was true. His touch soothed her. He clasped her wrist, palm up, and they both looked at the blister forming just below her forefinger.

He snorted. 'You don't have to be brave. I know how much a burn hurts.'

'It will be gone in a few days and not even leave a scar. This is nothing.'

'Is something else bothering you?'

She couldn't tell him her mother might return. The old stories would burst to life again.

Lily pulled her hand closer to her body, but he still clasped her wrist and moved with her, sliding his grasp to hold her fingertips.

Clenching the uninjured hand, she said. 'My father. Right now I wish the blacksmith would take his place.'

'Lily. Why aren't you happy that your father is the man who gave you his name?'

'I can forgive Mother easier, even with her theatrics. My father's game was more far-reaching. He says he didn't mean to deceive me. Didn't mean to let me think I wasn't his. And yet, when I think back, he accused her of so much without caring whether we heard or not. When they first lived separately, he would arrive unannounced. Quiet, with his eyes shouting condemnation.'

She exhaled. 'They saw each other more when they both had separate houses in London than when they were together. Father would visit regularly. I dreaded when he'd walk in the door.'

He'd arrive wearing his long back coat and carrying the leather satchel, and the house would erupt.

'I tried to keep things calm because I didn't think I belonged—it was the way I made myself be a part of the family.'

She braced herself and searched for the words, but when she tensed Edge moved closer, one arm falling around her in a touch gentle enough to calm a baby bird fallen from the nest.

This lie had been a part of her. But most importantly, she'd believed it. She'd been careful not to cause any upsets—not that she wanted to. She'd taken care of Abigail, the true daughter, and done the best she could to watch over her sister. Her duty.

She couldn't undo twenty-five years of believing something untrue about herself. And she'd so prided herself on looking at the situation the same way she would have if it had been someone else's life.

'Lily. The past is done,' he said.

He took her to the leather chair and sat, pulling her softly against him, letting her relax, except he still held the burned hand away from their bodies.

The past wasn't done. It was flaring into her heart, working its way through her over and over and back again. Not only could she not erase it. She couldn't keep it from growing in her memory.

'I hated being at my mother's house when she first left Father. It wasn't home. Finally, Mother fell into a new friendship and agreed to let us visit home. Once, when she had been crying and complaining for days and I couldn't stand it any more, I decided I must find a way to get us to Father's.'

'Your governess should have taken you.'

The woman would have had to get permission and Lily wasn't waiting. 'I sent a maid to tell the coachman to get the coach ready. It wasn't unusual for Mother to have me give the servants her instructions. Then I gave Abigail the task of capturing the coachman's attention. She wasn't to get in front of the horses, but to pretend. I told her to fall and act hurt. When he checked on her, I slammed the carriage door, called Abigail and told the coachman that the governess was already in the vehicle. Away we went to Father's house. We hid in the attic for two days and Cook had to know we were raiding the larders and taking all the food we could carry and buckets of water. No one looked for us and we became tired of hiding, so we moved to our rooms. We still laugh about the adventure. The governess was at Father's home by then and continued lessons as if we'd never been missing.'

'The adults let you get away with it.'

'The governess knew, and the other servants, but I never did know if my parents realised we'd taken it upon ourselves to relocate. My favourite childhood adventure. Abigail's, too. We even sneaked out into the garden to play during the day. Being ignored at Father's was a respite. But the escape didn't last for ever.'

Her mother just could not be alone long. She would be despairing and missing her daughters. 'Mother sent for us again. Back we went, unsure of what we'd find, knowing it wouldn't be sunshine and roses, but weeping or anger. She never took her anger out on us. Ever. But to see and hear her raging upset Abigail. Abigail would be in tears and Mother in tears and the governess would take Abigail to another room. I would stay with Mother. The maids would give us a wide berth.' She laughed. 'Mother's maids kept far, far away and wouldn't have ever turned their backs because they knew a shoe might be flung.' She laughed. 'My mother could not have vases or breakables on the shelves in a room with a fireplace. They made a dramatic crash.'

Lily touched Edge's arm. 'Once she told me never to be afraid when she threw something. She'd never hit me or Abigail. Her rage wasn't as out of control as I believed. The windows were never broken. The glassware was flung at the fireplace, unless there was a fire. Then she might pick up the poker with both hands and bat a whole tabletop of items on to the floor. Noise and drama. I'm pleased that was left out of the Sophia Swift *Memoirs*, although everyone who knows Mother knows how volatile she is.'

Only her mother did seem protective of Abigail. 'No mention of Abigail was made in the book. Everyone believes I am not my father's true child. My sister, though, no one doubts she's Father's. She has the dimple in her chin and the Hightower eyes.' Lily let a smile soften her words. 'My mother should have been an actress. She so enjoyed the performance and I so hated it.'

She looked at him. 'I felt so bad for days after I threw the biscuit at you. I swore never to throw anything again and I haven't.'

'I didn't mind.' He remembered the biscuit hurled in his direction and the surprise. His brothers didn't dare toss anything at him. Either a tutor was near, or he could use his size to easily put them to the ground and twist an arm behind their back.

He'd once made Steven say he loved Agatha Crump and wished to marry her.

Now, Edge held Lily's hand, absently rubbing her fingers, careful not to touch the burn.

'That moment I flung the biscuit, I saw myself becoming like my mother. I couldn't be like her.' She took in a breath. 'She exhausted and worried everyone around her. I even think she did the same to herself and that brought about the sadness.'

'You're worrying yourself a little more than you should,' he said. 'You're your own person, not anyone else.'

He put his face so close he could feel her breath on his cheek. 'I like you as you are.'

He admired her serious nature. She hadn't flitted around like a butterfly, waving a fan in his face, trying to catch his attention. But she'd not needed to after she threw the biscuit at him. He'd noticed her each time he saw her, but the instances were not often enough when they were young.

'All marriage isn't unhappy,' he said. 'If you look closely, the town is full of people who creak along at a sedate pace. The turtles, not the hares. They are much quieter than the unhappy people who complain of miseries. Overall, it's not polite to talk about how wonderful your life is, unless it is to mention the number of years married.' He paused. 'And even that is a risk because my parents had been married for quite some time.'

She met his eyes. 'I know.'

'I can't think of many good things you can safely mention without becoming a braggart. For instance, I cannot mention to anyone…' he put a thumb at her cheek '…tiny flecks of springtime green nestled in brown eyes.'

Tiny flecks that flourished bursts of awareness into him. She looked so perfect in his room.

She reached out and pushed at his chest, not moving him. 'Edge… Everyone has eyes.'

He heard her, but with her hand on his chest, forcing his heart into beating warmth throughout his body, he took a moment to find an answer. 'Not like yours. I would imagine no other eyes in the universe look exactly like yours.'

She'd left her hand on his chest, holding him captive, and she wasn't aware of it.

He was captive and captivated. Lips. Soft skin. Velvet eyes.

Edge pulled back so he could see her features.

He would like to see them on the face of a child— his child.

Before, he'd just thought her perfect for a duchess and rare because she wasn't awed by his title.

Now, he thought of her differently.

'Edge.' Lily pushed at his chest again and moved away. He didn't speak. She stepped to his window and looked out. 'Your house is so close to my father's. So close. I'd never be away from my mother.'

He watched her standing at his window. Awe trapped him silent and still. Rays of warmth flared into his body.

'Edge... Do you understand? I cannot bear to return to the misery my mother brings.'

'That's the past.'

He concentrated on her, wanting to understand and comfort her.

She shook her head. 'Don't diminish it. You can't brush away what happened with your father any more easily. And you—' She turned to him. 'You've only seen her from the outside.'

'I can help you if she returns. I've been on the inside of a scandal.'

'For a few years.'

'My father had been careful his whole life— as far as I know. But then he bought a new town coach and a phaeton, too, so he could race the younger men. He would have the valet prepare all sorts of scalp mixtures for his hair and he began taking Fowler's Solution from the apothecary. I only noticed when I saw the valet carrying an empty bottle and I questioned it.'

'You could reason with him, though.'

Edge snorted and shook his head. 'No. Not after— Not when— He changed completely.'

'She's coming back, you know. My father told me so. I swore, after she left, I'd never have her in my life again like that. You cannot keep ingesting poison and not expect damage.'

'I can keep it from you.'

Her head shuddered in disagreement and he had to take the lost look from her eyes.

He closed the distance and put his arms on her waist. 'I'll line the servants up elbow to elbow around the house if I have to. And I'll keep the supply lines open.'

Her lips turned up. 'The general has spoken.'

Sadness lingered on her face. She didn't believe him. He could tell.

He bumped his forehead against hers and

turned so that his face pressed at the top of her head. He savoured the wisps of her hair tickling him in a way that cascaded into him better than any hug he'd ever had.

'I wish you'd not burned yourself, but I'm pleased you're here,' he said.

His arms tightened and this time it melded them together, and he swept her backwards with him. He relaxed into the chair at his back, taking her along, moving his head enough so he could rest against the upholstery while savouring the flowery aroma of some hair mixture she wore that he could breathe in every moment of the rest of his life and never grow tired of.

He was having his first attic adventure. His first in his whole life. Lily took away the rules and structure and gave him a softness, but not everywhere. Just in the places he'd never felt soft before and he enjoyed the pulses of arousal mixing against the delicateness of her.

He hugged her close again, savouring.

'How is your hand?' he asked.

'It's fine now.'

'Let me see.'

She held up her hand.

'Closer,' he said.

She moved it. He shut his eyes.

'Against my face.'

Fingertips, softer than lace, touched his cheek. He could not imagine a bird having a softer wing tip. They stilled.

His hands tightened on her just enough to bring the feel of her completely into his body.

'I should have shaved.' He spoke aloud, both to himself and an apology to her.

'No.' Just a wisp of sound.

Then she touched his lips, following the outline, but the sensation strengthened beyond her caress. Her hands traced his whole body without leaving his face. He swallowed, opening his lips, and her fingernail gently grazed the skin.

'Why?' she asked.

'Because it feels better to me than to you.'

'It could not.'

He had botched the first proposal terribly, but he'd not been trained in it nor expected any resistance. But he wasn't going to botch the first real kiss. This was one he intended to remember longer than any orange biscuit.

He moved her slightly, turning her so he could savour every second and give her a feeling she would cherish.

'This is how it starts,' she said, whispering, shaking her head, turning away. 'It's not safe.'

'Yes. It is.'

He released her, but she didn't stand.

'One kiss,' he said, knowing it was likely the biggest lie of his life.

'No.'

But she didn't push away. She didn't move to her feet—she just sat and leaned closer against him.

'Half a dozen, then.' He didn't smile, again letting her hair brush his face. 'Twenty. And that's my final offer.'

He moved, seeing the grief flooding her eyes, or maybe it was fear.

'It's not— I just can't—'

He understood and he used the control that he'd demanded of himself so many times. He'd not botch the first kiss. The ones in the carriage had just been hints of what they could have together. 'We'll talk about it tomorrow.' He clasped his hand over her fingers and touched them again to his lips, and loosened his hold on her.

She slid to her feet, much in the same way a person might slide uphill.

He followed, sliding uphill, too, but with her

in front of him, it was no struggle. Their bodies remained as close as when they were sitting.

'You would like—' He caught her eyes and communicated in his gaze just how certain he was that it would be a pleasurable experience.

'I'm sure… But I might not want to stop.'

'You won't.'

Looking into the brown eyes, he saw sadness and all the feelings he felt at thinking he might never kiss her the way he wanted; might never again be alone with her. But he remembered how serious she'd seemed as a child, taking care that Abigail didn't hurt herself and playing the games her sister wanted to play. She'd even whispered to Abigail once not to bother him because he would have to go to university some day and it was full of lessons. Yet he'd never left his studies to talk with her. He'd only batted her away and she'd still drawn his name on the bench. *Lion Owl.* It made him smile, even now, to think of the moment he'd found it, scratched in pencil in her shaky, unpractised hand.

He cupped one hand to the back of her head and with the lightest touch, and the barest contact necessary so they could both have the utmost of control and no regrets for her—so he wouldn't have regrets—he pulled her so close their lips touched and then he just brushed against her.

'We'll talk again soon,' he reassured, trying to take the longing from her eyes and wish away the sadness.

She moved to the door and he stepped ahead, opening it for her.

She rushed out, running, he suspected, from her own feelings. She collided right into Fox's arms, knocking him against the wall and her stumbling along with him and, in true Fox-like fashion, he managed to land with both arms around her.

In one swoop, Edge pulled Lily from his cousin's grasp. 'Keep. Your hands. Off her.' Edge slammed the words out.

Fox raised his palms in surrender, eyes wide. 'She grabbed me first.'

'I did not.' She slapped him square across the face. Then her mouth made an O and she put both hands on her cheeks and ran to the stairs.

'One word to anyone and I will kill you,' Edge snapped to Fox, then Edge bounded after Lily.

'The path of true love is never smooth,' Fox called out in one of those *mother-knows-best* voices. 'I am available for advice.' The words faded from Edge's hearing and he hoped that Fox didn't say anything before figuring out it didn't matter whether he did or not because Edge was going to pound him anyway.

Lily almost made it through his garden when she remembered the lamp and turned back.

Edge rushed outside as she reached the bench.

'The lamp,' she called softly and ran, but her direction changed in mid-stride. She hurled herself against him, hugging him close. 'I'm ruined.'

'Fox will never say a word.' Edge's voice held command and reassurance.

'It doesn't matter,' she said, raising her face, looking at him, surrounded by a monument to strength. 'I'm ruined,' she whispered.

His eyes transferred something into her body, stilling her. The one look reassured and comforted. Erased everything that had ever happened to her. Gave her one moment of life that stretched eons.

His lips closed over hers in the kiss she craved, thundering her heart against her ribs. Her body woke, burned and soared.

She needed him so that she could stay alive. She needed his breath so she could breathe.

He pulled her against him and nothing hurt

anywhere, ever, in her whole life. Then everything chilled.

He pulled back, leaving her standing alone. He stood in front of her, but she was alone.

'I have to let you go,' he said. 'For now. Foxworthy has his nose to the window and the moonlight is bright.'

Thoughts were fragmenting before they could find their way in or out of her brain. She pushed herself to think of what Edge had just said and taught her lips to speak again.

'I've never liked Fox.'

'I imagine he figured that out when you slapped him.'

Edge stood motionless, a breeze teasing her with the scent of wool and leather, and tempting her to move closer so she could again smell his shaving soap from the morning. On another person the soap might seem floral, but on him, blended with his skin, the scent had a masculinity that pulled her. She couldn't step away because the air, without currents, held her, trapped, in place.

Edge moved. He calmly reached to the bench and took the extinguished lamp. Seemingly no different for their kiss, he indicated he would follow and walked her to the door. He handed her the lamp. Just handed it to her.

Irritation blasted, again fighting with the weakness that made words impossible.

He should kiss her again. Didn't he realise?

She stared at him. Feeling helpless.

'Goodnight, Lily.' His voice didn't sound the same.

Then she understood. The words came from the boy who'd sat all those years ago in the garden, unable to play and forced to remain at his studies.

He bent and kissed her again, his lips grazing her lips. 'Think of me tonight,' he whispered, and walked away.

'You were with Edge.' Abigail's voice jarred into Lily. Abigail stood at the top of the stairs, holding her own lamp, and effectively evaporating all the melty feelings inside Lily.

Lily stopped, staring upward. 'You were watching?'

'No. Fox heard you screech. He was on the way to see me and told me what he heard.' She crossed her arms. 'We waited and waited for you and when you didn't come out, I sent him to see if you were badly injured.' Her lips turned up in one of those *nabbed you red-handed* smiles.

Lily's chin firmed and she wondered what they'd heard. 'As you may have guessed,' she bit out the words and held up her hand, hoping she moved the one with the blister on it, 'I was injured.' She clasped her wrist, rotating the injured hand. 'And it hurts. Badly.'

Abigail clasped her own hand in a similar movement. 'I will remember to use that when I am courting.'

'Abigail, you can't ruin your reputation. You plan to wed and have a family.'

'And the sooner, the better.' Abigail fluttered her wrist. 'It probably wouldn't work on Fox, though. He's…' she laughed '…cunning.' Her eyes turned wistful. 'But if I married Foxworthy, I'd be a countess and you could wed Edge and you'd be a duchess. We'd both have children born into the peerage. Father would be in the clouds.'

'You'd better be the one to marry a peer if you intend for Father to be that happy.'

'You don't plan to marry the Duke?' She gasped. 'Lily. You're just—*meeting him*—privately. You've always hated— You know, people who act like—'

Lily brushed by her, moving up the stairway, but stopping as she moved even with her sister. 'I am not a woman *like that*. I am only friends with him and we have been acquainted since child-hood.'

'You weren't friends. You said he was uppity. And he is. At least Foxworthy is human. I'm not so sure about the Duke.'

'I slapped him.' They stood side by side on the stair.

'The Duke?' Abigail gasped, mouth staying open.

'Foxworthy. My hand. It was as if I had no con-trol. I'd been alone with the Duke and it was—I started turning into Mother. Just as I always feared. I'm like her. I slapped Foxworthy.'

Abigail's eyes widened. 'What did he do?'

'I stumbled against him and he caught me, but it was—I just—I was shocked and he had his arms around me.'

'Fox. Are you sure?' Abigail asked, her head moving turtle-like. 'Are you sure you didn't get them mixed up in the darkness?'

'No. No. No. I rushed out the door. I knocked him backwards and when he caught me, I didn't know what to do. I was not myself. The hall was dark and I just reacted. As Mother would have. With no thought.'

'Fox is adorable.'

Lily rolled her eyes. 'He says things he shouldn't, met you in the darkness, has too much fondness for married ladies and the only thing about him that's tolerable is his smile and his handsomeness, which he is quite proud of and makes him unattractive.'

'But that smile. It's perfect.'

'You can't let a weaselly little smirk be enough reason to be fascinated with him.'

Lily followed Abigail into her room and moved the newspaper aside so she could sit on Abigail's bed. Lily's recipe book still lay on Abigail's night table.

'Fox is handsome. I could kiss him all night.'

'I'm afraid to leave you alone in case you might sneak back out to visit Fox,' Lily said.

'No. You're afraid to leave me because otherwise you might trot back over to His Grace's house to ask him to kiss that burn better.' She peered across to her sister. 'I will remember to use that ploy. I bet I can end up with a marriage proposal within the hour.'

'I hope so. The sooner you're away and in someone else's care the happier I'll be.'

She couldn't read the recipe book in front of Abigail, so she slid from the bed and collected one of the lamps, lit it from the other one and put it on the table beside the bed. She picked up the newspaper.

Abigail moved to the mirror and touched the clasp of her jewellery case. She pulled out a necklace and held it in front of her. 'Perhaps I should spend more time with Foxworthy.' She turned to her sister. 'He is fascinating.'

'Go ahead,' she said to Abigail. 'Ruin yourself.' But she glanced at the mirror when she said those words.

'You're right about him, though.' Abigail smiled, admiring herself in the mirror. 'Fox is a rake.' She held the necklace closer. 'So, what were you and the Duke discussing?'

'I really think you should try to meet Foxworthy again,' Lily said. 'Now that I think of it, he has many admirable qualities.'

'I don't know that he's the one for me.'

Lily noticed that the necklace Abigail held wasn't her own.

Abigail put the emeralds to her neck. 'I like

Foxworthy, but I don't feel close to him. He's so flattering, but he keeps me at a distance—even when he is kissing me.'

'He should.'

'I could be any woman in his arms and he'd be just as content to kiss. I do like him, though. It's impossible not to. He's like one of your recipes that is quite good, but a person couldn't have it every day without getting sick of it.' Abigail laughed. 'Fox and I are getting to know each other better, but as we do, the chance of marriage gets more distant. I don't know what that says about us.'

'That you are thinking instead of following emotions?'

Abigail nodded. 'I'm not as emotional as you are.'

Lily sputtered. 'No.'

'It's true. Mother's outbursts bothered you more. You had to keep everything as correct as you could because it would upset you so.'

'Well, I'm not like Mother. She didn't keep anything correct and was always upset.'

'You don't like the outward explosions she liked. But you just keep them inside. You were always more upset than me. One orange biscuit would make everything fine for me and I'd forget about it. Not you.'

'I am not like Mother.' Lily ground out the words.

'Fine. You're not like her. You. Are. Not. Like. Her.'

'Don't say it like that.' Lily put her hands to her head.

'I could always fall asleep after our parents fought. But you'd try to get her to calm down, and really, it didn't matter that much. You even said to me it didn't because she'd put herself right back in a kettle of hot water every time. But you couldn't help soothing her because you felt you must.'

Abigail was wrong. But Lily knew she'd never slapped anyone in her life. Not anyone. Ever. But then she was being held by the Duke and her control was slipping away. When she saw Fox and he touched her, she'd just exploded.

Next she'd be throwing things. Like the time she threw the orange biscuit.

Abigail smiled. 'Don't look so distressed. It's been entertaining to discover what courting is like. We've both had our romance with a peer. We can casually mention some day how I broke

Foxworthy's heart before he became an earl and you broke the Duke's heart. It'll be a reminiscence we can have enjoyment with.'

'No.' Lily stood, took the necklace from her sister's hands and had Abigail turn so she faced the mirror while Lily fastened the jewellery. 'I don't ever want to jest about this. It's horrible. I am like Mother. The Duke makes me feel like her. No stronger than a butterfly and not able to do anything but flutter inside. I hate that. I am strong. Just not enough. Nothing makes sense in my thoughts when he is around.'

Abigail whirled around, eyes bright and beaming. 'Oh. I knew it. I could tell.' She grabbed her sister's arms. 'You truly like him and he is a peer, even if he is a bit distant. And he put the handkerchief out for you, didn't he?'

'It doesn't matter.' Lily pulled away from her sister's grasp. 'I'll not get into another one of those messes. If Edgeworth or I spent one moment dancing with someone else and it appeared we stood too close, it would be in the papers, just like the old lies. I don't want to live my life in the papers and I'm too muddle-headed when he's around to think properly.'

'You should never let people like Sophia Swift hurt you.'

Lily took a deep breath. 'I want to make sure you know that we are full sisters.'

Abigail rolled her eyes. 'I never doubted it. Who else could put up with me? You look exactly like the miniature of Father's aunt, anyway. I'd always thought it a painting of you until one day I asked where your picture had disappeared to and Mother told me it wasn't you.' She smiled. 'I did think it odd that you looked way older in the painting, but—' She shrugged. 'What do I know about art?'

Abigail patted the necklace. 'I think I will wear this when I break Fox's heart, if you don't mind.'

Abigail flounced to the doorway and looked back. 'We are full sisters. And sisters help each other. Remember that.' She twirled away so fast her skirt almost tripped her.

Chapter Eleven

'The cravat would pass any inspection,' Edge said. He leaned, looking into the mirror. The simple tie Edge had managed worked well enough for the meeting with his man of affairs.

'Are you sure you don't want your hair trimmed?' Gaunt asked for the second time.

'I most certainly do not.' Edge straightened, wishing his tone hadn't been so harsh, but the valet would have been nudged out of the way by a snail that morning. Still, Edge should have maintained decorum.

Gaunt put away the shaving supplies and his eyes didn't meet Edge's.

'I do appreciate your years of service, Gaunt.'

Gaunt paused suddenly. His lips turned up. 'Thank you.' But he didn't raise his head.

Frustration stopped Edge from saying more.

If anything, Gaunt seemed more distant, almost as though he was hiding inside himself, and now he took an extra moment wiping a cloth over the top of the mirror.

'Is anything wrong?' Edge asked, fighting impatience.

'No, sir.' This time Gaunt met Edge's inspection. The valet's eyes brimmed with mirth and then they darted to the window.

Edge's stare followed and then he saw the handkerchief across the way, caught in the window, hanging to the outside. 'Ah…' A welcome warmth flourished in his body and he took a second longer to look at the handkerchief.

'Does everyone in the household know?' he asked, curious, not upset.

'I would say you are the last person to be aware of it.'

'Everyone?' Edge read Gaunt's face.

A nod.

Edge put the towel by the wash basin. It would be a long time until darkness. Hardly seemed worth waiting if everyone knew.

'If they didn't notice the first…' Gaunt folded the cloth he used to dust, never taking his eyes from it '…they probably noticed the green one—

on the broom leaning against the corner of the house.'

Edge jerked his eyes to Gaunt's face, reading the truth.

'Or the third. On the front gate.'

Edge's grin tried to break through, but he kept it in check.

'I will collect the lower two and return them to their owner,' he said.

'If you collect the uppermost one—' Gaunt fought to keep his face straight '—I would take extra-special care.' Gaunt took in a quick gulp of air. 'Wouldn't want you falling from a ladder.'

'Your concern is taken in the spirit it is given,' Edge said.

'Thank you.' Gaunt walked out. An ally.

Instantly, Edge changed his plans for the day. He had some handkerchiefs to retrieve, although the one at the window couldn't be collected. Lily could bring that one to him later, after dark.

Edge walked into the sunshine, retrieved the linen on the broom. He kept himself from lifting it to his face, instead contenting himself to recall the mix of soap and springtime that made him think of Lily, of gardens and her childhood exuberance.

Then he folded the cloth and put it in his pocket. Next, he moved to the front gate and collected the one tied around the iron.

He took his time, fairly certain every window in his house had a face behind it watching him.

The butler at the Hightower residence received him. The butler had surely seen the handkerchief at the front gate. Had he not known what it was about, he would have instantly removed it.

Edge vowed that if he should have children, he would buy a small country hunting lodge for relaxation and have only one trusted servant about who lived in a nearby cottage, and he and his family would just have to get by. He imagined Lily and their children with him and wished he'd awoken earlier.

Edge looked around the Hightower sitting room. No portraits showed a perfect family. No intricate vases or books about. Just lamps, furniture and the one painting, the width of the mantel, of the Hightower bank. Lily's house reminded him of the studies of his childhood.

When Mr Hightower arrived in the sitting room, his pace was measured. He spoke, braced for unpleasant news. 'Everything going well, Your Grace?'

Mr Hightower didn't know about the hand-kerchiefs. Probably the only person in the two households who didn't.

'I wish to ask if I might call on your daughter.'

'Lily?' Hightower paused.

'Of course.'

'Well…of course.' Hightower collected himself. His face completely changed, lighting the room. He reached for the bell pull, snapped it so firmly that Edgeworth looked to the base to make sure it was still attached.

When Lily walked into the room her eyes were guarded.

'Your Grace.' She curtsied perfectly. Her eyes darted from him to her father and back.

'Edgeworth wishes to call on you, Lily,' her father informed her.

'He does?' She stared at him, seeming unable to take in the features of his face.

Edgeworth felt prickles of unease. 'Yes.'

Her jaw tensed. He wished he could read her thoughts. She definitely looked as if she were trying to tell him something with her face that she didn't want to say in front of her father, but Edge didn't think it the words he expected. Three handkerchiefs. Three.

Then Abigail pranced in behind her sister, her head bobbing a quick curtsy and her eyes alight. He would have thought she was the one expecting a— His gaze took in the sconce on the wall and he shuffled his feelings, and gave one censorious blink to the traitorous sister.

'Leave us for a moment, Abigail,' the father instructed.

Abigail's bottom lip quivered and she wavered, looking as if she tried to find some excuse, any excuse, to stay. She didn't budge. Expectation in her eyes.

Too many handkerchiefs. The father wasn't the only one who didn't know. Lily didn't either.

'Miss Abigail,' Edge said. He reached into his pocket and stepped to her, reaching out with the cloths. 'I believe you lost these in the garden.'

She took in a breath. 'Oh. Um… Aren't those yours, Lil?'

Lily's eyes changed from morning wonderment, to sunshine burn, and then to a storm's clash of lightning. 'They are Abigail's.' The last word snapped and ended on a hiss.

'Oh.' Abigail reached out, hand limpid, eyes wide, ever so unaware. 'I wondered where they'd gone.'

'And how did you end up with them?' Hightower asked Edge.

'They fluttered in my direction.'

Hightower stared at his daughters.

'Abigail,' Lily said, 'gets misguided and I'm sure while she was misguided, she lost them.'

'I suppose I should return them to my room,' she said. 'As no one here seems to appreciate them.' She flounced out.

Lily closed the door behind her sister, the click firm.

Lily moved to the sofa, careful to sit so her skirt wouldn't wrinkle. Edge sat across and her father remained standing.

'I had considered calling on you,' Edge said, irritated at the hesitancy in his voice. The one time he needed to feel like a duke and he didn't. In fact, perhaps the only time since his father's death that he didn't feel his title.

'I think it is a lovely idea, however…' She swallowed. 'I'm… I have a secret that I must tell you and I think when you hear it we will both decide to put the question aside.'

He waited.

'Yes. I didn't want it known…'

He raised his brows, watching her try to think.

Her eyes brightened when she settled on an idea. 'I'm in love with Foxworthy.'

'Lily.' Her father gasped, stepping back. Apparently he was hearing this for the first time.

'I didn't want to tell you, Father.' The words rushed. Guilt? 'I realised my true feelings recently. It has been a deep secret of mine. No one knows. Not even Abigail.'

'I understand your reluctance.' The father's lips moved to form more words, but he said nothing for a second. 'One wouldn't want to marry the wrong cousin.' His eyes raked over his daughter's face.

'Miss Lily.' Edge rose, stepped forward and held out his hand to her. She had no choice but to rest her fingers in his. The touch hit him to his boots. He'd been planning to let her off the hook, particularly since her scheming sister had set up the meeting. But Fox? Oh, hell, no.

'I completely understand. I care deeply for him, too. One can't help but love him,' he said. 'Does he reciprocate?'

'He will, I'm sure, eventually.'

'How could he not?' Edge's grip tightened on her fingertips. His eyes locked on hers. 'I did notice that intensity you had for him the last time we were together. You ran right into his arms and were overcome with emotion.'

'*Lily?*' Hightower choked out the word.

'Yes.'

He put her fingertips almost to his lips. 'I am completely at ease with that.' He kissed her fingertips, feeling the tug away. He released his grasp and her hand shot back almost to her shoulder, and her fingers were curled.

'The caress you gave him awed me.'

'*Lily?*' her father repeated.

'Yes, Lily,' Edge said. 'Please share with your father that moment so he will understand your deepest feelings.'

'I stumbled,' Lily said. 'Not ran. And I looked up into his eyes and his face, and I could not believe what I had just done. An error. Of monumental proportions.'

'No. It wasn't. Because of your deep devotion for Fox, then I don't see how being in his arms could be considered such an error.'

'Before. The stumble.'

'Again. Not an error.'

'You don't understand a woman's tender feelings.'

'Not for Foxworthy.'

'Lily,' her father said. 'You've never been a particularly good liar that I could tell. And you're not getting any better.'

She looked at Edge, her head cocked to one side, brows raised and her mouth in a straight line. 'Marriage... It's not for me.'

'Lily,' her father inserted, 'just because your mother and I didn't have the best of marriages, don't let it discourage you.'

His face tightened when he mentioned his wife, but so did Lily's.

Edge stood. 'I suppose I should be on my way. And, who knows?' Edge frowned. 'Perhaps you will change your mind about courting.'

She didn't relax at all.

He examined her. He walked forward, staring at her face.

Reaching in his pocket, he pulled out a handkerchief and put it in her hand, letting their fingers brush, before moving away. 'I believe you have something on your face. A speck of powder?'

She looked at the silk, ran a finger over the gilded embroidery threads and looked at him.

He touched a finger to his lip, at the same place the tiny scar appeared on hers.

She brushed at the area. 'Did I get it?'

He snapped his chin up a bare amount to give assent, noting the way her fingers kneaded the cloth in her grasp.

She held the handkerchief back to him.

He refused it with a wave of his hand. 'You can send someone with it later.'

'Yes, Lily. It should be laundered first. You know that,' her father said.

'I should take my leave. I just remembered that Fox and I are to go to White's tonight, and we tend to stay out until the early hours of the morning. So please don't be in any hurry to have it returned.'

She wore a spencer because of the chill in the air and arrived at the bench near one-thirty in the morning.

Edge stood waiting.

'How long have you been out?' she asked.

'Since the lights went out in your house. I didn't want an audience. I am sick of having an audience when I talk with you. I've sent Fox to Andrew's house. He's taken Mother for another portrait sitting with Beatrice and they won't be back for a few days because he values his life and I explained this is the easiest way to keep it. He owes me for the scrapes I've got him out of.'

She put her hands to her cheeks. 'I must apologise to Fox for slapping him.'

'I wouldn't,' Edge said. 'He had no business skulking around the house at that moment and he knew it. You can slap him again and I'm sure he'll have deserved it for something.'

'I can't believe I did that.' But she did. A side of herself she feared surfaced when she was around Edgeworth. Her emotions erupted. 'I shouldn't have met you tonight.'

'Yes. You should have. Did it occur to you that you could have just agreed to court and we could have just seen each other in your family's sitting room for a few times? Unless, of course...' He started that tickly thing again where his breath brushed against her cheek and warmed all the air around her. 'I prefer to court out here as well. Excellent choice, Lily. You're taking away the night chill quite well.'

'It would get Abigail's and my father's hopes up if we met in public. And what would we have talked about?'

'The weather.' He reached out, pulling her close, sending the right kind of shivers into her body. 'The world. The ships at sea. Just hearing your voice is conversation enough for me.'

'You sound like Fox.'

She felt the shake of his head more than saw it. 'Well, because of your deep affection for him, it should make you happy.'

'You know I just said that to try to discourage Father's hopes.'

'I've never sounded like Fox before in my life. If I do, perhaps I should remain silent.'

His cold nose pressed above her cheek and warm lips rested on her skin. 'I think silence now would be…pleasant.'

A chilled button from his waistcoat pressed at her thumb.

She tried not to let his words sway her. She needed to get back inside. She'd only ventured out because she'd not wanted him waiting and her not showing up. She would tell him they couldn't meet again. She opened her mouth to speak.

'Lean against my clasp,' he said, taking her in a light embrace, clasping his hands at the small of her back. 'I want you to see what I've recently discovered. Stars.' He took a step forward, bracing his leg, and holding her lower, so she could look straight up and into the sky. He held her completely and the stars glittered overhead.

'You're not like you used to be,' she said.

'I know. I almost died twice.'

He swung her side to side.

The stars shimmered and she closed her eyes.

He pulled her up and swirled her around and straight into him. 'I lived for this moment.' He paused. 'Or I almost died to find it.'

'You scared us all.'

'I went to check on my tenants because I wanted to do something away from what I'd done every day. I wanted to see what others' lives were like. The ale-addled man was so nervous having a duke watch him render lard that he stumbled and the hot fat covered the front of my legs. Then I was in pain and it was like the fever after my watery mishap. I didn't want to take the time to heal. But I did. And you won't even marry me. I got well for you.'

'You are only one of the many, many thousands of men I will not marry. And you did not get well for me.'

'To my next dying day, I will believe I did. And if there is another accident, there is one woman I would want by my side. One.'

She tried to make herself bigger—hug him closer to warm him. 'Don't talk about death.'

'Ah,' he whispered, 'I'm definitely alive now. Lily.' His voice rolled over her, sending waves of weakness into her arms and legs. 'Tell your father that you've changed your mind. You'll let me court you.'

'But…'

'But,' he murmured, his lips covering hers briefly before settling back enough to speak, 'we can still talk privately. At night. And you can always tell your father if you change your mind again. He'll adjust to it.'

He rubbed his nose against hers and the air warmed around them.

'We'll find out about ourselves. Together. I've been near death and I don't want to die without living.'

'What if I—?'

Lips trailed down her neck, not in kisses but in the firm slide of taking in the taste and feel of skin. Of her.

Tendrils of his hair brushed against her. Her fingers lingered in his hair and she could feel crispness where the strands ended and the trace of beard began. 'Later. You can always change your mind, later.'

He enveloped her in his arms and surrounded her with more than just his body, but his strength—and the scent of him, of maleness, and something else. She didn't know what. But she could have stayed in that feeling every moment the rest of her life and never pulled from it.

'You're not planning to make that possible,' she said.

'No.'

His forehead touched hers and their lips were so close. 'See how well we know each other already,' he said.

The kiss wasn't about taste, but sustenance. She needed him to keep her breaths moving in and out of her body.

His fingers tangled in her hair and loosened enough to skim her cheek. The lighter he touched her, the more she could feel each sensation.

Edgeworth spoke against her skin. 'You're not making it possible for *me* to change *my* mind.'

Her fingers rested at the side seams of his waistcoat, not pulling him close, and having layers of fabric between her palms and his skin. The fabric teased her. The soft silk of the back and the corded nap of a rougher fabric and then the friction of movement behind the cloth travelling through the threads to her fingertips. A shell covering the life underneath, but conveyed to her by the sensations of each flex of muscle beneath.

'Inside,' he whispered.

This time, she clasped his hand and he led her to the bedroom, the single lamp again burning at his bedside, but the wick had been turned down so it glowed hardly brighter than a candle.

He slid his coat off and she realised his cravat was already missing. He unbuttoned his waistcoat and tossed it aside. After untying the ties of his shirt, he pulled her near.

She'd worn a spencer to keep from freezing in the night air, but not fastened it. He put his hands at the sides of her neck, sliding his grasp down, his touch between her dress and the outer garment creating a friction that tingled inside. The spencer dropped to the floor.

Stepping closer, he pulled the shirt over his head with one arm and caught her against him with the other.

Her fingers traced the muscles of his arms, roving over the contours and absorbing the strength beneath the skin. Each dip and rise of him tempted and satisfied and did the same again.

He was more than the beauty she'd seen in sculpture and in art.

She brushed her face against his skin, taking in the scent of soap and his maleness. Opening her eyes, she saw his own stare, eyes darkened, lashes darker and lips parted on her name. He buried his face into the crook of her neck, pressing kisses against her. Her lips brushed his shoulder and her teeth grazed him and her mouth lingered with the taste of him.

Her fingertips could not take in all that she wanted. Her touch floated over him, absorbing all she could.

He undressed her with slow precision, putting a kiss at her shoulders when he pushed her dress to the floor, a hug against her back with his arms around her waist after the corset fell away, and when he grasped the chemise to pull it over her head his hands slid upwards, never letting his touch leave her body as he slipped the garment up and over her arms.

He kept her near, putting her on the bed and joining seconds after, returning to her again, the sensation of his hands over her bringing her alive and taking away everything in the world but her need to be touching him.

When their legs tangled together the roughness of his skin tingling hers surprised her, but she remembered the burns and knew the scars remained. Her heart created its own inferno, blasting relief throughout her limbs. If he'd not survived, she'd have died without ever knowing what his touch was like.

His kiss took her lips and cosseted her, and he rose above her and covered her with his strength, sharing it. His elbows braced on the bed and he hugged her, lifting her closer to his chest, holding her in a cocoon of his masculinity.

She slid from the bed, unsure of the room. Wondering how much time had passed and when it would be light. She must dash out before dawn. The lamp had gone out and the darkness hid her, even from herself.

A little inward rumble of breaths reminded her that someone else was in the room—a deep-breathing someone else—asleep. Totally unconcerned and unaware of her presence.

She stared at the sleeping form, unable to see more than the shadows that indicated the bed.

She would have liked to have been able to look at him, to study him—more than she could in the cave-like darkness of the room—but she preferred just to feel what was going on inside herself. To sort out the moment.

Her hair still was upswept, but only barely. She could tell because when she turned her head, it slid around. Reaching up, she took out the pins, letting the strands tumble. It didn't matter if anyone saw her with her hair down when she went back to her house because if she was caught returning home in the dawn—nothing else would really matter. She could be dressed with every last thread exactly as it should be and still the results would be the same. Nevertheless, with the pins pressed between her lips, she twisted her hair back into place and arranged the bun.

Somehow that made her feel a little more like herself.

Her bare foot rested on something soft and she leaned down, sorting out her chemise and pulling it over her head.

She had to touch him, but she didn't know exactly where her hand would land. Her fingers rested on his wrist, the little bone at the side, and his breathing changed—stopped being the softness of lethargy and became quicker puffs of awareness.

Her fingers traced his wrist in an ever-wider rotation, feeling hair, skin, bones and maybe even veins underneath. 'I need to leave,' she said.

Then his hand turned and caught hers. 'Stay,' he said.

Only he pulled her closer, back on to the bed beside him, and instead of using his fingertips to trace, he pulled her wrist to his face and used his cheeks and mouth to learn the feel of her arm.

'I really must leave.'

'I know. I'll help you dress,' he said.

The bed creaked, poking the littlest stab of guilt into her, like when she put her head down on a new pillow and found herself poked by the tiniest feather. It didn't hurt, but she felt it all the same.

He pulled something into his hands and stepped from the bed, the soft footfalls bringing him closer, and he stopped, a statue of a man. His shoulders stretched in front of her. Naked shoulders, all unclothed and unconcerned.

She let out a breath. His clothes had hid a lot.

'Here,' he said and she heard the bit of smile in his voice.

She moved quickly, trying to cover that moment of her stillness. She reached out to touch what he held. Corset ties tangled in her fingers.

He'd known right where it was. Or maybe he'd felt the garment with his foot when he stepped out of bed.

'Where's my dress?' she asked.

'Your dress?' Gruff tones reached her and maybe some humour. 'It might still be in the gardens.'

Relief put a smile on her face. He'd not been paying any more attention to their clothes than she had.

He reached out, finding her waist and giving her a nudge to turn. 'I'll get you laced up.'

He pulled at the strings, constricting her, not because of the tightness, but because he was adept.

'You've done this before.'

Movement stilled, then continued. 'Not in my home.'

'Oh.'

She waited a beat. 'Any children?'

'No.'

She heard the sound of her own breath being pulled in, but it wasn't from the corset. She hoped he thought so. She'd just forgotten to breathe. He finished.

'We'll marry if there's a child. Or, I hope, even if there isn't.'

'Have you proposed before?'

His body stilled. 'Only to you.'

She thought again of his mention of courting her. The words didn't sound quite so shattering now, but like delicious starbursts inside.

His arms slipped around her and his hands clasped in front of her. And his cheek rested alongside of hers and the hint of shaving soap she could have happily bathed in.

He held her. Not really hugging, or touching her except with the clasp, and at her shoulders and where his cheek pressed hers.

She thought if she didn't move he would hold her for ever.

She touched a finger to the back of his hand. 'My dress.'

He took a step away, reached down and tugged, and she felt the pull of the fabric from underneath her foot. She stepped aside. She'd not realised she stood on the clothing.

He lifted it over her head, letting it settle around her, and then he did the hooks. A lightning and thunder and windstorm exploded just inside her heart and she didn't move. She had to contain it quickly and quietly.

'I'd best be going,' she said, just like a nice governess would mention a lesson needing one last glance.

'I'll find my trousers,' he said.

It seemed too personal for her to watch him move about the room—after all, she was not some mistress.

Was she?

No, she wasn't. Mistresses didn't get courted or have discussions of marriage that they didn't start. Her mother's friendships had definitely made that clear.

The sound of wool sliding over muscles jarred her from her reverie. In the darkness, the sounds reverberated louder than any church bell.

She found her stockings and draped them over her arm, and pushed her feet into the cold leather of her slippers.

And then he reached for her arm. His shirt wasn't fastened and he didn't wear a coat.

'If we court in darkness,' he whispered, pulling her close, 'then we should also court in light.'

'But marriage. Everyone will expect it to lead to marriage.'

'Including me,' he said. 'But it doesn't have to. It's not a betrothal. It's a chance to know more about each other.'

He put a hand along her cheek, holding it. 'I expect you to like me, of course.'

'Does anyone dislike you?' she asked.

'They don't mention it if they do.'

'Well, no one dislikes me either,' she said.

She suspected the darkness was a truly wonderful thing because if she could have looked at him, seen the skin she'd felt against her, leaving would have been impossible.

Edge woke, thoughts of walking Lily home in the darkness bringing a peacefulness to him. He tossed the covers aside and looked at the swirling skin on his leg.

He felt whole again.

He'd been in so much pain after the accident.

Then the laudanum had nearly finished the job, and he'd not known about that until his mother told him later. Three times, he realized. He'd almost died three times, not just two.

After the burn, he'd taken some of the medicine at the tenant's home, but not nearly enough to stop the pain. And he'd been in so much agony when they'd finally managed to get him to his room and he'd been senseless. Gaunt hadn't known Edge had been given any laudanum and Edge couldn't think past the pain, then the tenant had arrived with the physician and the tenant had knocked the spoon from Gaunt's hand. A man who'd normally never be invited inside Edge's house had saved him.

He'd heard praying, lots of it, and he'd been certain he was in hell because the flames had been so intense and he'd wanted to tell them he'd not had time to do anything bad enough to deserve that because he'd been working just as he should and doing just as he should. Yes, there'd been slips, but he'd been human, after all.

Surviving had taken all his willpower, but now he had Lily, a woman who'd managed to grow up innocent and guileless in a world that would have engulfed her into its worst given half a chance.

He reached to ring for Gaunt, aware the man had been in the room earlier to open the curtains and awaken him. Edge had sent the valet away because he'd wanted to savour sleep and dreams of Lily.

Now Edge looked across the room. A blue garment lay draped over the arm of Edge's chair. A woman's coat that only went to her waist: a spencer. Edge hadn't placed it so neatly when he'd taken it off Lily the night before. It had surely been on the floor between the door and the window.

Edge cursed himself. Gaunt wouldn't speak of it, but he knew. It didn't matter at all to Edge, except he'd wanted to keep Lily's life private—for her. He wanted it to be a secret between them.

Chapter Twelve

Lily tried not to feel like the only splash of red in a painting when Edge arrived. Her father had summoned her and now she was officially courting.

Her father kept talking about the deposits in the bank, return on investment, and risk and reward.

Lily knew that her father was reminding Edgeworth that she was a wonderful investment, very little risk, and would be a rewarding wife. Words of high praise from him.

Edge nodded.

Lily relaxed while Edge and her father compared financial successes. She'd heard of her father's account ledgers many times. Even during dinner when she and Abigail were the only ones there.

Lily didn't even need to be in the room for courting, apparently.

Abigail appeared in the doorway. 'Has anyone seen my hair comb with the garnets on it?' Abigail asked, moving in to make herself comfortable.

'It's my hair comb and it's in my jewellery box,' Lily said quietly.

'Thank you,' Abigail gushed, sitting. 'I knew you'd find it for me. You're so organised.'

Now her father's conversation focused on the sturdiness of Lily's female ancestors who lived through droughts, plagues, famines and could manage a household of any size and could birth ten-pound babies without missing an embroidery stitch. And every moment or so Abigail would remind her father of the particular piece of jewellery that particular ancestor had passed down to Lily.

Finally, her father stood, straightened his coat, looked at Abigail and said, 'I'm ready for an ice at Gunter's. Abigail, why don't you go with me?'

He'd never ever before had an ice that Lily knew of.

'Oh, ices...' Abigail said. Her favourite. 'But who will chaperon?'

'I'll send the housekeeper to chaperon.' Then he shepherded Abigail from the room and Lily doubted he would speak with the housekeeper. She could hear him chatting with Abigail as they walked down the stairs. He'd spoken more words in the last hour than she'd heard from him in a year.

Her father, the banker. Twice he'd suggested matches Lily should consider, both of them wealthy and elderly. But he'd always had the Duke picked out for Abigail. Everyone had but Edgeworth, apparently.

She glanced at him and Edge shrugged, in a way to ask what else could she expect?

Lily reached to the pull and she rang for the maid to bring the tea she'd requested earlier.

Edge's eyes must have been rimmed by two rows of lashes. She'd never noticed it before because she'd not been able to get past the blue.

Her attention stayed on his face. No one's eyes had ever captured her as Edge's did.

'Lily?' Edge asked. 'Tonight, I'll have the little coat you left behind.'

'The spencer!' She recovered. 'Yes. Tonight. I can't believe I forgot it.'

'I can.' His eyes reflected a smile hidden deep. 'It was dark. You had something else on your mind.'

'True. It *was* dark.'

The maid walked in with the tray.

'Surprisingly warm for this time of year,' Edge continued. 'I don't think we've received enough rain though. I expect we'll catch up.'

'It makes the flowers look so pretty.' Was this what other people talked about while courting? If so, Lily could do without it. Flowers—pretty. Rain—wet. Sun—warm.

The maid left and he lifted an orange biscuit from the platter. The blue blazed right through her, spiralling a warm trail to the tips of her toes.

'My favourite,' he said.

She picked up a biscuit. Courting. It wasn't all about the weather. 'Mine, too.'

Only a few words here and there kept the conversation going because sitting with him answered a question inside her, letting her know they could have quiet moments together.

When it became time for him to leave, he kissed her softly and told her goodbye.

So soon after he left that the delivery had to have been waiting, a maid walked inside the sitting room, carrying a vase of lilies so abundant that the flowers obscured the woman's face.

Lily ran a finger along the flower. She'd been wrong. She loved lilies.

At two a.m. she arrived in the garden, her shoes quickly growing damp from the earlier shower that had left the grass wet. She could see her breath in the moonlight. He stood, holding the spencer open so she could tuck her arms into the sleeves, but he didn't release it and closed it around her. Holding her.

'Have you been here long?' she asked. He sheltered her. The air had to be freezing. The collar of his woollen coat brushed against her neck. She shivered, but not from the cold.

'No. Only since the rain stopped.'

The weather. What was it about the weather?

'Let's go inside,' he said.

Just that simply. Maybe the weather meant something she didn't quite understand. A euphemism. But, no, she would have learned it from her mother. Her mother believed that Lily should be told all about the intimacies and agonies of life so she would be prepared. She'd meant well, Lily realised, trying to protect her daughter from mistakes that would hurt.

It hadn't prepared Lily. It had terrified her. The stories about the shredded hearts and unconcern of the men, and about how once you started with the passions you couldn't ever contain them. They controlled you.

But Lily didn't feel controlled. Life surrounded her. Looking at Edgeworth made her feel safe, wrapped in security, and alive.

She rotated in his arms and now she faced him. 'It is freezing.' But it wasn't really. Not when he was near.

He released her, then took her hand and draped it over his arm in the same way he would have led her into a dance at a soirée.

He took her inside his house.

The warmth of his home flowed over her and she imagined it hers, and walking into it with him as her husband. A small lamp sat on a table, giving enough light so that she could see him. Even now, she couldn't read his thoughts or even imagine them. His eyes guarded him, she realised. One could hardly look into them when he had that cold, ducal stare he usually had. The stare that warned a person to tread lightly. Only he didn't have it now. She couldn't even remember how many days since she'd seen it.

Perhaps she was good for him and he realised it.

'Andrew and Bea are going to Drury Lane tomorrow,' he said. 'We could go with them. She could be your chaperon.'

'Beatrice?' She'd never thought of Beatrice as quite suitable for a chaperon. 'Didn't she attack someone's carriage with a parasol once?'

'It was her parasol and her carriage. When it broke, she took her husband's cane to it. She shouldn't have done that.'

'You think she's a suitable chaperon?'

'Yes.'

'Going to the theatre with the three of you would be the same as a—an announcement of sorts?'

'Oh?' His brows popped up in a way that told her how well he understood that.

'I don't know.'

'What concerns you?'

The words couldn't make him understand. Beatrice had had a bad marriage once. At the time, she'd been constantly talked about. The thought of Beatrice's escapades reminded her of the way love could take over a person and turn them into frozen glass that could shatter so easily, or into water so hot the bubbles turned into steam and nothingness.

But his gaze softened her; it didn't spear. She didn't feel unsteady—just stronger as if she could gain strength from him. This wasn't the same volatile union her mother warned her about. Yet a duchess? Oh, it would be grand, but it would be difficult, too.

But she could confide in him.

'The eyes on me,' she said. 'People would be watching everything I said. Everything I did. I hate that. I hate even being at the dances and moving across the dance floor and most of the time I know no one is watching, except my partner. And he doesn't care if I make a mistake, but I don't like it.'

'You could have a dancing tutor.'

She moved to the side and rubbed her hands over her arms. 'It's not the dancing. It's the eyes watching to pick me to pieces. The voices of other people. Mother's friends would sit hours—days—discussing everyone else. Laughing. No one did well enough for their spiteful stories. I've already been mentioned in the rubbish Sophia published.' She stopped rubbing her arms. 'The words feel like they're branding marks on the skin in a way you can't feel it, but which sears into you just the same.'

'Some people are like that—even if you stand at the corner, they will tear you apart anyway. You may as well do what you wish.'

'I like being alone. I do like it.'

'Not always. As a duchess you'll learn to be comfortable with others. After a time, the people you're around will often be the same ones and you'll form close friendships.'

He took the lock of her hair that had escaped her bun and twisted it around his finger, then pulled free and continued, outlining her chin and barely touching her throat, tracing her collarbone, but staying over her spencer, stopping at the shoulder and letting his hand fall away. He made it so hard for her to think.

'I can't,' she said. 'I never have been able to feel comfortable when eyes are watching me.'

'You didn't have any trouble trying to catch my attention when we were young. And I'm sure I stared blades at you.'

'I wanted you to play,' she said, touching his collar. 'Another person for our games. You did look so—miserable. Abigail and I had each other. You never played with your brothers that I saw.

If you joined our games, you could have been the pirate we captured.'

'You wanted a victim.'

'Yes.' She heard the laughter in her voice. 'It would have evened the odds somewhat. The two of us against you. I was bigger than Abigail. I had to lose on purpose. With you, we could have gone all out to defeat you and you might have lost. I was fine with that.'

'I would lose on purpose for you.' He reached to interlace their fingers on both hands, then he raised them high and stepped backwards, and backwards, and landed against the wall, their clasp still joined. He gave a tug and she tumbled against him, raising their joined hands.

'See, you've captured me. I surrender.' He bent forward, breath touching her cheek. 'You may claim your kiss now.'

She did. A peck. Nothing more than a dart to his lips.

Her spirits lifted. Unburdened. 'I don't think it would bother me to dance again,' she said. 'If you were my partner.'

Standing near him, she felt she didn't care what anyone ever said, or wrote about her. She'd finally put the past behind her. The mistakes that guided her didn't matter any more after being in Edge's arms.

'I will be,' he said. 'I think we should practise now.'

His hands fell from hers and rested on her waist. 'Miss Lily, may I have this dance? Or better yet, a kiss?'

His lips touched hers, and she tasted him. His strength surrounded her and she fell against him—safe, knowing he would catch her.

Abigail flittered around Lily, working again with a strand of her sister's hair. When she reached for the perfume bottle, Lily held out her hand. 'No more.'

'I only put the barest drop on you.'

'Yes. And I love it. But I don't want to choke the horses when I walk by the carriages or smell like a cheap woman.'

Abigail sniffed the air, then moved closer, still sniffing.

'You don't smell cheap,' Abigail said. 'You smell quite costly.'

Lily slapped her away.

'My sister.' Abigail's eyes glanced to the ceiling and then her gaze floated back to Lily. 'The wallflower Duchess.'

Lily stood, turning, the skirt of the dress twirling around her feet. 'It's not being a wallflower when you're observing other people. I prefer to be at the side.'

'You do?'

'Perhaps,' she said. 'I thought about it a lot lately. I like to watch others. I really don't like them watching me. Standing at Edge's side, I won't be alone.'

She wanted to be with the Duke. Was happy to be with him. She couldn't keep the smile from her face. The only time her happiness faltered was when she remembered the tale of his half-brother being published, but he'd put that behind him. Lily forced herself not to think of it.

She could imagine the Duke standing beside her. His shoulders twice the width of hers, and standing just enough taller. His eyes would be distancing ice, but she would know the softness of them. With him at her side, stalwart, strong and an iron duke in his own way, she didn't need to even think about anything but his presence.

He would ask her again to marry. She was certain. And she would say yes.

Happy shudders bubbling about inside, she pulled on the gloves. She had her opera glasses, a fan and, of course, her handkerchief. But she wouldn't need it tonight.

Edge waited in the sitting room with her father. He rose—the contrast of his gold-silk waistcoat against the black of his coat and blue of his eyes causing her to forget everything in the world but him.

She doubted the carriage wheels would even touch the ground on the way to the theatre. She felt like a duchess and it wasn't the heaviness she'd expected, but light and grand. Her corset ties didn't feel tight and her shoes felt feather-light.

She looked at Edge and she could tell he'd just shaved. A duke and he'd just shaved for an evening out with her.

Her father had insisted on attending and, deep inside, she suspected it had to do with investments, but she didn't care.

They walked to the ducal carriage and she stepped inside.

As they rode along the Duke's appearance must have affected her father as he sat stiff backed in the carriage, his neck high and a serene smile on his face except when he gave Edgeworth approving smiles.

The carriage moved slowly, avoiding every single bump in the road. She didn't know or care if she imagined the smoothness or it was real, because the night was the most perfect of her life.

She alighted from the carriage, her hand resting in Edgeworth's and then he tucked her hand over his arm. If she'd not been watching close, she wouldn't have seen the merest wink before the emotionless façade took over his face again.

They were almost at his private box when a voice dripping with a throaty charm called out, 'Edgeworth.'

He stopped and Lily's eyes rested on Genevieve. Genevieve, and her heart-shaped face and heart-shaped mouth, and the disheartening misfortune of being widowed at the age of twenty-four.

'Edge,' she said again, walking towards him as if he'd not heard the first time and turned in her direction. She'd called him by the same name his family and closest friends used.

Her ruby bracelet slid up her glove when she raised her hand, reaching out to brush his arm before her hand slid back to her side. Genevieve's face remained animated when she took in Lily and her father, the dark eyes showing large against the perfect complexion.

'Genevieve,' he said, turning to include Lily and her father in the conversation. When Edge-worth moved his head in Genevieve's direction, Lily watched his face. She wished she hadn't. He greeted his former mistress with a whimsical smile Lily hadn't seen before. Years fell away from his face and reminded her of the boy she'd seen in the garden.

Then the eyes shuttered again, the Duke returned and he greeted the man with Genevieve.

And there was no wall for Lily to stand against to make herself invisible. The man with Genevieve was introduced. Lily saw the barest recognition in his eyes the moment the man connected her name to Lily's family heritage.

'The younger Miss Hightower?' he asked.

'The elder.' The words flowed easily from her lips. She'd said them before.

'My elder daughter,' her father inserted. She felt him step closer. 'I've never attended the theatre with her and I decided it was time. I work too much.'

'Don't we all,' the man with Genevieve said.

'But she insists I take her out.' He gave a sideways glance at Genevieve and her cheeks reddened.

Again her glove moved and the bracelet sparkled. 'You insisted you wanted to take me to the theatre tonight.' She tucked her hand around his arm. 'Didn't you?'

'Of course. Of course.' He shook his head slightly. 'I always insist I want to do exactly what you want to do.' He included the men in his half-smile, half-jab at himself. 'Well, we must be moving along. Want to take our seats before the play starts.'

In the brief moment when Genevieve said goodbye to Edgeworth and walked away, the muscles at his mouth relaxed and his eyes softened again.

'Genevieve Carson. Her father and I purchased some property together once. Good man,' her father said. 'Head for finances. Lives in Nottingham now, I believe.'

'Leicester,' Edge corrected.

Lily's corset ties bit at her waist and she tried to match the easy strides of Edgeworth and her father.

'Bad when her husband died,' Lily's father said. 'Though he was quite sickly when they married, and couldn't rub two pence together without losing one. You remember him, don't you, Your Grace?'

'Yes.'

Lily ignored the pain her slippers caused. Irritated that she'd chosen them. Wishing her father would speak of something else, and unable to stop him because she wanted to hear every word.

'If she married him for his funds, she was sadly misled.'

'No. She didn't,' Edge said.

Her father paused, eyes wide. 'You knew them well?'

'Well enough.'

'The man she's with now, though, I would recommend him.'

Lily knew what that meant.

Edge didn't speak.

She examined his face, trying to gauge his thoughts, but she wasted her time. Another man called out to him and he turned, giving greetings. Everyone knew Edgeworth. Everyone.

Lily tried to push the insecurity aside.

She had no true claim to Edge and no claim at all on his previous actions. Genevieve was his mistress. *Was.* The past. It didn't matter. Edge was at her side.

The past didn't matter at all. Her slippers mattered. They made her feel too tall and too wobbly. She should have worn something flatter. Something that helped her hide just a bit more.

Edge talked with the man, and then with someone else who wanted a moment of his time.

Lily moved a half-step back, keeping her gaze level and eyes serene, and wishing for all the world she'd worn something more comfortable. She felt as if she was wearing another woman's clothing. She shouldn't have worn the new dress. She should have stuck with something plainer.

The man mentioned meeting Edge again for a chance to win back the losses of their card game.

Edge nodded, ever polite, and when the talk ended, they moved to the box.

Beatrice was already seated, but she jumped up when they entered and her eyes welcomed Lily.

'Lily,' Beatrice called out. Her voice could crack glass, eggshells and possibly the inner workings of an ear. Her arms stretched to include Lily and her father. 'So happy to see you.' Beatrice didn't just rush to them, her movement exploded inside the box, like the fluttering of dozens of birds' wings moving as one flock.

Andrew stood, a bemused smile flitting across his lips.

Lily didn't have to look out over the theatre to see necks craning and eyes examining, but this time she could disappear behind the flurry of Beatrice.

After greeting them, Andrew spoke softly to his brother. 'If I'd known you were going to be here, Your Grace, I might have chosen another night.'

'Andrew.' Beatrice slapped at her husband's arm. 'I told you he invited us.'

'That you did,' Andrew said, laughter infusing his voice. 'I thought it a clever ruse on his part to make sure our paths didn't cross.'

'It was,' the Duke answered, sending a nod of acknowledgement to his brother. He spoke in a tone which barely carried. 'I thought you'd be certain to avoid tonight if I let you know I planned to attend.'

Andrew laughed, giving a brief bow of surrender, and Beatrice rolled her eyes. She turned to Lily. The observers' attention stayed focused on Beatrice and even across the theatre, patrons stilled.

Beatrice's words wouldn't have carried beyond the five people. 'If the brothers ever speak kindly to each other, they're angry. Watch out for that.'

Relieved laughter bubbled from Lily.

Then Beatrice turned around with a flourish and wiggled into her seat at the front of the box, leaning forward to wave to a lady wearing an oversized plume in her hat. 'I wonder where she found that,' Beatrice said, speaking to herself. 'I must find out later. It's adorable.'

'You didn't bring Mother?' Edge asked his brother.

'No,' Beatrice answered for her husband, looking over her shoulder at Edge. 'She's had enough of me for one day, but she was too kind to say so. Her portrait is going wonderfully. And I'm giving her art lessons now.'

'Mother?' the Duke asked, his brows up.

'Certainly.' Beatrice wiggled around in the seat again so she could wave at someone else. Her eyes remained on the audience. 'Your mother has a natural talent for art.'

Andrew looked at his brother and his shoulders

quirked in question, letting him know this was the first he'd heard of their mother's skill.

'Isn't this a lovely night?' Beatrice absorbed the attention from the other theatre patrons, taking it in the way glass absorbed the sun's rays.

'Absolutely,' Andrew said.

Beatrice turned to Lily, speaking quietly while they were taking their places. 'He says that all the time. It means, *Whatever you say, Beatrice.* Or, *I really wasn't listening.* Or…' She turned to him. 'An agreement on enlarging the sitting room.'

He groaned. 'Absolutely.'

Beatrice looked across and called out to another patron, smile beaming, waving, 'Agatha…'

Andrew's head tilted down, hiding his expression, but Lily saw the smile.

The Duke took in a breath, but didn't speak. He sat beside Lily.

Beatrice spoke without moving her lips. 'Everyone's going to be talking about this. *Oh, my. Oh, my. Edgeworth was at the theatre with a woman of marriageable age…*'

'I'm aware.' The Duke's voice barely reached Lily's ears.

'Oh, I bet you are,' Beatrice said. She looked at Lily. 'Andrew and His Grace—' her brows bumped on the word '—are very stuffy.' Then she whispered, 'Don't let that naked portrait you've heard about fool you. Andrew didn't really pose for it.' She clucked her tongue.

'I hope they mention my hair.' Beatrice might have been talking to her husband. 'I had to sit an hour to get it curled just so.' She patted the ringlets hanging around her face. 'It's natural, but not quite this natural.'

Without turning her head, Lily looked in the Duke's direction while Bea continued describing the moments of hair preparation.

The Duke glanced over the other theatregoers. Lily knew he'd expected his mother to be with Andrew and Beatrice. A family outing. His and hers. An announcement of sorts, with Beatrice along to make sure everyone noticed.

She pulled her thoughts deep inside herself, ignoring the spinning feeling in her head. Edge put the actors on his stage exactly where he wanted them. She tried to pay attention to the actress speaking on the theatre's stage, but she couldn't keep her mind on it. Lily realised she didn't even know what the play was. It hadn't mattered. Nothing had settled in her mind earlier except that she would be spending the evening with Edgeworth.

Beatrice's arm flashed out, the large ring she wore over her glove visible. The one on her left hand. Lily looked at her own gloves. No rings were even under them. Then she looked across at Edgeworth's hand. He was wearing the ring on his little finger again. The Lily one.

He caught her looking and she could see behind his eyes. A smile.

She couldn't help herself. She gave a tiny shake of her head.

One little flicker at the edge of one brow argued with her. She turned her head precisely, staring ahead. Ever so lightly, he moved in his chair and tapped his foot.

She glanced at him again.

He raised his brows in question and touched the ring.

She squeezed her eyes tight, looked over the audience and shrugged.

He let out a breath, loud enough for her to hear. When she turned his way, he tapped the ring again.

This time, she nodded.

She saw it. He grinned.

Beatrice leaned forward in her chair, laughing

at something onstage. The sound carried as well as the actors' voices, or better.

Eyes turned to them.

Edge was aware. He turned to Lily, pulling the attention Beatrice had called their way. His head was only inches from hers. 'Are you enjoying the play?' he asked.

'I'm enjoying the performance,' she said.

The actress onstage paused for a moment. Even she turned her head in their direction before resuming her role. Edgeworth laughed softly.

Lily examined the faces looking in her direction and it didn't matter. Being watched wasn't so bad with Edgeworth at her side.

Then one man from the pit around the stage tipped his head to her. She took in a breath. She forced her face emotionless, but acknowledged him with a nod.

Edge caught the movement, eyes appraising her and back to the man. Edge shot the man a quelling glare. 'That scandalmonger wrote the article about my father.'

Abigail lay on Lily's bedcovers, sound asleep. The jewellery box lid was open and the contents scattered around it. A lamp lit the room.

Lily shut the door, hard.

Abigail jumped into a sitting position, rubbed her eyes and said, 'What did you think of the play, Your Almost Grace?'

Lily shrugged, smiling, pushing aside the memory of the man she'd seen watching her.

Her sister swung around on the bed. 'So did Edgeworth propose?'

'That would be a personal matter.'

Abigail grunted. 'I guess I'll ask Father. Or better yet, just listen and, if I hear him shouting it from the rooftop, then I'll know. Not that it matters to him one way or the other as long as we're happy.' She stood and stretched. 'And wealthy.'

'Leave,' Lily said.

'No. I'm your sister and I know you plan to take a stroll later tonight into that unhealthy night air. But I'm not making it easy for you.'

'You can stay in the room,' Lily said, waving a hand. 'Keep the light on for me.'

Abigail examined her fingernails. 'You will have to marry him if you start meeting him so often.' She patted her stomach. 'You'll start looking plump.'

'Be quiet.'

Abigail shook her head. 'No. I've listened to

enough warnings from you. It's your turn. I'm concerned for you. Besides, I brought Edgeworth right to the front door for you with the handkerchiefs.'

'I'm still not finished with you over that.'

'I did you a favour.'

'No. You didn't. Whenever he wishes to find me, he knows where I live.'

'He certainly does. You're making a trail in the grass. At night.' Abigail crossed her arms. 'I'm saying the exact same to you as you've said to me. Start out like Mother—end up like Mother.'

'Be quiet.'

'You hated it more than I ever did.'

'I'm not like Mother. At all.'

'Well, you're not acting like yourself.' She walked to the door and pulled it open. 'Do as you wish. You will anyway. But you'd certainly be angry at me if I met Foxworthy—in his house.' She opened her eyes wide. 'Not that you're doing that, of course.' Then she pointed to the third finger of her left hand and left.

Lily smiled at the memory of the ring on his little finger.

She understood why he'd asked her now that she'd seen Beatrice gathering all the attention.

Edge wanted someone who... Edge wanted someone who didn't pull everyone's attention. He wanted a proper duchess, one who could sit quietly and watch the others around her.

Touching the last necklace she wore, she ran her finger over the chain. A simple one her mother had tossed into the waste bin because she'd not thought it grand enough. The only one Lily liked.

Her mother had warned her. *Once you start releasing your passions you can never call them back. They control you.* At the time, hearing the admonishment had irked Lily because her mother hadn't followed her own words. But now Lily understood. Her mother had been trying to keep Lily from following in her footsteps, the same way Lily tried to keep Abigail from erring.

But the Duke didn't have the passions of her mother's friends. He put his duties first and planned what he did. He would never turn on her like her parents had turned on each other. Never.

She could hardly wait until she could be with him again.

After her own house had settled into sleep, she left through the back door, kicked off her shoes, slipped her stockings away, tossed them to the ground and dashed through the dewy grass.

She ran to the door, touched the wood and then the knob.

He'd said he'd be waiting. He'd told her the door would be unlocked.

Inside, she tiptoed and ran up the stairs, making no more noise than a mouse might.

Right before she knocked on his bedchamber door, it opened. He pulled her inside, into his arms and against the chest that took up her whole vision.

'I've missed you,' she said.

'You can't have missed me much,' he said. 'We just parted.'

'A whole hour ago.' Being a mouse was pleasant when one got to burrow into the chest of a lion and feel his arms securing her in an embrace that lifted her from her feet.

The door clicked shut and he stepped into the middle of the room with her. 'So tell me,' he said into her ear, his breath sending ripples of shivers into her, 'what have you been doing since we last met?'

'Thinking of you.'

He touched her face. 'I've been thinking of you.

I enjoyed being out with you. And I'm pleased you could tolerate Beatrice.'

'I like her.'

'Good.' He gave her a squeeze.

Joy thrummed through her heart. She felt beautiful. The only place in the world that she didn't want to be a wallflower was in Edge's vision. She stood in the centre of the room and the most important eyes in the world were on her.

He stepped away and gazed at her feet. 'Where are your shoes and stockings?'

'I left them at my door,' she said. 'I knew they'd get wet with the dew and I didn't want the maid to notice.'

'You cannot run around barefoot. You'll hurt yourself,' he said.

'I'm fine,' she said. She twirled around and managed to stop against him, and rest in the shelter of his arms.

He slid the shoulder of her dress and her chemise aside, just enough to put a kiss in the hidden location, then moved his lips up her neck, through all the shiver spots, and stopped at her lips.

He lifted her and moved her to the bed, sliding down beside her.

* * *

Edge held her in the crook of his arm, knowing she slept. Absently, he rubbed the top of her fingers.

He couldn't describe her. Innocence. Softness. Holding pleasure against his chest and inside his chest. Fragile. Gentle.

She stirred, waking.

'Will your father be home tomorrow afternoon?' he asked.

She rolled against him, burrowing closer. 'I'm not sure.'

'I'll be courting you again. I'd like to speak with him. Would you let him know?'

'Yes.'

She squeezed him, but her breathing didn't relax as it had.

He would let her father know they planned to marry. Lily hadn't yet spoken the yes, but she surely would, and this time he would ask her in front of her family. He wanted to marry soon. He'd already taken his brothers aside and told them not to be surprised if he should wed, and his mother had told him she'd not be surprised if she had a new daughter.

Lily felt perfect at his side. Holding her now,

the woman he'd dreamed of, made his life feel complete.

He kissed her hair, letting his lips rest against her and savouring the floral-scented hair and the warm, alive, comforting scent that radiated from her.

Sitting at the theatre with her, he'd been proud. He'd noticed the difference between her and Beatrice, who was one hundred per cent Beatrice and perfect for Andrew. But Lily fit her name and fit into his world in a way he'd not thought possible.

The question of her parentage could be ignored or easily dealt with. He could bring the subject up, quietly, to the right ears and the right mouths, but really it didn't matter what people believed.

The night couldn't have been better, if not for seeing the publisher. The vulture who'd published the rubbish about Lily and then later the story about his father. He could hardly believe Lily knew the man, but then her mother stayed one step from total ruin after she'd parted from Lily's father.

The peacefulness Edge felt evaporated at the thought of the publisher. The man had hurt Lily, destroyed Edge's family and called Andrew's wife a beast. Andrew had spoken to the publisher afterwards and the stories had changed.

But Edge had said nothing to the man earlier when the story was printed about his father. Nothing. His mother hadn't wanted more attention and Edge agreed. When he'd discovered the words were true, he'd spent his time dealing with the repercussions in the household.

The lie about Lily was different.

Edge realised where he must start with correcting the story of Lily's birth. He knew how to get the word out—the same place the lie had started.

He would think of how he wanted the story told and if the scurrilous publisher wished to live in London—if he wished to be able to continue to publish his paper—then he would find a way to make one very sincere correction to the past.

Lily would shine. As she should. He knew she didn't truly like to stand out from the crowd, but this time would be different.

Lily listened to Edge's breathing. Rhythmic. Relaxed. She scooted away from him and he moved his arm. Her sleeping lion.

She slipped from the bed. She took one look back at him, then took a second glance. She wanted this to remain in her memory for ever. Lamplight shadowed his face and she could see the lashes resting at his cheeks. A softness in the repose of his lips.

This was the portrait no one could ever capture. The man, innocent and vulnerable in sleep. She hoped Genevieve hadn't seen him so relaxed and was fairly certain she hadn't. Lily doubted he fell asleep easily around others.

She looked away—an unease creeping into her. She moved, trying to dislodge it from her body.

She dropped a kiss in the air over him, knowing if she touched him he'd wake, and she didn't want him to feel he had to dress and walk her home. Just a quick dart across the way and she'd be there.

Chapter Thirteen

Edge stepped inside the Hightower residence and noticed the reddened cheeks of the butler. The man's face showed no recognition of Edgeworth, and he didn't waver from his role, but his movements were too quick. He hurried, as if he wanted to rush away.

Looking up, Edgeworth saw Lily standing, hand on the end of the bannister, watching.

No welcome shown from her eyes, and yet, she waited for him.

'What's wrong?' he asked, not caring if the servant heard because whatever it was, the butler already knew.

'My mother's here.' Lily searched his face and then looked over him when she continued. 'She'll disrupt everything. Every day.'

'Her presence doesn't change anything, except

she should know your future plans.' He walked into Lily's line of vision.

His face locked into an impassiveness. Lily didn't flinch, so he knew she couldn't see the irritation that sparked in his chest, causing his hand to tighten.

He took Lily inside the empty sitting room, led her to the sofa and released her arm from his and, with her hand in his, guided her to sit. But he didn't join her. Instead he moved to the chair across. He started to sit, then changed his mind. 'You're using her as an excuse not to court or marry. What is the real reason?'

'You can't know what it is like to live in the same house with her.'

'I'm not asking her to marry me—I'm asking you. And we're not going to live in this house. Just next door.'

'She'll meddle. She can take one little grain of something and she feeds on it. Think of a piece of dropped bread and how the ants appear from nowhere and surround it.'

He didn't speak, letting the silence ask the question he wanted answered.

She put her hands on the upholstery at each

side of her. 'I didn't know what peace was until my mother left.'

'Peace above all else?'

'I don't know.'

'Think about it. Think about how you felt in the past. Do you want to return to that?'

'Never.'

She glanced down and then at Edge.

She rose and moved to him. 'If you ask me to marry you, you'd better be certain it's what you want. I'm going to say yes, and you'll be acquiring a wife and her mother will be next door.'

'Doors have locks.'

She smiled, but it didn't linger. 'I just worry that you'll be involved in her theatrics.'

He took her hands. He would have a few words with the newspaper publisher. He wouldn't let them say anything about Lily because of her mother. If her mother wished to run naked in the streets and the man reported it, Edge wouldn't complain. But the newspaper had best not mention Lily in any connection to her. His and Lily's family would stand alone and rise above everything on their own merit.

'Send for your father.'

'He's here. I'll get him.'

In seconds, Lily returned with Mr Hightower, a stout man who Lily overshot in height. The thought bounced through Edge's mind that she really didn't resemble her father. He could understand the tales. Mr Hightower glanced at Lily while she watched her father's face. In the two profiles, a similarity appeared in the directness.

Her father's attention returned to Edge.

'Lily and I plan to be married.'

The years seemed to fall away from her father's face. 'You're both old enough to know your own mind. It will be nice to have you in the family, Your Grace.' He lingered on the words, letting Edge know he valued the title. But then his eyes changed into the steely glare of an equal. 'I'm not concerned about the fine points of the marriage settlement. Draw up the papers as you see fit. If anything should happen, I will provide well for both my daughters.'

'I arrived just in time.' Lily's mother rushed into the room, her eyes as bright as her red-stained lips and her laughter forced.

Lily's fingers loosened from Edge's tender clasp when she noted her mother's face.

'Welcome to the family,' her mother said,

beaming at Edgeworth. 'I always knew you and Lily had a fascination for each other. Childhood sweethearts.'

'I thought you were shopping,' Lily said.

'I am on the way,' her mother said, 'but I had the carriage return for a moment as I wished to change bonnets. The one I chose had been in the wardrobe for quite some time. And had a definite musty odour.' She waved a hand in front of her nose. 'I feel like letting every servant in this house go because, without me here, I can tell how much they've shirked in their duties. Perhaps my husband asked for my return because his daughters were of marriageable age and he wanted someone to oversee the housekeeper.'

'It would be easier to hire a new servant,' her father said.

'I wish you had.'

Lily glanced at Edge. No movement on his face.

'Lily,' her father spoke quietly, walking towards her and motioning with an arm to move Edgeworth along. 'Why don't you and Edge go for a walk? I'm sure you have plans to discuss.' As he ushered them out, he reached for the small chain hanging beside the door.

Before Lily realised what her father meant to

do, she and Edgeworth were standing on the other side of the door and she heard the key click the lock.

'He and your mother wish to be alone,' Edgeworth said.

Lily watched the wood, half-expecting it to splinter at any moment. 'He's never done that before.'

'Their daughter is getting married. They're reunited. Their lives are changing. Don't think about it because it'll only worry you.' Edge took her arm and moved her along.

She didn't speak, but walked in the direction Edgeworth guided. Her parents had never locked themselves in a room together. One had always stormed out, usually her father because of the objects being hurled at him.

They stepped outside, the scent of honeysuckles touching the air and giving the world a false sense of sweetness. Lily realised she'd just agreed to marry. And live next to her mother. The two things she had vowed never, ever to do.

'Lily Hightower. Your future husband is standing beside you. Act impressed, or at least aware,' Edge said.

The sound of breaking glass—a window—reached Lily's ears.

'No thud,' Edgeworth said. 'A good sign.'

'She's never broken a window before.'

He gave a one-sided shrug and touched a finger to her arm, stilling her.

'Edge—'

'I tried to control my father. I did a fair job of it at the end.' He shook his head, words moving out on a breath. 'It's not worth it.'

'But you see what she's doing right now… And your mother—the Duchess—lives within hearing distance. And everyone around us—everyone has lived in these houses much longer than my father has and they are all like—' She stopped, lowering her own voice. 'Like you.'

'Like me?'

'They've been born into this world. They didn't buy their way into it.'

He tilted his head to hers. 'Lily. Do you realise how much it costs to buy into this world?'

She didn't budge. 'It's not the same as arriving by birth.'

'I agree. A few people in the area might even wish that they had the funds to purchase a place here instead of arriving by birth.'

A screech blasted in the air.

'I cannot bear this,' Lily said, flexing her fingers.

He leaned close. 'But you didn't hear a word I said which means we're as good as married already.'

'I cannot bear it, Edge. I am serious.'

'Perhaps you shouldn't be.'

He held out his arm for her to clasp and she did. They stood on the front steps of the mansion.

Another screech shot through the air.

They heard the back door slam, shouts to the coachman and in moments the carriage rumbled by with her mother in it.

'At least Father let her leave when she wanted.'

'Perhaps he was locking us out.' He opened the gate for her. 'And you should let them level it out amongst themselves.'

'She'll be back,' Lily said, walking with him to the front of his house. 'They just can't seem to let each other go. It's unfathomable. But if Abigail and I both speak to our father, perhaps he will reconsider.'

'Don't alter the course of your parents' lives.'

She shook her head. 'It's my life I'm concerned with.'

She wasn't sure she even liked her mother most of the time. And to see her next door, daily, and to know that she could become like her, concerned Lily.

'Perhaps if they were your children you could decide to let them live their own lives. Think of it like that.' He'd spoken quietly, but she felt the judgement.

'It is for their own good.'

'I thought the same thing and now I'm not so sure. When the story was published about my father's actions, I took complete control of my father's life. He couldn't disinherit me so his hands were tied in that direction. He never expected me to go against his wishes so he didn't expect the actions I took. He could only shoot me in the back and he had no weapon.'

She turned her head, not wanting to hear.

'I planned it more methodically than any chess game,' Edgeworth said, taking her arm and walking with her to his house. 'I refused to lose or give in. Our family would remain intact. I leveraged everything I had against the man who raised me to take control of his heritage—only he'd never imagined me doing so while he still lived.'

The Wallflower Duchess

'You did what you felt right, and who is to say it wasn't? No one can blame you for trying to hold your family together.'

Inside the entrance to Edge's house, the butler vanished from sight as soon as he realised he wasn't needed for anything.

'I understand that if the story didn't appear, things would likely have moved along with my father supporting the other woman and his child. I would have found out when he died and kept it from my mother. I would never have let those words be printed if I had known of them. But once my mother knew and it wasn't a whisper any more, I acted. That's what I was trained to do—take control of the family and work to make things better. But I should have left my parents' marriage to them.'

'You did it for your mother.'

'I could have spent more time trying to bolster her up, instead of taking lives and moulding them to my wishes.'

He touched the ring finger of her left hand, resting the tip of his finger on the empty spot. 'I'll be there for you. I'll help you with your mother, but not as an audience, and you must keep yourself from being one as well. Few actors perform when the spectators have left.'

'What if she breaks out a window in your house—with your mother in the room?'

'I will have her escorted out and have the window fixed. My mother can withstand a lot. She had no choice the last years of my father's life. He didn't blame me for the loss of his mistress at first—he blamed his marriage and my mother.'

Her throat hurt. She shut her eyes. If she could go back and change one day, one moment of her past, she knew exactly which one it was. The one when she spoke with the newspaper man. She'd hurt the Duchess so much and Edgeworth. She'd brought the same grief into their lives that she hated for herself.

He squeezed her hand.

Edge looked at the jewellery box on the table. He'd soon be putting the ring on Lily's finger. Supposedly the tradition started because of a connection to the heart, but he didn't care how it began, as long as Lily wore his ring. They'd set a date.

He heard clattering and knew, without a doubt, the footsteps belonged to his cousin Foxworthy.

Fox burst into Edge's sitting room, his laughing call to Edge preceding him. He held a newspaper in his hand.

Edge frowned. He really didn't care what intrigues his cousin was involved in.

'Look.' Fox held out the paper, grinning. 'I did it. Twentieth time I've been mentioned...' he held his head to the side '...and I'm not counting when I was given credit for that little inaccuracy about being challenged to a duel.'

'I couldn't care less,' Edge said, lifting the box to his hand.

'Twenty times. Andrew said I couldn't do it.'

Edgeworth frowned. Andrew should be throttled for challenging their cousin in such a way. 'You realise Andrew won whatever the outcome.'

Fox's hands stopped, but then he continued opening the paper, folding it to the page he wanted. 'See,' he said to Edge. 'Name spelled right. All events true.' He examined it. 'They do need to get a better engraver though. I look like a wolf. And the ladies all look like plump chickens, but...' He waggled his head. 'Twenty times. I did it.'

Edge glanced over the hideous drawing and pushed the paper back to Fox.

Fox read. 'Yes. Sophia's in this edition, too. It's hard to get noticed more than a courtesan. Blast it.'

He tossed the paper to the spot where the box had rested. 'Well…' He straightened his jacket, nodding. 'I accomplished my goal. But I plan to be written about another five times before the end of the year.'

'Did you think that might be foolish?'

Fox picked up the paper he'd just relinquished. 'I like being written about. The ladies all ask me if the events are true and I tell them I admit to nothing. And then I usually admit to everything.' He glanced at the print and recreated the grin from the drawing. 'It really doesn't look a thing like me.

'Oh, and it says Mrs Hightower is in London again,' Fox said, reading.

Edge tossed the box to the table and seized the paper.

Fox shrugged. 'Nothing of particular note. My story was better.' He waved to Edge. 'You can keep that one. I have extras.' He left, his feet thudding down the stairs as he left.

Edge read, suppressing the urge to charge to the publisher's immediately.

Mrs Hightower had returned to London in fine style, according to the words. She'd apparently spent a considerable amount of money on her shopping trip and captured a lot of notice with parcels loaded over the top of her husband's carriage, if the tale were true.

And then, just a reference to 'indiscretions in her past' and another suggestion that she'd been quite good friends with Sophia Swift, although the only current actions written about were over-abundant shopping.

News indeed.

His jaw and hands clenched, but nothing else moved except for the vibration of the paper he held.

He would personally throttle the publisher of the paper. No, he would have the man investigated because surely someone so spurious in writing about others could not have lived an exemplary life. Edge could open a competing publishing house and give the news away for a pittance.

When the words had been about his father, his mother had begged him not to make matters worse. To let the news fade away.

The paper in his hands ripped, surprising him. He'd not known he held it so tightly.

This refuse would be addressed and he would use every ounce of his authority to stop this damage.

Lily's whole existence had been affected by this type of scandalmongering. He couldn't let it continue.

As he left his house, his footsteps made no noise. If the publisher wanted to play a game of chess, Edge would engage. He thought of the favours he could ask returned and the financial motives he could give for people to see things his way.

They would treat his wife and her family with respect, and if that wasn't possible Edge would make them suffer. Dearly.

Edge rode to the publisher's office. He'd passed the butchers and the nearness to rotting entrails suited the location well. A dank little building, better for holding corpses than anything else.

Edge walked inside. Ink and paper scented the air as if he'd stuck his head deep inside a book. A rhythmic clanking noise from another room and a desk—possibly a desk—sat near one corner, fronted by stacks of newspaper and more to each side. An ink-splotched man stepped from the back room, but the clanking continued. Edge recognised the man from the theatre and he looked more like a caricature than a person, yet he'd dared to lash out at Edge's father and hurt Edge's mother.

Edge kicked the stack of newspapers, scattering them about. They fluttered off the walls. 'I will not tolerate my family being written of again.'

The man looked at the jumbled papers and then at Edge, studying his features. Then he looked to the doorway. The ducal seal was on the side of the carriage parked just beyond the window. Recognition flashed on the man's face. 'You'll be getting a bill for that, Your Grace.'

Edge leaned forward. 'I might be getting several. One for whatever is in the back of your shop as well. But don't expect the funds to arrive promptly.'

'Why in Hades do you care one half-damn about what that rake Foxworthy does?'

'You attack families.'

'Ah, yes. The old Duke.' He snorted. 'Don't think you're the first peer that ever walked in here with a threat on his lips. Doubt you'll be the last.'

He picked up a knife and used the blade to clean the ink from under his fingernails.

'Your Grace, I put ink on paper.' He scowled. 'Good ink. Good paper. Good stories. Bad people. And sometimes good, when a person dares enough to show it. I print what is already there. News.'

'News? News?' Edge raised his hand. 'You disgrace everyone. You're a vulture picking at the bones of others even before they're dead. You pushed my father to his grave.'

The man gave a dry chuckle. 'Oh, yes. It's all coming back to me now. I'd forgotten about seeing you at the theatre with a lovely young woman. Practically an announcement of a betrothal to come. But I didn't print it. I'm rather impressed with Lily Hightower's tenacity. And she is more respectful than you are.' He moved his head to one side. 'I admire her. She looked me straight in the eye. Not many can do that.'

The publisher pulled a rag from his waistband and wiped at the smears on his hands, and scowled at Edgeworth. 'Every single time you read a report of someone saying they have been defamed by the press, every time you read a report of someone saying lies were printed about them—their rebuttal could have been ignored. Their side is being told—in black and white. They're getting their say. A print run is being given to them to tell how print runs defame them. Not many businesses would do that.'

'They shouldn't have to say it in the first place. Don't try to make yourself a paragon. Because you are not.'

The publisher snorted, stopping the scrape of the knife against his fingernails, and his face angled so that only one eye looked at Edge. 'If you think I'm bad, think how it would be if I wasn't here. Without this—' he pointed the knife tip to the jumble '—only those in power would have a voice and they wouldn't even need a voice because they could conduct business with the signature of a pen. The people with the biggest houses could stuff their pillow coverings with pound notes and prey on the weaknesses of the people who near-worship them.'

He turned, picking up a paper, never taking his eyes off Edge. 'People disgrace themselves. People. Disgrace. Themselves. I write it. I write the truth. All of it. In fact, I mentioned Lord Andrew's wife for the next edition.'

He opened the paper, smearing ink, and folded

it open to a page. He stuffed it towards Edgeworth. Edgeworth let his breath ease out so he could force his hand forward to take the rag. He studied the ink, controlling his thoughts so the words made sense.

Beatrice was quoted. Something about her having an art showing with all the sales to benefit families losing their income because of the loom factories.

'So it is one instance of good you mentioned. It doesn't take away from all the bad.' He thrust the rot at the man, but the publisher stepped back, refusing to accept it.

Edge slammed it into the air at his right. The publisher's eyes narrowed.

'You look at the paper,' the publisher said. 'My paper. It isn't one instance of virtue or one story of vice. It is one instance of this town. I have many stories of people doing good, as it happens. I print stories. Whatever they are. And people, being so sickeningly perfect, search for the bad ones and remember them far longer than any mention of art. It will not be my fault when someone doesn't read the story of Beatrice, but hunts for a report of your cousin Foxworthy proposing yet again in public to a married woman.' He choked. 'I get so tired of his antics. I only print them on the slowest days now.' He held up the knife, casually bobbing it. 'The man should be nipped.'

'You know he only does it for the scandal. The notoriety.'

'Yes.' He pointed his weak chin in Edge's direction. One fist could have killed the man. 'And I print Fox's escapades for the nonsense it is. I do not print the stories of the maids who prepare countless meals or empty countless chamber pots. It is not news. It is boring.' He tossed his knife to the disarray on the desk. 'And sometimes those people who scrape up the refuse left by the wealthy—someone reads my words about the foibles of their superiors to them and they feel a little better about themselves.'

The publisher rapped his knuckles against the desk. 'Your Grace. Lord Edgeworth. I know your name and so do most of the people in this town. Not just the ones on St James's Street, but the ones on Cheapside as well.'

'You also wrote of my father's mistress.'

The man unrolled his half-white, half-inked sleeves. His eyes blackened, but his lips smiled.

He moved to his chair, sat, leaned back and put interlaced fingers behind his head. 'I did. Didn't I?'

Edge took a step forward. They would not hang him but once.

The man's eyes narrowed. 'You have no idea what I did not tell.'

The words slashed into Edge's brain. Every bit of blood inside Edge's body stilled, until he took in a breath, allowing himself to continue living.

The man raised his brows and his voice hardly rose above the clanking. 'So you stand there, basking in your fury. Your self-righteousness.' He shrugged. 'Be thankful I have a good heart.'

'Liar.'

The man's posture changed. He sat straight, picking up a pen, waving it in rhythm with the shaking sideways toss of his head. 'No.' The pen paused. 'I rarely print an error and when I am told of it and it's shown to me, I correct it with the same emphasis, if not more, than I wrote the mistake.' He stood. 'I right my wrongs, Lord Edgeworth.' He crossed his arms. 'I do not pay them to go to the Americas.'

Edge stared ahead, hiding the inward flinch. He'd been so careful when handling the transaction.

'And just this morning, I had another decision to make. Another one. And...' he stared into Edge's eyes '...you are making it so much harder. So much harder to keep quiet...' His voice faded and he examined the pen.

'If you print one more word about my family, I will kill you.'

'Well—' he shrugged '—I suppose I should write fast then, as she is not currently your family.'

Edge stepped closer, his hand in a fist.

'Your Grace. Such behaviour from a peer.' He clucked his lips. He tapped the nib of his pen on to the paper in front of him. With the nib still on the paper, he looked at Edge. 'Who do you think told me of your father's mistress?'

The words hit Edge just below the ribs, knocking him a step back.

'Yes.' The publisher nodded. 'And she was at Sophia Swift's house this morning.'

A lone drop of perspiration ran down the side of Edge's face and his temples throbbed redness into his vison.

If the man lied, Edge would take the shop from him and destroy his livelihood. The man would beg for crumbs.

He slammed from the room. He could have walked the globe in the time it took to get to his carriage. If he'd stayed, he would have ripped the man into the same pieces as the smallest print. But he had to leave. He must find out the truth.

Lily.

A lie. It had to be a lie.

But there'd been flint in the man's eyes. And he'd known about Edge sending the woman away. Edge had taken such care to keep it quiet.

And the publisher had recognised Lily at the theatre.

How dare she?

She'd—

His family.

His manners barely held when the butler greeted him at the Hightower residence.

'I'm here to see Miss Hightower.'

The butler studied Edge, thought for a moment, then showed Edge to the sitting room.

Edge didn't sit, but stood at the window, studying the recent repair. The sill had been repainted. The room reeked of paint. He touched the sill. Wet. He took out his handkerchief and wiped away the smear on his finger.

He didn't wait long before he heard her voice. 'Edgeworth?'

'Lily,' he answered, not turning and still jabbing at the repair. 'Were you at Sophia Swift's recently?'

He didn't have to see her. He could hear the truth in the silence.

'I was searching for my mother.'

'I have just spoken with an acquaintance of yours—a newspaper man.'

She didn't speak.

He turned on one foot.

She still stood in the doorway, but when their gaze met, she stepped inside and shut the door.

'It's tempting.' He shook his head. 'It's tempting to break the window again. But then your butler would send someone to summon the man back who repaired it and your father's man of affairs would get the bill, and the sum would be deducted from the accounts and it would mean absolutely nothing.'

He blinked. 'You couldn't send a messenger to Sophia Swift's?'

'I wore the old clothing. No one saw me. I know it.'

'Someone did.'

'Only Sophia could have known of it, which is no doubt how you came to hear of it. She sent for me. Mother was there. She thought Sophia owed her for the trouble she caused in the book and the fact that they'd been friends. But, really, Mother had nowhere else to go but there or here.'

'Your father could have gone for her.'

'I didn't want him to know. I didn't want more things thrown.'

'You ignored my words to let them sort their problems.'

'You should leave.'

'Before you throw something at the window or before I do?' His eyes locked on her face.

'Does it matter?'

'One thing does above all else. You knew. Of the mistress. All along.'

'Yes.'

His head recoiled an inch. She could have hit him full on with her fist and he wouldn't have moved that much.

'Well, so you did.' His lips moved in the direction of a smile. 'Why did you not tell me?'

'You were the... You were your father's son. I couldn't tell you such a thing. "Thank you for rescuing my kite. Did you know that my sister and I are not at my mother's house today because my room was needed as a rendezvous place for your father?"'

He raised his chin. 'Are you telling the truth?'

She nodded. 'Yes.' Her words barely reached his ears. 'Your father had quite the airs, walking about as if he could do no wrong and yet he had a mistress. My mother and his mistress were good friends. Your father visited my mother's house to meet her.'

Lily remembered how it felt. The old Duke had a mistress nearly the same age as Edgeworth and he'd looked at Lily and Abigail like so much dirt under his heels since he'd found out they knew of his secret.

And Lily had marched to the publisher herself and asked why he printed so much about her mother and ignored the Duke and his baby.

The man's jaw had dropped and Lily realised he'd not known about the Duke. He'd apologised to her. He'd been nice.

But the Duke's youngest son, the illegitimate child, had been mentioned in the next publishing. And she'd known. Known it was her fault. She'd only wanted the publisher to ignore her family, but she'd got angry and betrayed the Duchess and Edgeworth. The two people in the *ton* who'd treated her with respect. Who'd been nice.

Edge's eyes pierced her. She knew how it felt to be plucked from the earth by a hawk, talons piercing the soft skin, and being rushed to a nest above the earth with the finishing insult of being torn into bite-sized pieces.

'I cannot undo what I did,' she said.

He stood at the window. He took one fingernail and scraped away a dot of the new paint on the glass, before facing her again. 'When we were children, you acted as if you cared. You acted fond of me,' he said. 'You didn't seem to know I was different than everyone else.'

'I thought you fascinating. Your perfect family. The vast garden separating my imperfect one. Yet later I discovered my family was more honest in its outward appearance than your father was.'

'When my father was foolish, you showed it to the world.'

'It's better to hide?'

'It's better to do the right thing. But you completely avoided that path when you spoke to the publisher and destroyed my family.'

'Your father did.'

'No.' Edge put the force of his size into the quiet word. 'Our family might have been imperfect, but we were still a family until those words blasted into our faces and into the rooms of everyone who knew us and many who didn't.'

'My parents didn't hide them behind a façade.'

'It wasn't a façade for me. And that doesn't make you less at fault because my father did wrong. My father died with a rift between us that can't be solved—ever. I will go to my own death knowing that our last words were bitter.'

'It is not the newspaper story that caused your father's deceit.'

'I will grant you that. But it doesn't change what you did.'

'No.'

'You purposefully destroyed my family.' He closed the distance between them, his eyes showing an intensity she'd never seen in anyone before.

'Not on purpose.'

'You could not hurt him without hurting us. And Mother felt the pain most. The woman who'd had you to tea so many times.'

'How could you not have known unless you closed your eyes to it? When you went to the family that summer, your father stayed behind and spent days and days with my mother's friend. I knew because I was sent here and he didn't appear the whole time.'

'I did not know. I can assure you, he kept it from us.'

She had to turn away and she saw the open door, and wondered how much of their conversation had carried. Just a betrothal had turned friends into enemies. 'You believed a lie because you didn't open your eyes and ears. The servants had to have known.'

He shook his head. 'No. The servants didn't know.'

She whirled around and let the pause lengthen, disputing his words with her eyes.

'He said he stayed at the club often while we were gone. They would have thought him there.'

'I suppose.'

His chest rose. 'The club. Because the house felt so alone without us.'

'I would say he didn't like to be alone.'

The glance had more strength than a slap. 'I don't know how you could look my mother in the eye.'

'No one had trouble looking at me when my

mother's indiscretions were the talk of the town. They had no trouble with their eyes and their chins would go up or their noses would point my direction and they'd squint.'

'I never did that to you. Never.'

'No. Your nose was already up in the air because you were the heir. Your nose stayed there for everyone so I was equal in your eyes to all the people around you. And it was a game to try to pull you from being the heir. And you seemed to like it. You even seemed to like me. And I thought you special not because of your birth but because of your actions.'

'I had a role to fulfil and I knew it.'

A clash of eyes.

'You did what was proper,' she said. 'Always. Always. Rescuing the little girl's kite. Sending the girls back to their governess. Studying your lessons. Always so proper.' She turned away. 'I thought you a saint, of sorts. The one who might walk by us with a kind nod as he went to do his great works. Who could walk alone on the uppermost clouds. I believed you better than everyone else. Just as you did. And do.'

'I did not have a choice. I couldn't make one mistake on my lessons. I had to be perfect. I could not risk an error that I could catch. Because if I didn't learn to excel, then how could I be the leader I needed to be? Even at the clubs, I could not drink more than two drinks. I could not do anything that others might remember later and talk about. I had to be the future Edgeworth.'

He raised his hand shoulder height and clenched the air. 'And you know what happened. My father was out ruining the family name while I was doing exactly as he told me I should do.'

'But you're blaming me.'

His eyes stared into her. 'For the publication only. All my life, I accepted that I could not swear, have another drink, or have anything but the best of manners unless I was alone in my room. I upheld the name. You splashed dirt on it.'

He moved closer. 'I wanted to be like my father. It would have been nice if I could have believed he didn't live a lie just a little longer. But even if I'd realised he was betraying my mother—I would not have hurt her with it. I wouldn't have displayed it for everyone else to judge. People should respect their leaders. It gives everyone something to believe in and more ability to trust in the decisions. And they must trust the decisions. The people are working all day to eat and they do not have extra time to study every law and every decision that can starve or feed them.'

She flicked her brows in response.

'I learned how much mistakes cost when I sent the woman and her child away,' he said.

'You didn't have to do that.'

'At the time I thought I did. And it fixed nothing. Nothing. I wanted that ducal family more than my father did for us. And I couldn't get it back.' He snapped his fingers. 'Gone. One little voice in the right ears and my family shattered.'

'Nothing changed. Except you knew.'

'Except everyone knew. Everyone who could read or listen to someone who could.'

'You said your brothers knew.'

'Foxworthy told them.'

'But he didn't tell you and they didn't.'

'No. I had a role to fulfil and no one could even tell me the truth of my family. Or they wouldn't tell me. That was why I needed to find out what it was like to be a common man. I realised an invisible wall stood between me and the people I want to serve.'

'You are the perfect Duke. Too perfect to listen to imperfection.'

'When I almost died, I realised I wasn't doing

enough. All I have ever done in my life is follow the path designated.'

'You did have time to meet Genevieve.'

'Yes. I did. That was scheduled as well. Once a month. I could not spare more or I'd risk letting my heart be involved. I did not have time for that.'

'And you chose me.'

'I was dying. And you brought life into me. I lay there recovering and I remembered that you had once asked me to play dolls. *Dolls.* You had thrown a biscuit at me and didn't care who I was. You must have spent an hour trying to fly that kite on to my head before it finally caught in the tree. You even brought a handful of half-mashed strawberries out to share with me one day and I told you I didn't want them—but I did. No one ever dared serve me anything not carefully prepared. And, yes, I noticed the little heart drawn with a pencil on the bench. The one with the words *Lion Owl* inside it. I looked forward to walking out to the gardens to do my studies because I could see the words you'd written. After they'd faded, I still looked for them.'

'I forgot about the heart.'

'You forgot that. But you remembered how my father looked at you and you took your revenge.'

His words slowed and he closed his feelings away. 'Don't misunderstand. I wouldn't trade away my birthright. Or sell it. I have a chance to make a difference in the world. It was worth the lost pleasures. To keep the country as best that it can be for the blacksmith, his family and the daughter he *didn't* have. And people who would smear my family name into all the mud they can throw.'

He moved to the door, but he kept his path wide around her and he spoke in his perfect, calm tones. 'I came over to tell you the betrothal is off. I know that a man cannot call off such a thing normally, but in this case I'm putting aside my role and doing as I wish.'

Then he left.

Chapter Fourteen

Edge walked to his bedchamber. He'd been betrayed. Lily had cut out the heart of his family, sent his mother into spasms of pain and helped push his father into the dark box of death.

She'd made the people who disliked his family smug.

His father had done wrong. Edge had no doubt of that. But Lily had taken the wrongness, sharpened the tip of it and shoved it into all the people he loved. Every. One.

He'd known his brothers and his friends had kept the truth from him, but he had expected Lily to be different. She'd suffered from her own mother's deceit, just as he'd experienced his father's.

But she hadn't been different; only more wrong.

Now he saw Lily through the shades of her deceit. And she'd known all along. Lily.

His mother had invited her for tea and Lily had arrived, knowing how she'd decimated an innocent woman's marriage.

And he'd let her into his house and taken her to his bed and put his heart at her feet. He'd wanted her to have his children. His name. And be at his side. He'd wanted to whisper with her in the night and let their touches soothe everything else away. He'd wanted them to be a part of each other.

And like all the people who'd known about his father's mistress and not told him; she'd had her own secret—every moment she was in his home.

He would find a way to forget he had known her.

Abigail's voice took up all the empty spaces at the dining-room table. Their mother had left after picking at the food. She'd hardly spoken.

Lily stared at the lemon tart she couldn't finish. She'd taken one bite of the confection which had the texture and flavour of creamy glue covered with a sprinkle of sawdust.

All Lily could think of was when she'd stolen a pencil from her father's desk, taken it to the bench and written the letters her governess had taught her. She'd already known how to make a heart. And learning to write *Lily* had been much easier than learning the words *Lion Owl*. She'd thought it his real name and the grandest name she'd ever heard. The governess had been snickering while she taught Lily the letters, but Lily didn't care. Then the governess had mentioned her own lofty background and told Lily that dukes didn't care for little girls with less breeding than their staff.

Then the governess had pulled Abigail's hair one day and Abigail was such a baby she didn't have any hair to spare.

Lily had thought about it before she went to sleep that night. She'd remembered her mother telling the nice cook to leave. And the ladies' maid.

Her mother might have ignored that the woman pulled Abigail's hair, but she'd never overlook the mention of having less importance than the governess, Lily knew.

But now Lily stared at the pastry and she couldn't bear to lift the fork to her mouth. She didn't even want to move from the table. She was turning as morose as her mother.

Abigail mumbled some nonsense and Lily nodded, still looking at her plate. Lemon wasn't as good as orange, but she couldn't bear to think of orange more than one second. In the past few days, everything had tasted like ash.

'I just told you I am going to run away with Fox and become a courtesan.' Abigail waved her fork so close in front of Lily's face that Lily jumped, her mind warning her she could be rapped on the nose. She leaned back, shoving aside her sister's arm, but didn't speak.

'I'm going to have Fox's child,' Abigail said.

Lily looked again at the mound of yellow on her plate. 'Best of luck to you.'

'I was just seeing if you were awake,' Abigail said. 'I'm not going to have a baby.'

'Probably for the best. Especially if it had his chin and your whiskers.'

Abigail rapped the fork against Lily's knuckles.

'You're about to have lemon-scented hair,' Lily stated.

Abigail reached over and scooped up the yellow confectionery from Lily's plate. 'You've not sneaked out to the gardens in days. Not since—I don't know—the theatre? What happened at the theatre?' Abigail said. 'You have to tell me. You don't keep a diary.' She took another bite. 'You really should keep a diary for those days you don't feel like talking.'

'I'll start if you'll promise never to speak to me again.'

'So, what did happen with the lofty Edgeworth?'

Abigail took the last bite from Lily's plate.

'I was going to eat that,' Lily said.

'No you weren't.' She swallowed. 'So what happened?'

'Nothing.'

'That tart was good.' She paused. 'Wonder if there is more?'

Lily didn't answer.

'Fox didn't even know you and Edgeworth are avoiding each other, but I told him.' Abigail still held her fork. 'I thought you'd want him to know.'

'So kind of you.'

'He said Edge is acting like a lion with a thorn in its paw and when he told Edgeworth that he'd be glad to have the thorn, Edge shouted at him. He said he'd never seen Edge shout and he didn't even know Edge had a temper, and apparently Edge has a monstrous temper. Then Edge said he was going to the country because he could not stay in this town another second.'

Abigail tapped her plate, making the most annoying clicks. 'I'm going to have Fox ask Edge's mother what has happened.'

'You do that.' Lily stood.

'There's fleas in your bed. I put them there.'

Lily shrugged, leaving. 'No different than when I shared a room with you.'

Lily knocked on her mother's door, but didn't wait for an answer. Her mother sat, eyes red, head down, hair scattered about her face, the butterfly hairpin she preferred lying on the dressing table. She looked up. 'Lily, there's something wrong with me.'

Lily leaned against the open door. 'I know. There always has been.'

Her mother brushed back a tangle of hair, but it fell forward again. 'I'm so happy some moments that I can hardly stand it and the next, I weep for days.'

Lily walked over and took the last pins from her mother's hair, letting the locks fall, and gathered the brush, running her hand over the bristles. 'Yes.'

'Your father. He said he loves me.'

'Well, there's something wrong with him, too.'

Her mother sighed. 'Thank you for bringing me home from Sophia's.' She gazed up at Lily. 'I wanted to know why she did that to me. She said she shouldn't have done it, but I could tell she wasn't sincere. I'd thought we were true friends. Not that she was using me to find out information for her memoirs.'

Lily brushed her mother's hair. Then twisted it up into a knot and put the pins back in.

'I hate being here. Everyone remembers, and really, I didn't do the things they say. At least— not all of them. I thought Sophia wouldn't judge because she's a courtesan, but she's false.'

She sniffled and reached for a handkerchief. Lily's eyes followed the white cloth.

'I was happier in the country and I wasn't upset all the time,' her mother continued. 'And no one visited and tempted me to go out.'

'No one will visit you here now. Since you left, no one calls, and if someone visits, the butler can say you're unwell.'

'Your father wanted me in London. And I did miss my girls terribly. So I had to leave the plants I'd tended for years. And I had a goat named

Samuel Johnson and he ate the vegetables I grew. I left him behind.'

'You grew the vegetables or your gardener did?'

'I didn't have a gardener. Didn't want one. I got up early and, if I couldn't sleep, even at night, I worked in the garden. In the winter, I would make plans for the next season. I even had turnips because I could feed them to the horse. And winter onions. And I don't like onions.'

'And did you have a beau?'

'No. I stayed away from men. Without your father getting upset it seemed pointless.'

'Did you throw things?'

'No. Your father wasn't there.'

'He can be irritating.'

'You're so sensible, Lily. You're nothing like me.'

'Are you sure?' Lily waited for the answer even before she'd finished asking the question. She studied her mother's face.

'I'm positive. I would know.' She grimaced. 'Even before I married, I was rather dismal and sad most of the time. When I met your father and felt better, I thought that would fix everything. It didn't. But he had a lot of money and he didn't mind that I was taller than him.'

The older woman turned in her chair. 'What of Edgeworth? Abigail said you were going to marry him and now you're not.'

'No, I'm not.'

'Why?'

'Several reasons. And he makes me feel all fluttery and insensible.'

'That's just at the beginning when you get attached to someone. It goes away. Then your mind returns and you look at him without any pretensions. That's when the funds are handy.'

'Mother. If you liked the plants, why don't you grow them here?'

'Nothing will grow here. It's all shaded.'

'What about in front of the house?'

'Your father would have a temper. What will everyone think if I start digging around in the dirt?'

Possibly a lot nicer things than they'd said before, Lily thought. 'When the flowers grow, they might think you're happier. Perhaps you could tell Father you won't break any windows if you have a garden. And if he lets you have a cat, you'll not shout.'

'And if I can cook confections in the middle of

the night when I can't sleep, it will be so much better.'

'Then just start digging up the dirt and cooking when you want and tell Father to go to the devil if he doesn't like it.'

Her mother smiled and tossed the handkerchief aside. 'I'm so pleased you're not like me.'

Lily leaned to the table top and took the butterfly pin. She tucked it into her mother's hair.

She bit the inside of her lip to keep it from quivering. She wasn't telling her mother that she'd been crying for days and had only been able to stop twice since Edgeworth had called off their betrothal.

In her room, with the door latched, Lily hugged her pillow to her chest. Edge was in the country. But it didn't matter.

She would never, ever let herself feel this way again. Memories of her mother's despair flitted through Lily's mind. She had to stop herself from making the same mistakes. If it felt this way the first time, she could not bear a lifetime of it. She'd seen the devastation in her mother's face so many times. Lily's choice to be a spinster had been the right one and when she'd forgotten it, the world had crashed, hurling all sorts of blades into her.

She'd not known the inside of a person could hurt so much more than the outside.

She'd tried crying it out, pounding it out with a fist into her pillow, and forced herself not to throw things because she'd already seen that accomplished nothing. But neither did anything else.

Edge had turned her mind both wrong side out and wrong side in. Her numb skin did nothing except work as a container to hold the aches neatly locked inside her body, and keep her raw and throbbing with each beat of her heart.

She'd walked to the window. And then she'd realised—she was watching for Edge and she wasn't even at the right window for the view. Slamming the window shut, she forced herself to turn away.

A hundred times she'd seen her mother go through this, but her mother had lacked the strength to deal with it. Lily clenched her jaw. She might not have the willpower a second time. A second time would bring her to her knees just as it did her mother. Each time her mother gave in quicker to the feelings, sinking deeper and losing herself, and recovering a little less than she had the time before. And it had only taken a lifetime for her mother to discover her mistake. Lily couldn't live like that another twenty-five years.

The door clattered as someone knocked and then tried to get in.

'Go away,' Lily said.

'I can't,' Abigail answered. 'I care about you. I need you healthy so some day you can repeat all those frightful talks you've told me and then explain them to the children I plan to have. I want them to *like* me so I can't tell them all that folderol about how you hiccup and a baby pops out of your mouth.'

'I corrected that error.'

'Yes. I preferred the hiccup story, by the way. Much more sensible.'

'Then stay. I'm not opening the door,' Lily grumbled back. 'I have food and water in here, and when I come out, don't forget, I'm taller and I outweigh you.'

'But I can run faster.' Abigail's voice faded, but kept its shrillness so Lily knew her sister walked away.

Against her wishes, but unable to help herself, Lily walked to the window. She couldn't even see

much of Edge's gardens because her room faced
the back of the house. She'd have to go to Abigail's room for the best view because she wasn't
leaning out her window and turning sideways.
But she did feel closer to him when she looked
outside. Then she noticed the barest reflection
of her face in the glass—all of her that was left.

Edge stepped from the rear door of his house.
Going to the country hadn't solved anything. Lily
owed him an apology and an explanation. He
couldn't sleep for thinking how she'd betrayed
his family and kept it from him. She knew. She'd
been in his home and she'd known how she'd
tossed his family's secrets out into the wind, letting them scatter like thistle pods to open and
spread their seeds to carry on for ever.

He didn't move forward. At least the window
across from his garden was the sister's. The one
at the back of the Hightower house, near the corner, almost hidden and looking over the shadows,
was Lily's.

He looked to Lily's sister's window, remembering the handkerchief, irritated he'd ever let that
get started.

Movement caught his eye and he stepped closer to the other house.

Abigail marched underneath the window, with two workmen trudging along hefting a ladder.

She looked over, shook her fist his direction and kept walking.

Edge couldn't help it. He moved where he could see the window at the back of the house—Lily's. Damn Lily for reducing him to someone no better than the reader of a scandal sheet. Although he didn't think anyone could avoid watching a neighbour with a hammer in her hand caterpillar her way up a ladder while trying to hold her skirt close to her body so the two workmen below would not be able to see her woman parts.

Abigail made it to the top and used the hammer to tap on the glass and raised the tool high. A true daughter of Mrs Hightower. The window opened and a splash of water dowsed her. She tossed the hammer inside and dived in behind it.

'Out,' a screeching voice shouted.

He couldn't hear the answer.

The workmen looked up, one of them moving his head in the same manner of a new reader following a line of words.

The hammer flew out the open window, barely

missing one of the men, and he half-expected Abigail to follow, but instead she stuck her head out, waved to the men below and shouted, 'Thank you. We're through for the day.' Then she disappeared inside.

The one on the left looked to the one on the right and they remained, looking up, listening.

Edge walked closer to the men, stuck his arm out, pointing to the road. They bobbed their heads at him and left without even taking the ladder.

He went back inside and swore not to look at the house beside his. He would not. He would stick both legs into flames before he walked her direction again and he would not let his eyes betray him either.

Two days later, Gaunt appeared at his door. His face flicked between sadness and perhaps amusement.

'A woman to see you.'

Righteous indignation swirled in Edge's body. The apology. Not that it would matter. Lily had destroyed his family.

'She's dressed in mourning,' Gaunt said, seeming to bite the inside of his lip to keep a calm demeanour.

Edge's shoulders stiffened. He would not make this easy for her.

Edge walked into the sitting room. The visitor sat, her face covered with the mourning veil.

She lifted her handkerchief, a plain one. Her shoulders heaved a bit and she lifted the veil enough to put the handkerchief to her lips. Her voice quivered and the deep breaths made it sound as if she sobbed, and her voice came in high-pitched, muffled, warbling sniffles.

'I most sincerely apologise,' she said.

'For what?'

'Everything.'

He spoke softly. 'But, Abigail, you've done nothing to me.'

She flipped the veil up. 'I'm here on behalf of my sister. She sent me to apologise.'

Like hell.

'Accepted,' he said and turned on his heel.

Just outside the door, he huffed a breath and turned back. 'But thank you for your efforts on your sister's behalf.'

She stood, walked up to him, pointed her nose in his direction, eyes narrow slits, and said, 'I'm really here on your behalf. She's too good for you.'

With a snap of her wrist, she pulled the veil down. 'I don't know what happened, but I hope you rot.' She took a step and turned back. 'She can't sleep.' She took another step and then turned back again, the mourning clothes swallowing her. 'You destroyed her. I hope you're happy.' She put her hand on her hip. 'She won't even read her cookbook any more.'

He stood silent. He should have stayed in the country, but he'd just not been able to.

'And she won't eat. Not even those hideous orange things she likes.'

She could leave any time now.

'I had Cook make her favourite orange biscuits and you would have thought I was trying to poison her when I took them to her.' She was quiet for a second. 'I thought she was going to cry.' She raised her head higher, pointing a finger to the ceiling. 'And my sister does not cry over biscuits.'

'You may leave now.'

'Edge...' The Duchess's voice.

He turned. His mother stood on one side and an addled woman on the other.

'What *is* wrong?' the older woman asked.

'Nothing. Just a matter I'm clearing up.'

'Ha.' Abigail didn't lift the veil. 'He destroyed my sister. Took a knife to her tender emotions and stabbed her through with all his might.' Then she whirled away and ran out the door.

His mother clasped her throat. 'Edge. What did you do?'

'That was Miss Abigail Hightower.'

'Oh.' The Duchess looked to the doorway, emotions fading from her face. 'Takes after her mother?'

'I would guess so.'

His mother appraised him. 'And what did she mean by your taking a knife to her sister? I thought the two of you were courting.'

His teeth together and jaw locked, he shook his head, the weight of the movement taking all his strength.

'Well…' she reached out, picking a piece of lint from the sofa, but still every bit the Duchess as she emphasised her words with a shake of her head '…I told Lily you could be difficult.'

'Mother, I do not doubt that I can be difficult, but the woman—' He turned away from his mother, not wanting her to see his face. 'You cannot believe what she is truly like.'

'Fairly quiet, I would say, except when the two

of you are together. Never heard a peep from her when she was growing up, unless you were outside. Then I could hear *"Lion Owl"* being shouted,' she mumbled. 'If I had named you William, perhaps, that would have been best. Your father wanted you named Lionel.' She stopped. 'A very lovely name.'

'She should have addressed me properly.'

'Booby-head?'

'You listened?'

'I'm your mother. It's what I do.'

He watched as she moved the fripperies around on the mantel, arranging them in ways that made no discernible difference. Then she picked up a book and put it under her arm.

'Have I given you any advice lately?' she asked.

He huffed a breath. 'No. And I know what you're going to say. Forgive. Forget. Rise above. Duty. Heirs.'

'I was going to say don't be a booby-head, actually. Same thing, I suppose, but sounded better the way you said it.' She stood back and examined the room. 'Could you help me move the chair? I think one of the servants has it a little crooked.'

He stared. A footman should do that. But then

she pressed her lips together and pointed to the furniture.

He picked up the arm, moving it just the amount she indicated. 'Nice and tidy. Perfect. Just the way your father would have liked it. And he certainly wouldn't have liked the thought that Lily Hightower would be a duchess in this house—at least, not at the end.'

'She's not going to be.'

She examined the chair. 'He was a good man, your father, but not at the end. Not at the end. Sad. A whole life of doing the right thing and then—' She snapped her fingers. 'Just threw it all away.' She tilted her head. 'Don't do that.'

'You have to understand.' His voice thundered. 'Lily told the newspaper about Father.'

She put a hand to her cheek. 'So is that what this little crisis is all about?'

'I'm surprised you're not more horrified.'

'It was all a long time ago now, darling.'

'Mother. She destroyed our family.'

'Give your father some credit there.' Her eyes pinched. 'He did his share where that's concerned.' She gave a dainty kick to the leg of the chair. 'He changed in one year into a stranger.

He was irritable and not himself. I think he was getting ill and didn't know what was wrong.'

Her eyes narrowed. 'Don't think it was easy, but I forgave him. We did talk at the end. About the woman. About how his mind didn't seem to work right any more and he couldn't think. I believe he couldn't live with what he'd done to me and our family, and that's what finished him off. He went downhill so rapidly after everything came out. He was angry at Lily, of course. He felt I should be angry at her, too.' She nodded while speaking. 'But he really brought that on himself.'

'You knew all along?' He questioned his mother with his eyes.

The Duchess nodded. 'Your father was furious, as I say. It ate him up inside. After once letting everyone know he had Abigail Hightower picked out for your bride, your father began telling everyone that those two girls were practically raised in a brothel. That they were following in their mother's footsteps. Lily was of marriageable age and think how that sounded in the minds of the women planning events, particularly coming from the Duke of Edgeworth.'

Edge looked aghast at his mother while she continued. 'Whatever Lily did to this family, whatever slip of the tongue led to your father's secrets getting out, your father made sure she served her sentence. Lily didn't betray this family, Lionel, your father did.' Her voice faltered. 'Your father betrayed his own values and broke his own heart and mine, too. Must more hearts be broken over this?'

Edge dusted the cuff of his coat, not that he needed to. He couldn't be more alone than he was. His friends made his head ache. He'd snapped at Gaunt twice and he couldn't believe that the tiny burr on the inside of his trouser seat had magically appeared. Someone had to have put it there.

Make that three times he'd snapped at Gaunt, but that time the man had deserved it.

His burns were even hurting again with the warmer weather and riding in the countryside had irritated them anew.

He reached to his waistband and gave a tug to pull the trousers back to his waistline. Gaunt needed to take in the trousers, but Edge was afraid Gaunt would forget and leave a needle in.

Lily Hightower owed him a full and frank conversation and he would have it. He was tired of waiting for her.

He strode from his house and walked to the front of the Hightower residence and the butler greeted him by name.

'Miss Hightower,' Edge said.

She was at home. He'd watched since the morning. Their carriage hadn't left.

Five minutes later, Abigail flounced by. Then in moments, she returned. She smiled, one of the lopsided ones. 'My sister accepts your deep concerns about her. I told her you are here, weeping with remorse over not seeing her. And that you are little more than a skeleton. And your hair has fallen out.' She whispered her next words. 'I thought she'd have to see for herself.'

'Will she?'

Abigail shook her head. 'I regret to inform you that my sister says she is contagious.'

'What might she have?'

'She claims a festering sore that will not go away. She claims...' the word dragged on and on '...she caught it in the garden.' There was total innocence in her face and he had no idea whether Lily had said those words or they were Abigail's invention. It didn't matter. The statement was right. The sore wasn't going away.

'That is fine with me. I wish to talk with her.'

Abigail didn't speak. 'I will check with her again.'

Half an hour later, a maid walked by and did a double glance.

'I'm here to see Hightower,' he stated.

'Certainly,' she said.

A few minutes after she left, Mr Hightower arrived.

'I would like to see Lily,' Edge said.

Mr Hightower leaned a bit closer. 'Haven't you been meeting her every night in the gardens?'

'No.'

'I don't know what to tell you.' He scratched his nose.

Edge didn't speak or move.

Mr Hightower said, 'Lily is— She's always been a bit— Well, she has a mind of her own. I can't talk any sense into her.' He nodded. 'She's her mother's daughter.'

Rage flared, but Edge pushed the boil into a simmer. 'I would assume she is her father's daughter as well.'

Hightower's chin rose. 'To what are you referring?'

'I would say we all have a mind of our own, Mr Hightower.'

His eyes narrowed even more. 'Yes, I do.' He inclined his head at Edge. 'Good day.'

He stalked from the room and Edge wondered if Hightower's valet had put a burr in his trousers as well.

Hightower stopped outside the door and looked over his shoulder at Edge. 'The pull's there. Ring for a maid if you wish to see Lily.'

Edge took a step nearer the fireplace and reached to the pull, giving it a tug.

In seconds, a maid rushed in.

'Please tell Miss Hightower I am leaving.' He blinked once. 'I am sure you know to which Miss Hightower I am referring.'

The upwards bobble of her head told him he was right and she disappeared from the room.

He contemplated tugging on the pull again, about five times until someone got tired of it and tugged Lily from her room, but he was a duke, after all, and it wouldn't be correct. Or mannerly.

Chapter Fifteen

'I'm fine,' Lily told Abigail, pushing her sister out the door. Then she put her head on the wood, eyes shut, palms flat against the door, holding it shut and holding herself inside.

Edge was only steps away. In her house, to see her.

But she couldn't go to him.

Pushing from the door, she crossed her arms over herself, holding her thoughts at bay. She refused to think. She'd made it through a day and she'd make it through another and another and another after that. And if she went to him she might never make it through the one after that.

When she was younger, Lily's mother had laughed, danced and then wept on the floor. She had existed only to dissolve into a man's smiles and later drown herself in despair. And she'd taken so long to learn from her mistake.

But now she was dashing around, digging up the garden and the happiest Lily had ever seen her.

Lily must learn from her mother's actions. Learning from her own cost so much more.

Edge paced the floor and kept thinking of the ladder against the window. He didn't even know if he could climb a ladder. Dukes' sons didn't need tools or even need to know where they were stored on the property.

And he could never have climbed a ladder in his youth. He was watched too closely to get near one. What if he had suffered injury?

At thirteen, though, he was allowed to select any horse he wanted. They'd even steered him towards the stallions. But he'd selected a spotted mare with a bite out of its ear. He'd loved it the moment he'd seen it. The horse would have taken a bullet for him.

It didn't have the same lineage as the other horses and was a hand shorter, but if it came down to it, he would have taken a bullet for it, too. It had neatly sidestepped a runaway carriage and hadn't balked a bit when caught in the lightning storm. But after it had died, he'd bought the perfect stallion. The one who'd tossed Edge into the water and nearly caused him to drown.

He didn't know if Lily was more like the spotted mare or the stallion, but he suspected she was a bit of both. But he'd just have to get on the ladder because he couldn't live like this any longer.

He turned. Tools. Gaunt would surely know.

His hand paused at the bell, but he rang for Gaunt anyway.

Gaunt opened the door, his face impassive.

'I need a nail,' Edge said.

'Certainly.' Gaunt changed no more than if Edge had asked for a glass of brandy and, when Gaunt returned, the nail lay unmoving, probably cleaned recently, and lying in the middle of a silver tray.

Edge picked it up and didn't remember if he'd ever held a nail before. He met Gaunt's eyes. 'Thank you.'

Gaunt left without questioning the request.

Edge left the room immediately after Gaunt. He wondered if his footfalls were heard on the floor below and how quickly his servants could communicate to each other.

Stepping into the back garden, he walked around the house until he stood under Lily's window. The ladder had fallen on to the ground. He bent and lifted it, feeling the muscles in his arms tighten. He'd not expected the weight. But it didn't matter. He put it against the window, thumping it into place, testing it.

He forced himself not to turn back and look towards his home, suspecting he'd feel like a daft stable boy instead of a duke. Regardless, he wouldn't be able to see the eyes watching him. Yet all it would take would be one pair of eyes to inform the others. He expected his servants to be watchful of the things going on outside his household. They were paid well to do so. Sometimes he wished otherwise. He wasn't meant to be the one they watched, not that it really mattered, not now, at least.

He found the hammer resting nearby and began to climb the ladder. His stallion had felt sturdier.

The ladder gave a bit, springing under his weight, but Edge reached the top. He braced his boots on the rungs and used his weight to steady himself, and pulled the handkerchief from his pocket. Then he flourished the white flag in the air. No sense in making someone strain their eyes.

Next, he pulled out the nail and with two raps quickly secured the handkerchief into the frame where it would flutter in front of the window.

Dropping the hammer to the ground, he descended. Feet on firm ground, he looked up. A breeze fluttered the handkerchief across the panes. He took the ladder and put it near the Hightowers' front door and told their butler to be sure it was put away.

Edge's shoulder leaned against his own window frame. He was lost in thought until a rap on the door surprised him. He raised his head and looked to the doorway. 'Enter.'

Gaunt walked in, again carrying the tray, only this time it had a white cloth. 'Your mother sent one of her handkerchiefs,' he said, lifting it and bringing a medicinal smell into the room.

'Thank you.'

Gaunt turned. 'Best of luck to you, Your Grace.'

'I appreciate that, Gaunt.'

With that, he left.

Edge raised his hand, palm up to the heavens. *Now,* his staff could confide in him and tell him what they thought.

The handkerchief didn't lighten Edge's spirit. If one didn't work, then a dozen wouldn't work.

An hour later, he strode to the door and peered around the corner of the Hightower house to inspect the neighbouring window sill. The cloth was gone.

He didn't wait until complete darkness to move to the bench. It seemed pointless. He took a stroll in the gardens, then made himself comfortable on the bench. If her servants were as helpful as his, perhaps they would also give her a message.

He heard the door close, but didn't know if the steps he heard were truly hers or if his imagination filled in the sound for him.

She walked around the hedge and he stood.

'I'm returning this,' she said of the handkerchief. 'It has a hole in it, however.'

He took it between two fingers, then clasped his other hand around it and tugged it through the circle of his hand until he reached the end of the cloth, and he pulled it, bandage-like, around his knuckles. 'Why did you do it?' he asked, watching her through the fading light. 'Why did you tell the newspaper of my father's child?'

'The newspaper printed another tale about

Mother's life, this one false. The publisher was hurting Abigail. Abigail wanted to marry and the stories were making it harder for her to meet eligible men. I'd had enough.'

'I didn't know.'

'Agatha Crump had visited to commiserate with me about how she'd heard the news that the old Duke had said he wouldn't be inviting the Hightower sisters to any more soirées at his house. I knew he'd not wanted the risk of us saying something in society to reveal his secret life. Before his words, we'd been invited to many different places, but afterwards only a few invitations arrived. I didn't know at first why people stopped inviting us.'

'He wasn't himself at the end. He'd had stumbling spells a few years before he died and he never seemed quite the same after.'

'I didn't go there planning to hurt your family. I only wanted the publisher to stop hurting mine,' she said. 'I truly thought the man had heard about the baby since he knew so much about my mother. I *was* angry that the newspaper kept saying so many bad things about my mother and father, and yet your father was meeting his friend at Mother's house so often. They'd

spent the summer together and it seemed everyone knew. At least, all my mother's friends did.
Then when I said the words about the baby being
on the way and him not caring—I saw the look
on the publisher's face. No one had told him.'

She reached out, putting her hand on Edgeworth's, her touch shooting through his body.

'I couldn't take it back. It was too late. And then
I read the words. And your mother had been so
kind to me. And you as well. I felt bad for that.'

She stepped back, removing her hand, opening
a chasm between them.

'Lily?'

'I can't live like my mother and I can't live in
the world of—' She held out her hands, palms up.
'Your world. The people who watch your every
move.'

'Lily, your movements are reserved. Not the
kind to pull unwanted attention.'

She turned away. 'Nevertheless, I don't want
to be watched so carefully—to have my movements noted and examined. To have my words
repeated and possibly twisted. When a person
errs, and it's talked about, the person deserves
some of the words, surely. But when the truth
is twisted, as it was with my birth—I didn't de-

serve that. Your mother didn't deserve the hurt of the words said about her marriage. It was bad enough she was betrayed.'

'Perhaps that's why my father's situation was so difficult. The public nature of it. Perhaps it bothered me most because of that.'

She closed her eyes and tried to explain it to herself as much as him. But she didn't even want to hear the words from her own lips.

'It's just...' She paused, putting a hand to her chest. 'I feel the eruptions inside me. The flutters and...other things. I feel differently when I am with you and then when I am away from you it feels that I'm lost. I have to be near you to feel alive. And I cannot bear a lifetime of such feelings inside my body. I saw what they did to my mother.'

'I certainly hope those feelings are normal, because I have them, too. It's love.'

'*Love?* But it doesn't feel good. And I so fear being like my mother.'

'No. You're nothing like her.'

'How do you know? You were away at school and she hardly ever was here.'

His voice softened. 'I remember her once, shouting at your father. I'd never seen such a thing. A husband and wife shouting at each other the same as the street urchins. "You're not her," he said. "I know that. And I am not my father. I know that.'

He stepped forward, pulling her hands into his and holding them. 'The difference we have is that we've both seen how things can go wrong—very wrong. And the destruction and pain the disruptions cause. And we've liked each other. Always.'

He put the lightest kiss to one cheek and then one on the other and brushed a third at her lips. 'I know you love me and you don't want to. But you do.'

'You're so certain?'

'Yes. Will you marry me? You'll have a lifetime to grow used to the idea of a different kind of marriage than what you've seen. A marriage unique to you and me, and not like either of our parents' unions. Perhaps that is why I've taken my time and not married in the past. I was waiting for the time when it was right for you and me to wed.'

He pulled her hand to his lips, palm flat, and kissed it. She let her hand remain and the smile behind his lips flowed through his fingers into her heart.

Lily reminded him of orange biscuits, of laughter, and of caring in the way she mothered her little sister. She reminded him of a world that almost existed and possibly could. 'You don't make me think of your mother or father. You make me think of you.'

While looking into her eyes, he spoke, and even in the darkness she could see something in his face she'd never seen before.

'Lily. I love you more than I love anyone. More than all the people of my past put together. Let's start new today and move onward with only the memories we build from now.'

'The memories will always be there.'

'Only as reminders of the past and not a part of who we are going to be.'

He pulled her close, then closer still, finally enfolding his arms around her. 'I might like hearing how you feel about me.'

With the fortress of his chest connecting them, as if their blood flowed through each other's hearts, she said, 'I may have not entirely told the truth when I searched you out to ask if you were going to court my sister. I hoped she'd wed someone else and I hoped to spend the rest of my life a spinster, living next door to a duke who never married, and sometimes we'd meet in the gardens. You were the silent knight I dreamed of, reading his lessons so he might some day conquer the world.'

'All I care about at this moment is if I conquered your feelings.'

'You hold them in your hand.'

Epilogue

Edge was dressed in black except for his white shirt and cravat as he waited for his wife to finish her preparations for their night out at Beatrice's charity art showing.

His hand touched the handkerchief in his pocket.

'Did you order the handkerchiefs?' he asked Gaunt, who walked a little to one side and frowned.

'Yes, all the servants have received the new silk ones.'

'Thank you, Gaunt. I appreciate that and the service you provide to me, and the way you watch over the others in the household.'

'I could not work in a better household,' Gaunt said and his voice wavered. Then he smiled. 'And don't be surprised when I knock, and pause, before waking you on future mornings.'

'I suppose that will be much easier for you than waiting until I return from escorting Lily across the way.'

'You were getting later and later, sir. It's a good thing you married today, otherwise the secret of your visits might have slipped out. Because none of the servants, of course, were aware of the trail to her garden in the morning dew or the earring the scullery maid found, and the request for twice as many orange biscuits as you'd eaten before.'

'I was hungry,' Edge said.

'Of course, it often sounded as if voices could be heard talking when you were alone. I've told the others you walk in your sleep and had selected a gift and lost part of it. The voices in the early hours are merely ghosts because a tragedy happened on the grounds long before the house was built and it was too terrifying to be even spoken of by the living and the only way I know of it is that I overheard one of the spirits swearing when he hit his toe in the dark—which makes no sense, but I won a pence for being able to come up with the best explanation the quickest.' He lowered one brow and lifted the other. 'But I'd expected the need to explain, as I tend to notice things before the others do.'

'And did you give that one pretty maid two silk handkerchiefs?'

'Yes.' Gaunt nodded, trying to puzzle out the reason the maid was given an extra gift.

Edge shrugged, but he didn't turn away. Gaunt bowed and, when he did, a concerned look passed over his face. But he left without another word—walking as if a maid had put a burr in his trouser seat. Edge smiled. Soon Gaunt would be preoccupied with a romance of his own and Edge would tell Gaunt that they were even.

When he left, the connecting door opened.

Lily walked in, lips upturned. 'Are you ready yet?'

'Yes.' He nodded and noted the ring on her finger, which didn't sparkle as much as her eyes. He'd never thought about how wondrous a gold band could look until he saw it on his wife's finger.

Together they left for Andrew and Beatrice's house. Along with the charity event, Andrew and Beatrice were unveiling his mother's portrait.

When they arrived, Edge's hand at the small of Lily's back lifted her courage and she was pleased to walk into the centre of the room.

Beatrice bounced over, her heels clattering, and she whispered to Lily, 'I even invited my very worst friend, Agatha Crump. She tried to shred me under her talons when I was at Drury Lane once and I decided to repay her evil with kindness. And poison her punch.'

She handed Lily a glass. 'This one's safe. But really, the best way to swipe at your enemies is to be kind to them—if you don't poison them. And it's much more enjoyable to see them cringe at your happiness.'

Then Beatrice turned and whispered, 'She's heading this way. A perfect chance for me to grab the poison.' And she darted away.

Agatha Crump joined them, holding her own glass. She sniffed the air. 'So much romance and happiness around,' she said. 'Does me good to see all the love floating about. Life's dust motes that give us hope.' She took a drink. 'Lovely portrait of your mother, Edge. Lord Andrew's wife is quite the artist. I've yet to see the portrait of Andrew, though I did see the engraving. From what I hear there is no foliage in the original. Is that true?'

'I've not seen it,' Edge said.

'I hear it is what caused their love to blossom.

His posing.' She looked at Edge. 'And when did you fall in love?'

'I don't remember the moment,' he said. 'I remember working on my studies and thinking quite highly of her, so perhaps I fell in love early on. Or perhaps it was when we were children and she gave me an orange biscuit.'

Crump's brows lifted. 'How inspiring. And did you fall in love with him at that moment?' Crump turned her attention to Lily.

'I cannot say the exact moment. But I did wish to eat all of those orange biscuits and I shared them, so perhaps I loved him even then.'

'Let us not bore everyone with our private life.' Edge turned from Lily to Agatha. 'Have you a particular favourite among the paintings?'

She shook her head and lowered her voice. 'Teeth should not be shown in a painting. Lawrence doesn't do it.'

'Happiness showing on a face brightens the portrait,' Edgeworth said.

'Some of us don't have as much to be happy about as others,' Crump said, chin going up. 'I've heard she painted a very indecent Boadicea and displayed it Somerset House,' she stated, shuddering.

'I didn't see it,' Lily said. In fact, she'd not even heard of such a painting by Beatrice.

'I particularly like the way Beatrice captured Mother's earrings,' he said. 'Though I thought them a little sedate.'

Crump's eyes widened, she nodded and walked away.

After the guests left, the men remained in the ballroom.

Now Edge's brother Andrew sat across from him and his cousin Foxworthy perched on a chair arm. He didn't understand how his mother's sister could have produced such a rogue. Well, yes, he did. Fox's father hadn't instilled the necessary responsibilities in his son. The earl had raced off on some quest and hadn't returned.

'What is the fondness for these biscuits?' Foxworthy asked. He stared at the one in his hand, eyes narrowed as if looking for a bug. 'Lemon. Lemon is good. When I stayed with Edge—every day, I would see a plate of orange biscuits somewhere about.'

He tossed the treat in his mouth, swallowed and put one palm flat to his chest, and with the other patted in semblance of a beating heart. 'My two cousins, Edge and Andrew, have been smitten by Cupid's sword, straight through the nether regions, I would assume.' He rested one hand on his knee.

'You should be so lucky,' Andrew said and immediately turned to his brother. 'So how did it happen?'

'The usual way.'

'I actually brought them together,' Fox said. 'At that event a few months back. I danced with her and the jealousy rampaged through Edge. I could tell. His eyes moved. That's how I know when he's jealous of me.' He paused. 'See,' he said to Andrew. 'His eyes moved again.'

'Next it'll be my fist.'

'Aunt Ida didn't instil proper manners in the two of you, I'm afraid,' Fox said. 'You're both always wanting to resort to fists or rude gestures. I rely on looks alone and, of course, my good nature.'

'Not intelligence, obviously,' Edge said.

'I'm happy for Edge and Lily,' Andrew said. 'Beatrice is hoping to paint a portrait of the two of you soon.'

'Um…' Fox looked at Andrew. 'Has she mentioned when she plans a portrait of me?'

'Yes,' Andrew answered. 'Not planning it any time soon. Afraid to paint you. Says her true feelings show on the canvas and she's concerned you'll end up looking like a flea-ridden rodent.' He studied Fox. 'Even if her feelings didn't show, you'd end up looking the same.'

'Beatrice has the right view of him,' Edge said.

Andrew eyed his brother. 'But you didn't answer how this marriage came about.'

'He doesn't have to,' Fox said. 'Time to marry. Produce the offspring.' He swung his head to the window. 'The sad lot of inheriting a title. Must continue on with the line. I have to consider the same path.'

'Perhaps you should make an exception, cousin,' Edge said. 'All of London would thank you.'

Fox crossed his arms. 'Eyes moved again, Edge.'

'Don't mistake disdain for jealousy.'

'You should both be so happy as I am.' Andrew stood and smiled. 'But I do want to wish you well, big brother.'

'And I wanted to offer condolences,' Fox said, 'as I hope you'd do for me.'

'I'm extremely happy with Lily as my wife.'

'I think she's an excellent choice.' Andrew moved to the door.

'Me, too,' Fox said. 'I should have asked her to marry me. I just didn't think of it. But I could ask Abigail.'

'Don't even get near Abigail,' the Duke ordered. 'I've been introducing her to eligible men who will treat her well.'

Fox smiled. 'That advice usually doesn't stop me.'

'It will this time,' Edge commanded Fox.

'I was just having a jest.' Fox laughed. 'You've always been Edgy.'

'You are forbidden to court the Duchess's sister.'

'Blast,' Fox said. 'I just realised. If I inherit the earldom, the former Miss Hightower—Lily—will outrank my wife should I ever marry.'

'Don't worry about that. Beatrice has been a countess, but she says I'm better than any peer that ever walked the earth.' He strode to the door, then stopped, and his eyes brightened as he added, 'I must say, I think she's the smartest woman that ever walked the earth.'

A chuckle sounded from the hall, and Beatrice walked into the room, followed by Lily.

'Marriage turns men's words into gibberish.' Fox meandered behind Andrew, but bowed to the ladies and gave each a kiss on the back of the hand. 'But had my cousins not found you two gems first, I would be pleased to ask either of you to be my bride.'

At that moment, a scuffling noise sounded in the hall. Jakes, Andrew's valet, walked into the room carrying a squirming brown bundle of puppy at arm's length.

'And did I mention that I have a present for you, Beatrice?' Andrew said.

Jakes put the puppy on the rug and it ran underneath a chair. 'Sir. He put a very rude puppy deposit in my room.' He dusted his hands. 'But I was able to clean it with your cravat.'

'As long as it was one of those you left scorch marks on when you ironed,' Andrew said.

'That could be any one of them.' Jakes shuddered, removed a hair from his coat and sprinkled it to the floor.

'You can grow to love a cuddly little beast quite quickly,' Andrew said.

'Not me,' Jakes said, turning to leave. 'Nothing that bites.' Then he shuddered and left.

Andrew glanced at Edge while Beatrice tried

to coax the puppy from under the chair. 'I heard
that you were carting around a ladder, trying to
find your lady love's window the other day. Stairs
broken?'

'The ladder was faster,' Edge said. 'I wanted
to present her with a handkerchief as a token.'

'So you climbed a ladder to hand her a handkerchief?'

'Yes,' Lily said. 'And it was a special handkerchief. His.'

Fox put his hand to his head, gripping, eyes
shut. 'Blast it, Lily. A man can't be climbing lad-
ders to give a woman his handkerchief. Stairs are
much more durable. Love and marriage turn a
man's mind to mush.'

'You should *not* find a wife, Fox,' Lily spoke.
'It is not for you. You would wither and die. All
your man parts would fall off. Vultures would
swarm, thinking you dying because of the
agonising screams coming from your lips.' She
looked at Edge. 'Have I left anything out?'

Fox answered for his cousin, 'No. I think you've
convinced me.' He bowed. 'I believe I must leave
now. It appears that I must go somewhere to wash
the sight of all this happiness from my mind.' He
left, whistling.

'Why did you tell him such?' Edge asked.

'To save some unfortunate miss whom he might propose to.'

'Foxworthy will not propose willingly until he is so old the miss can happily look forward to becoming a widow.' Edgeworth looked at Lily. 'I should have told him that you'd planned to marry me since you were a little child.'

'I did not, Your Grace.'

'Sweet.' He clasped her hand and pulled it to the crook of his elbow. 'I remember. You and your sister were playing and you told her you were going to marry a handsome man who had a big spotted horse.'

She grinned. 'So I was half-right. You don't have a spotted horse.'

'I once did.' He led her to the hallway.

She looked deep into his eyes. 'Truly?'

With a quick flick of his wrist, he pulled her against him. 'Of course. At the country estate. I thought, well, if Miss Hightower thinks a spotted horse is quite appealing, then I should have one.'

'I have no particular fondness for spotted horses and can't remember ever saying such a thing. But I do have a fondness for a certain handsome duke.'

'A fondness?'

'Yes. Mixed with love, it is quite a pleasant feeling.'

'Ah, I like pleasant feelings,' he said, rocking her in his arms. 'And you're the most pleasant feeling ever.'

She looked into his eyes and saw the lightness reflected back, and he smiled and she knew it was with his whole heart.

* * * * *

THE WALLFLOWER DUCHESS
features characters seen in Liz Tyner's
THE NOTORIOUS COUNTESS.

And don't miss these other
great reads from Liz Tyner!

THE RUNAWAY GOVERNESS
(part of THE GOVERNESS TALES *quartet)*
SAFE IN THE EARL'S ARMS
A CAPTAIN AND A ROGUE
FORBIDDEN TO THE DUKE

MILLS & BOON®
Hardback – August 2017

ROMANCE

An Heir Made in the Marriage Bed	Anne Mather
The Prince's Stolen Virgin	Maisey Yates
Protecting His Defiant Innocent	Michelle Smart
Pregnant at Acosta's Demand	Maya Blake
The Secret He Must Claim	Chantelle Shaw
Carrying the Spaniard's Child	Jennie Lucas
A Ring for the Greek's Baby	Melanie Milburne
Bought for the Billionaire's Revenge	Clare Connelly
The Runaway Bride and the Billionaire	Kate Hardy
The Boss's Fake Fiancée	Susan Meier
The Millionaire's Redemption	Therese Beharrie
Captivated by the Enigmatic Tycoon	Bella Bucannon
Tempted by the Bridesmaid	Annie O'Neil
Claiming His Pregnant Princess	Annie O'Neil
A Miracle for the Baby Doctor	Meredith Webber
Stolen Kisses with Her Boss	Susan Carlisle
Encounter with a Commanding Officer	Charlotte Hawkes
Rebel Doc on Her Doorstep	Lucy Ryder
The CEO's Nanny Affair	Joss Wood
Tempted by the Wrong Twin	Rachel Bailey

0717 GEN STD HB

MILLS & BOON®
Large Print – August 2017

ROMANCE

The Italian's One-Night Baby	Lynne Graham
The Desert King's Captive Bride	Annie West
Once a Moretti Wife	Michelle Smart
The Boss's Nine-Month Negotiation	Maya Blake
The Secret Heir of Alazar	Kate Hewitt
Crowned for the Drakon Legacy	Tara Pammi
His Mistress with Two Secrets	Dani Collins
Stranded with the Secret Billionaire	Marion Lennox
Reunited by a Baby Bombshell	Barbara Hannay
The Spanish Tycoon's Takeover	Michelle Douglas
Miss Prim and the Maverick Millionaire	Nina Singh

HISTORICAL

Claiming His Desert Princess	Marguerite Kaye
Bound by Their Secret Passion	Diane Gaston
The Wallflower Duchess	Liz Tyner
Captive of the Viking	Juliet Landon
The Spaniard's Innocent Maiden	Greta Gilbert

MEDICAL

Their Meant-to-Be Baby	Caroline Anderson
A Mummy for His Baby	Molly Evans
Rafael's One Night Bombshell	Tina Beckett
Dante's Shock Proposal	Amalie Berlin
A Forever Family for the Army Doc	Meredith Webber
The Nurse and the Single Dad	Dianne Drake

MILLS & BOON®
Hardback – September 2017

ROMANCE

The Tycoon's Outrageous Proposal	Miranda Lee
Cipriani's Innocent Captive	Cathy Williams
Claiming His One-Night Baby	Michelle Smart
At the Ruthless Billionaire's Command	Carole Mortimer
Engaged for Her Enemy's Heir	Kate Hewitt
His Drakon Runaway Bride	Tara Pammi
The Throne He Must Take	Chantelle Shaw
The Italian's Virgin Acquisition	Michelle Conder
A Proposal from the Crown Prince	Jessica Gilmore
Sarah and the Secret Sheikh	Michelle Douglas
Conveniently Engaged to the Boss	Ellie Darkins
Her New York Billionaire	Andrea Bolter
The Doctor's Forbidden Temptation	Tina Beckett
From Passion to Pregnancy	Tina Beckett
The Midwife's Longed-For Baby	Caroline Anderson
One Night That Changed Her Life	Emily Forbes
The Prince's Cinderella Bride	Amalie Berlin
Bride for the Single Dad	Jennifer Taylor
A Family for the Billionaire	Dani Wade
Taking Home the Tycoon	Catherine Mann

0817 GEN STD HB

MILLS & BOON®
Large Print – September 2017

ROMANCE

The Sheikh's Bought Wife	Sharon Kendrick
The Innocent's Shameful Secret	Sara Craven
The Magnate's Tempestuous Marriage	Miranda Lee
The Forced Bride of Alazar	Kate Hewitt
Bound by the Sultan's Baby	Carol Marinelli
Blackmailed Down the Aisle	Louise Fuller
Di Marcello's Secret Son	Rachael Thomas
Conveniently Wed to the Greek	Kandy Shepherd
His Shy Cinderella	Kate Hardy
Falling for the Rebel Princess	Ellie Darkins
Claimed by the Wealthy Magnate	Nina Milne

HISTORICAL

The Secret Marriage Pact	Georgie Lee
A Warriner to Protect Her	Virginia Heath
Claiming His Defiant Miss	Bronwyn Scott
Rumours at Court (Rumors at Court)	Blythe Gifford
The Duke's Unexpected Bride	Lara Temple

MEDICAL

Their Secret Royal Baby	Carol Marinelli
Her Hot Highland Doc	Annie O'Neil
His Pregnant Royal Bride	Amy Ruttan
Baby Surprise for the Doctor Prince	Robin Gianna
Resisting Her Army Doc Rival	Sue MacKay
A Month to Marry the Midwife	Fiona McArthur